THE ROYAL BASTARD

NICOLE BURNHAM

The Royal Bastard

by Nicole Burnham

Cover design by Patricia Schmitt

Edition: May 2022

ISBN: 978-941828-05-2 (paperback)

ISBN: 978-1-941828-04-5 (ebook)

For more information or to subscribe to Nicole's newsletter, visit nicoleburnham.com.

For my great uncle, Harley Magee, an adventurer, athlete, ice cream aficionado, and gifted storyteller.

CHAPTER 1

FIVE HOURS after Rocco Cornaro buried his mother, having tossed the last shovelful of dirt over her grave while wishing her a swift ascent to heaven, Satan knocked at his front door.

More accurately: Satan's driver rang the bell at Rocco's wrought iron security gate.

Rocco stood at a second story window in his Dubrovnik villa, seething at the gall of the woman hidden behind the tinted windows of the rented black Mercedes. The uniformed driver hadn't given his client's name, but Rocco knew. Her appearance was inevitable after she'd phoned two days ago and he'd hung up after informing her that he had no interest in anything she had to say. He'd thought she'd at least give him the day of his mother's funeral in peace, but apparently royals did what they wanted when they wanted, and to hell with anyone else.

Rocco took a seat in his late stepfather's favorite worn leather chair, kicked his feet onto the windowsill, and dragged his palms over his face. Keeping it together while delivering his mother's graveside eulogy was the toughest thing he'd done in his life. Despite the emotion that threatened to overwhelm him, he'd made it through, his voice resolute as he addressed the small gathering of friends and family. He finished a heartbeat before spying his wife watching from the shadows of a tree near the edge of the cemetery. There was no mistaking Justine's stature, still lean and tight as any Olympic athlete, nor the fact she recoiled as he glanced in her direction. He hadn't invited her, and she hadn't intended to be seen.

What was it with women showing up where they weren't wanted today?

Thank God his siblings hadn't noticed Justine standing alongside the trunk of the thick oak. Double thanks that they hadn't accompanied him back to his residence to see the sleek Mercedes now parked outside. It would've spurred even more questions than his wife's appearance.

Rocco leaned forward in his chair to take another look outside. The driver spoke near the Mercedes' cracked rear window, nodded, then returned to the gate and folded his hands in front of him in a show of resolve. On the roadway behind the Mercedes, a red BMW belonging to Rocco's uphill neighbor slowed as it passed on its way to the heart of the city.

"Damn it all to hell."

"Sir?" Kos Horvat stood in the doorway of Rocco's study. Twice Kos had informed the driver that Rocco was not available. Twice the driver had insisted that Rocco would wish an audience with his passenger and that they would wait.

Rocco swirled the amber liquid inside the crystal tumbler he clutched in one hand, then took a long, slow sip, savoring the burn as it made its way down the back of his throat. If anyone could be deterred from darkening Rocco's entrance, Kos was the man to deter them. Not only did he manage Rocco's properties, he had extensive security expertise and a build as powerful and unyielding as Dubrovnik's ancient city walls. But Queen Fabrizia, whose husband ruled the wealthy Mediterranean island nation of Sarcaccia, apparently wasn't one to be put off by a burly, sour-faced Croatian with a voice rough enough to intimidate men twice her size. Nor was she one whose mood would improve with the delay.

"Talking to myself, Kos." Rocco rose from the chair and turned away from the window. "Allow the visitor to enter, but the car and driver stay outside the gates. If this person is so anxious to see me, they can walk."

The corner of Kos's mouth twitched. It was as close to a smile as the big man ever revealed. "Of course."

"Then go home. You've been here around the clock for the last two weeks and worked overtime before that." During those long days, while Rocco's mother had been ensconced in the guest room waiting for the end to come, Kos had been a godsend. "You're due a vacation."

"I've no need of a holiday."

"And I don't need you for the next few weeks. It's April now. The weather should be beautiful. Go while you're able."

Kos regarded him for a moment, then gave a slight nod. "I'll leave once your guest has departed."

"No need to wait. I'll gladly provide a personal escort from the premises when we're finished." Then he could sink into the solitude he desperately craved. He could mourn. He could rattle about the villa with no witnesses, no looks of concern, and none of Kos's silent watchfulness.

"When shall I resume my services?"

"Take two weeks. No…take three. Your wife deserves a vacation as much as you do. She's been incredibly patient while you've been here."

"As you wish." Gratitude flared in the Croat's eyes. "Again, sir, my condolences. Your mother was a great woman."

"She was. Thank you."

As Kos's steps faded, Rocco spun away from the door and set his half-empty tumbler atop the wide mantel that crowned the room's stone fireplace. His mother always described Queen Fabrizia as a worthy opponent. Better he wait to finish his liquor until the woman departed.

With any luck, it'd be his first and last confrontation with her, and it wouldn't take long.

He ran a hand around his waistband, ensuring his shirt was securely tucked in, then straightened his tie. He couldn't imagine what the queen could want that warranted a face-to-face visit. She was one of the most sought-after women in the world. Arriving on his doorstep unnoticed couldn't have been easy.

He sensed Fabrizia's presence before he heard Kos announce, "Sir, your visitor."

"Thank you." Without looking over his shoulder to gauge Kos's shock—for surely he knew the famous face—Rocco said, "I trust your walk up the driveway was a pleasant one? The gardener did a spectacular job with the annuals this year."

She waited until the door closed behind Kos to answer. "You've made a beautiful home for yourself, Rocco." The voice sounded just as it did on television, warm and well-modulated, the Italian accent hearkening to the queen's Sarcaccian home.

"Pity you felt the need to travel so far to see it. I've had an exhausting week and am not in a position to play host. On the other hand, I didn't feel I could leave you at my gate. You never know who might wander by with a camera and I suspect you don't want your visit here noticed."

"You suspect right, though for more reasons than simply exposing our...link."

He turned then, taking in the sight of the elegant queen as she lowered a scarf from her head to her shoulders. He'd grudgingly found her attractive whenever he'd seen her on television and magazine covers, but those images paled compared to the real-life woman. Despite knowing her to be in her mid-sixties, Rocco would've guessed her age closer to fifty. Golden hair cut in a sleek, modern style emphasized her high cheekbones and full mouth. A light spray of wrinkles radiated from the edges of her bright, intelligent green eyes, but her taut physique, fitted black and white silk dress, and matching black studded leather handbag gave her the overall appearance of a younger woman. She held a pair of sunglasses he guessed she'd worn with the scarf to mask her identity.

More than her attractiveness, however, it was her dignity that surprised him. She didn't require a crown to demand attention and deference.

"I don't believe your man recognized me." The queen approached as if she were being introduced to him at one of her palace garden parties, her hand extended and a cordial smile lifting the edges of her lips. "It's a pleasure to finally meet you in person."

He couldn't bring himself to be so rude as to ignore the proffered hand, nor could he pretend graciousness by responding in kind. He kept their touch brief and businesslike. "Fabrizia."

Her eyes lit with a mixture of curiosity and amusement. "So much like your parents."

He merely raised his brows in response. The queen might hold power in Sarcaccia, but not in his home. So long as they stood in his home, in his study, discussion of his parents was off the table.

"Like Teresa, you don't use my title," she added as she slipped the sunglasses into her handbag.

Good for you, Mother. "Titles should be earned. I've never much cared for them."

She moved past him, her fingers trailing across the back of the study's plush gray sofa as her gaze flicked around the room, taking in the tall windows and the clean-lined navy curtains that framed them, then the hefty desk and leather chair he'd inherited from his stepfather, before settling on a framed photo of his mother at one end of the mantel. "For you, on this occasion, I'll grant a pass. You are loyal to your mother and I find that honorable."

"Why are you here?"

She laughed, a true, bubbly laugh that surprised him. "Now that is your father's trait. For better or worse, you prefer to get to the point, rather than learn about others through discussion."

"My father died five years ago. You never met him."

The queen paused near the mantel, then slowly turned to face him. "Jack Cornaro may have married your mother and raised you, Enzo, and Lina, but it's King Carlo's blood you carry in your veins." She lifted Rocco's crystal tumbler and swished the contents beneath her nose. Her eyebrows lifted. "You drink Aberlour."

"I do."

"Interesting. So do my husband and twin sons."

He took a long, quiet breath, waiting for her to get to the point.

After he finished that glass—*if* he finished that glass—he'd find a new brand of Scotch.

"You look like them, you know. It's uncanny, the resemblance between you and my twins." The softness of her voice snapped his gaze to hers. She was studying him in the same calculating manner as she'd assessed his decor.

"Not surprising, as we share a sperm donor." Her damned husband. The man who'd taken advantage of his mother all those years ago, then abandoned Teresa for the aristocratic, wealthy Fabrizia.

Rocco's harsh words didn't deter the queen. "I can understand why you feel that way, but I assure you, King Carlo considers you far more than the result of…that. As do I."

"Don't." His tone made it clear he expected her to state her business and leave.

She set the Scotch on the edge of his desk. "Teresa and I had our differences. Strong differences. However, she was a good mother to you. King Carlo would have been a good father to you, if he'd had the chance—"

"I had a good father."

"Yes, you did. But now you have neither Jack Cornaro nor Teresa. You have soundly rejected King Carlo. Therefore, your care falls to me."

Care? "I'm a grown man, Fabrizia. Older than *your* children, in fact." Including the children Carlo fathered with the queen while still involved with Rocco's mother, the son of a bitch.

"You're a grown man in trouble, whether you know it or not. That's why I'm here."

"Say your piece, then I shall wish you a safe and speedy journey home."

She swept a hand toward the sofa. "May I?"

"You weren't stopped by my gate or my property manager. Why stop now?" He'd never before spoken to a woman in such an abrasive tone, let alone a queen, but dammit, he'd buried his mother today. And he still had the matter of his wife's graveyard appearance to confront.

The queen perched on the edge of the sofa, her back straight. Rocco remained where he was, arms crossed over his chest.

"You remember last year, when every reporter in the world seemed to be searching for my son, Alessandro?" At his grudging nod, she continued, "Your mother called King Carlo and said you were approached at a farmer's market in Dubrovnik by a man who asked if you were Alessandro. Teresa was very concerned. She claimed that the man followed you to the market from your wife's apartment."

"My wife is none of your business."

He regretted the outburst as comprehension flashed in the queen's eyes. She knew she'd pricked his Achilles' heel.

"You handled the situation well by telling the man he was mistaken. However, the incident gave me pause. I put a tail on you to ensure no one inquired further and discovered the truth of your parentage."

"You…*what?*" Fabrizia had been spying on him? Had his mother known? No…she couldn't have. She wouldn't have stood for it.

"It was for your own protection."

"Let's be honest about who needed protection here," he shot back. "It wasn't me." If the world discovered that King Carlo had a stealth paramour and children during the first years of his marriage to Queen Fabrizia, it would severely damage both the king's popular image and the queen's reputation as a savvy, intelligent woman.

"I would do anything to protect my family. Choose to believe it or not, but I include you and your siblings in that group. If your parentage were to become public knowledge, your life would be forever changed."

"So would yours."

"Then we're on the same side, aren't we?" She exhaled and shifted her position on the sofa. "The man who approached you that day in the market was indeed a reporter. He moved on to another story when my son returned to Sarcaccia the following week. However, while investigating the reporter I discovered something far more disturbing. He wasn't the only one watching your movements."

She opened her handbag and withdrew a cell phone, then turned the screen toward Rocco. It displayed an image of a sidewalk café located on a busy street a block from his wife's apartment. "Have you ever seen this man? Do you know him?"

Taking the phone from her, he zoomed in on the face of the man seated at the outdoor table. The man's hawklike nose, lean build, and curly dark hair were familiar. "I don't know his name, but he rents one of the offices above mine."

Rocco first noticed him several months ago when they'd stood in line at a local newspaper kiosk waiting to make purchases. A teenage boy mouthed off to the owner for refusing to sell him cigarettes. The man in the photograph had told the youngster to move along, much to the relief of the elderly kiosk owner. Since then, Rocco caught glimpses of the man from time to time, usually as he ducked in or out of the building's elevator or followed Rocco through building security. He carried a worn, black leather messenger bag and walked in quick steps with his head down, as if he were late for an appointment. If not for the incident at the kiosk, the man would've escaped Rocco's notice entirely.

"Who is he?" Rocco asked.

"Viktor Radich. Twenty-eight years old. Tech expert. His specialty is surveillance equipment." She aimed a glance at the upper corner of Rocco's study, where a security camera was mounted, its form partially obscured by the woodwork. "Mostly custom-designed, high-end systems like yours for a variety of clients around the world."

"You're quite observant."

"It serves me well in my position." A tentative smile lifted the edges of her mouth. "It also doesn't hurt that I live in a residence with superior security. I've made it habit to look for both cameras and exits upon entering a building. A member of my staff once told me he always has a minimum of two escape routes in mind when I'm in a room. I've never needed them, but his words stuck with me."

Rocco suspected the queen was the type to have more than two escape routes in mind, and not because she'd been instructed to do so. Teresa had once described Fabrizia as a wily survivalist camouflaged by designer labels. He didn't doubt it.

"Radich's parents divorced and his mother emigrated to the United States with Viktor when he was a small child. Under the custody arrangement Viktor spent summers with his father in Moscow...at least when the man wasn't being held by the authorities." Her look was hard. "Russian mafia. No charges that stuck long enough to keep him imprisoned indefinitely, but he's still questioned frequently. Radich hasn't been back to Russia since he finished high school. He went on to study electrical engineering and computer science at MIT. Graduated near the top of the class."

"So he's intelligent."

"Very. No criminal record, either, which is necessary if one wishes to work installing security systems. He started his own business right out of college and had several high-profile clients in the United States before moving here, ostensibly to open a second office."

"He didn't install my system, if that's your point."

A twitch of the queen's lips made it plain she already knew that fact. "Tell me, Rocco, how far is your office from your wife's apartment?"

He frowned, unsure where the queen was heading with the abrupt question. "A ten-minute drive without traffic. Twenty with."

"Every other Tuesday, Radich dines at the same restaurant where your wife meets with her girlfriends, about three blocks from her apartment. He arrives a few minutes before they do, like clockwork. He sits at different tables each time, but always in the same section where the women have their standing reservation. He's done it for at least three months now."

Rocco returned the phone to the queen. He forced a calm expression, though a sense of unease prickled the hairs on the back of his neck. "Coincidence. Many people who work near my office live in the same district as my wife. It's a popular neighborhood."

"That's what my people thought...at first. But on alternate Wednesdays, the morning after Radich has eaten near your wife and her friends, he leaves the office building you share to have lunch at this café near your wife's apartment, despite the fact there are any number of places to eat near your office."

"Perhaps he has a standing meeting."

"In fact, he does." Fabrizia turned her phone to show Rocco a different image. "Ever seen this man?"

"No. Never." Taken at the same café, the photo showed a barrel-chested, middle-aged blonde man with a military haircut and dark sunglasses. His face bore bright, raised scars on one cheek, the edges stretched and shiny, as if he'd suffered excruciating burns. The scars extended from beneath the lower edge of his sunglasses and down his jaw to his neck, then disappeared in the collar of his dark leather jacket. A camera sat on the table in front of him as he leaned toward Radich. The pair appeared to be studying the screen of Radich's laptop.

If Rocco had ever encountered this man, he'd have remembered. The guy dwarfed Radich, and Radich, while lean, wasn't short. A scarred man with such a massive build stood out in a crowd.

"His name is Anton Karpovsky."

"Doesn't ring a bell."

"He was honorably discharged from the Russian army after being injured by an IED in Chechnya. He developed a reputation among his men for his patriotic single-mindedness. Very driven, very inflexible. Very unforgiving of the Chechens…or anyone who rebels against Russia, for that matter."

The queen returned the phone to her handbag and met Rocco's gaze. "Karpovsky resented the fact that his injury cost him his military career. His parents hired him to work at their grocery store in Yeka-terinburg, which he considered beneath him. Then one night, he shot his wife three times in the head and chest when she arrived home late from work. He claimed he thought she was an intruder, but his wife's sister alleged that Karpovsky was engaged in illegal activities, having become acquainted with members of the Russian mafia while sourcing inventory for his parents' store. His wife had planned to report him to the authorities and file for divorce. The sister-in-law believed Karpovsky killed his wife to keep her from going to the police and testified to that at his trial. He served two years in prison for manslaughter before having his conviction overturned when the sister-in-law recanted."

Rocco spread his hands wide, silently asking what the beefy Russian's presence in Dubrovnik had to do with him.

"The sister-in-law disappeared a few months later while vacationing in Bali. Whether there was foul play or not, I haven't been able to determine, but the woman's claim that Karpovsky is involved in illegal activities is true. Publicly, he once again handles inventory for his parents' grocery store in Yekaterinburg. Privately, he is a gun for hire."

The queen stood, leaving her handbag behind on the sofa as she strode to the window and looked out at her driver. When she turned back to face Rocco, her brow was furrowed. "I believe they intend to kidnap your wife."

CHAPTER 2

Rocco's first instinct was to laugh. The idea that Russian thugs would kidnap Justine, whose life these days was as routine as they came…it was as outrageous as the plot to a bad television movie. Only the fact the queen appeared to be holding her breath in anticipation of his reaction stopped Rocco from saying as much aloud.

"Since you've been following these two men so closely, I assume that your—your employees, I suppose I should call them—overheard them make a specific threat against my wife?"

Her expression told him the answer was no before she spoke. "They've been unable to hear more than snippets of conversation between Karpovsky and Radich. But Karpovsky wouldn't have come to Croatia unless there was a large amount of money involved, and you, Rocco, have that money. And I suspect you may have something more valuable." Her voice lifted at the end, as if she were asking a question. Rather than address it, he waited for her to continue.

"I don't know what you're doing in your office. Your security is tight and I've kept my—my employees, as you call them—at a distance."

"Thank you for respecting my privacy."

She heard his sarcasm, but ignored it. "If there's anyone in the world capable of piercing your security, it's the man renting the office space directly above yours. I doubt that's a coincidence. If those two want your money or whatever it is you keep in your office, all they need to do is get their hands on your wife."

The sense of unease that pricked at him earlier evolved into alarm. He'd been extremely careful to keep his work quiet, but that work, once complete, would be worth millions. His earlier projects—projects that saved thousands of lives while making him wealthy enough to purchase this villa and take care of his mother—would pale in comparison.

He forced himself to keep a calm countenance as he regarded Fabrizia. "You realize that my wife and I are separated. If those two men are watching us, they know it, too."

"The separation works to their advantage. It removes her from your web of protection." Her eyes narrowed as she studied him. "After a year apart, you aren't divorced. While I have no wish to pry—"

This time, he couldn't stop a bark of laughter at the irony of her statement.

"—she clearly means something to you. While she's never returned to this villa, you've visited her apartment more than once and stayed overnight. I'm also told she visited your mother's grave after you left the cemetery this morning."

He'd scanned the cemetery following the service and failed to spot Justine again, so he'd assumed she'd left. The idea that she'd stayed behind, hidden, and visited Teresa's grave made him wonder what could be going through her head. The two women had never been close.

He pushed thoughts of Justine aside—he'd consider them later—and started to tell the queen that his relationship with his wife was out of bounds, but the royal held up one well-manicured finger to stop him.

"If I believe that you and your wife still have a connection, they're likely to believe it, too."

A *connection*. He supposed that was one way to describe his relationship with Justine.

"Radich skipped the Tuesday dinner week before last as well as his Wednesday meeting with Karpovsky. Nor is Radich at the restaurant this evening. He's staying late at the office."

"Unbelievable." Rocco scrubbed a hand over his head. "You're following her right now."

"Of course." She waited until Rocco met her green-eyed gaze before continuing. "My people believe that the Russians' surveillance is complete. Whatever Radich and Karpovsky plan to do, they'll do it soon. When you wouldn't take my call, I decided to see you in person. It was difficult to schedule private time so I could slip away without being noticed by the press or my staff, but I needed to warn you."

Thanking her didn't seem appropriate. Part of him knew he needed to heed her warning—too much of what she said tripped his internal triggers—but another part hated to acknowledge that his mother's enemy had done him a favor. Or what it meant if the queen was right.

"Warning taken. I'll look into it."

"What do you plan to do?"

It was a demand as much as a question. "I'm sure you have suggestions, but how I handle this information is none of your business. And on that note, I would appreciate it if you'd cease following me and my wife. Immediately."

Surprise flickered in her eyes. He doubted she often heard demands in response to her own.

She shouldered her handbag as she stood. "I can agree to that. In exchange, I would appreciate being informed if you involve the police or other law enforcement. King Carlo deserves to know if your relationship might become public."

"I'll consider it." The man hadn't done him any favors...not that Rocco would've accepted any.

"My children have no idea you, Enzo, or Lina exist. No matter your feelings toward King Carlo, put yourself in their shoes. I would appreciate the opportunity to inform them before they hear about it on the evening news."

"You've never told them?" The Barrali siblings were known to be tight-knit, and close to their parents, as well. The enormity of the secret would devastate them.

"It was a decision the king and your mother came to years ago. They felt it was the best way to protect each set of children." Her gaze went to the floor as she lifted the scarf to disguise her hair. "I've honored their decision."

"Your husband doesn't know you're here." The realization sent a jolt of power through him. "I bet he doesn't even know you've had me followed."

"And I bet your mother would want you to protect yourself and your wife, promises be damned." She met his eyes without flinching. "On that note, I'll take my leave."

"I'll show you out."

The queen nodded before rounding the sofa. She paused near Rocco's desk and studied a framed photo of his mother and Jack Cornaro on their wedding day. "I'm deeply sorry for your loss. Teresa loved you dearly. I'm sure your instinct is to spend the evening in mourning, but your mother was nothing if not practical. She'd want you to take action rather than sit here cradling your Scotch."

Fabrizia opened her handbag and withdrew her sunglasses. After donning them, she pulled out a flat, cornflower blue velvet box, the type designed to hold an expensive pen set or jewelry. "King Carlo has had this for years. It belonged to your mother."

Rocco eyed the box as the queen set it on his desk. "Whatever it is, I don't want it."

"It belongs with your descendants, not mine." She tapped the lid and smiled. "It's also my excuse for the visit today, should my husband ever inquire. Oh, and I almost forgot." A soft white business card joined the box. "My private cell phone number, should you need anything at all."

A few minutes later, Rocco watched from the front door as the Mercedes made a U-turn in front of the gate, then disappeared from view, carrying the queen back to her private jet for the short flight across the Adriatic and southern Italy to the Mediterranean island she called home.

He wasn't sure what to make of the woman's visit, other than knowing that his mother would roll over in her freshly dug grave were she to know Fabrizia had crossed his threshold. He trusted his mother, and his mother hadn't trusted the queen.

Rocco placed a hand on the closed door to his mother's bedroom as he passed it on the way to his study. Watching his mother fight for her life these past weeks had worn his emotions to a nub, leaving only a hardened center. Approaching Justine was the very last thing he should do, given his current state.

He shoved Fabrizia's blue box into his bottom desk drawer, reached for the glass of Scotch, and downed it in a single gulp.

THE POUNDING at her front door could only mean one thing. The devil had come for his due.

Justine Cornaro turned away from the kitchen sink, where she'd just finished washing out her ice cream bowl, and adjusted her nightgown. Resisting the hospitable impulse to turn off the flamenco guitar music echoing from her speakers, she moved to the front door. Sure enough, a glance through the peephole revealed her spouse.

Correction: her soused spouse. His head was down and his hands were in the pockets of his slacks, a pose that signaled a rare overindulgence. So rare she couldn't remember the last time he drank that much. Perhaps the night of their wedding.

He raised his fist and pounded again, the first blow striking the thick wood before Justine could jump away. "Justine, let me in. I know you're awake. It's important."

She placed a palm flat against the door, then counted to three. "Rocco, it's after midnight. I'm not in the mood for a booty call." Though truth be told, after the day he'd had, she understood why he craved female companionship. Physical activity was Rocco's preferred method of clearing his brain, with certain agonies better treated by heart-pumping sex than a heart-pumping hour in his home gym.

Satisfying as the physical release might be for Rocco tonight, she wasn't sure she could deal with her own emotions afterward.

"Not why I'm here, honey." She looked through the peephole again to see him roll his shoulders, then stare at the door as if he could open it by willpower alone. He'd grown a close-cropped beard in the month since she'd seen him last. It lent him a dangerous air that unsettled her.

She wondered if he knew she was watching him. Probably. And if he wasn't here for sex, it meant he'd spotted her at the cemetery and was here for a lecture.

Great. Sex would be easier.

She slid the chain and flipped the deadbolt, then stepped back to wave him inside.

"Get dressed."

Well. Definitely not sex.

"Nice to see you, too." She closed the door behind him. "It's too late to go out and I've had a very long day. Another five minutes and I would've been in bed."

"Alone?"

"None of your business."

"Is there anyone else in the apartment?" He looked toward the speakers, as if the music was a clue.

"You're not off to a good start, Rocco." She folded her arms, then realized her mistake as his gaze drifted to her breasts, now high-lighted by the thin, tightly pulled fabric of her baby blue nightgown. Thank God she still had on her bra.

He lifted his eyes to hers. Dark rings beneath his light brown eyes attested to his lack of sleep, and his thick hair appeared to have been finger combed, adding to his menacing aura. "I'm asking for a reason, Justine. I have cause to be worried about your safety."

"I'm alone." She frowned as his words registered. "Why in the world would you be worried? I'm perfectly fine."

He sucked in his lower lip, as if he hadn't considered how he'd explain himself, which wasn't like Rocco at all. The man didn't plan a step ahead; he planned five. Nothing was done on the spur of the moment.

On a blown-out breath, he said, "It's tough to explain, but you need to leave the apartment. At least until I'm sure you're not in danger."

Teresa's death must've gutted him. It certainly explained the fact he still wore the dress shirt and slacks he'd had on at the cemetery, though the jacket and tie were gone.

Justine spoke in a soft, calming tone. "Rocco, I'm in one of the safest parts of town. I have neighbors downstairs and across the hall if there's any problem. The only way *you* got into the building is because I gave you a key." Her neighbors weren't the type to buzz in strangers. Even so, she kept her door both chained and deadbolted, a habit built by years spent in hotels.

"The building is three hundred years old. The windows are vulnerable. I could smash the glass on the entry door and be up the stairs before your neighbors even rolled over in bed, if I were so inclined." He angled his head and planted his hands on his hips. "For once, could you humor me? Come stay at the villa or let me get you a hotel room."

She wanted to touch his arm to reassure him, but fought the impulse by moving to the small dining table in the corner near the kitchen and taking a seat. "Today was a difficult day for you and I can tell that you've been drinking." She held up a hand to stop him from arguing. "Not that you're not entitled. Go home. Get some sleep. We'll talk tomorrow."

"Have you noticed anything unusual in your apartment? Items moved? Come home to lights on that shouldn't have been?" He surveyed the room before returning his attention to her. "Anyone in the building who doesn't belong, or anyone new you keep bumping into at the grocery store or restaurants?"

It was as if he'd never heard her suggestion that he go home. She stifled the urge to roll her eyes, knowing it'd only make him more agitated.

"No one is following me, Rocco. Why would they? Only a few friends know who I am. To everyone else here, I'm anonymous." Years ago, it would've been a different story. When she was go-get-'em Olympian Justine Flyte of Lake Tahoe, not boring Justine Cornaro of Dubrovnik.

His eyes darted to the kitchen window.

"It's locked," she said. "So's the one in my bedroom. I'll turn on the alarm if that makes you feel better, but I'm not going to pack up and leave just because your imagination is running away with you. It's not like I could find a hotel room at this hour, anyway."

Besides, she had business to attend to tomorrow. If plans went her way, it could turn her life around. No more hiding out in a tiny apartment a continent away from home. No more late-night visits from a man who could never truly love her. A man with secrets he refused to acknowledge existed, let alone share with anyone aside from his mother and siblings. Even Kos didn't seem to know his longtime employer's true nature.

"How'd you get here, anyway?" she asked. Her apartment was near the edge of Dubrovnik's medieval old town, which made finding a parking spot akin to winning the lottery. "Is Kos circling the neighborhood, waiting for us to come out?"

"He's on vacation. I walked."

"That's three or four miles. Are you crazy?" Or was he that intoxicated?

And since when did Kos take a vacation?

"As you said, it was a difficult day for me. I needed the air and time to think. I'll get a taxi back to the villa, but only if you come with me." He gave her a long look. "It's probably an overabundance of caution, but it can't hurt. Please?"

She wasn't sure whether it was the rare "please" or the concern in his soft brown eyes that did it, but she pushed back from the table. "Fine. But separate bedrooms, and I need to be out early tomorrow."

"Why?"

"You don't get to ask why."

"Justine, it's a matter of—"

"Safety. I know, I know." He should be damned grateful she'd agreed to come at all. She'd had her reasons for moving out, and Rocco's desire to know all about her while revealing so little of himself topped the list.

Pain shot through her left leg as she pushed to stand, but she waved off Rocco's assistance as he leapt to help her. It happened from time to time, especially when she'd put in a tough session at the rehab clinic, as she had this morning. And that was before standing for a solid hour at the cemetery and then going out to dinner with her girlfriends.

"You quit taking your pain meds?"

This time she did roll her eyes. "I agreed to come with you. I didn't give you permission to play twenty questions. Now let me pack a bag before I change my mind."

Rocco grumbled his irritation, but strode to the sofa and seated himself to wait. He began dialing his cell phone—presumably for a taxi—so she turned and went to her bedroom, closing the door behind her for a moment of privacy. The man was blindingly attractive, even in his current state. It was in her best interest to spend as little time in his presence as possible.

She walked through the darkened bedroom to her bathroom, flicked on the light, and arranged her essentials in her makeup bag. After mentally running through her morning routine to ensure she had everything she needed, she returned to the bedroom to change out of her nightgown and grab the clothes she'd already laid out for tomorrow. Rocco would wonder why she packed a suit, but she'd deal with that in the morning.

She reached for the bedside lamp at the same time a floorboard creaked behind her. She spun to see a man step through her bedroom window from the fire escape. She jerked, her hand halfway inside the lampshade as she reached for its pull chain, and inhaled to scream for Rocco.

"Don't make a sound. And don't turn on that lamp."

Shocked, she let her hand fall to her side. The man was huge, his voice rough and low. He remained in the shadows near her window, rendering his features unreadable, but there was no mistaking the dark barrel of the gun he held.

It pointed straight at her chest.

CHAPTER 3

TERROR THREATENED to buckle Justine's knees. "Who—"

"Not. One. Sound." The accented words were dark, lethal. The man stepped closer, affording Justine a better view of his face. Savage scars riddled his left cheek. The lack of light kept his eyes too shaded for Justine to read, but the set of his broad jaw proved he meant business. "We are going out the window and down the fire escape. A car is waiting at the bottom. You will get in the back seat. You will move to the center. You will put on the seat belt. If you resist at any point" — his shoulders lifted— "you will die on the street and I will throw your bloody body into the car myself."

The manner in which he uttered the instructions made it clear he meant every word. As if he'd done this a dozen times and knew every thought going through her head, could thwart any argument, could anticipate every escape attempt.

"Do we have an understanding, Mrs. Cornaro?"

She nodded, then held her hands palms out in surrender before pointing to a pair of sweatpants she'd left on the corner of the bed. He tipped his head, giving her permission to pull on the pants underneath her nightgown. Despite the mind-numbing fear that sent tremors through her entire body as he watched her step into one leg, then the other, she forced herself to dress slowly. The self-defense experts she'd seen on television said to do anything possible *not* to climb into a car with a potential assailant. Once you did, your odds of surviving dwindled.

Not that stalling would help her. The streets were empty. No one would see the man shove her in a vehicle. Her neighbors were likely asleep and wouldn't hear her on the fire escape. Screaming was out of the question; she'd be dead before they could react.

Then there was Rocco. He wouldn't hear a thing over the music playing in the living room. If he knocked on the door to hurry her along, what could he possibly do other than get himself killed?

She swallowed hard as the gunman angled a look at the window, silently instructing her to climb out. Was this the danger Rocco warned her about? Was Rocco *responsible* for this man's appearance in her bedroom?

Justine took a step toward the fire escape, sliding her feet into the moccasin slippers at her bedside without asking. At least with the moccasins on, she could try to flee when she reached the street. Two years ago, she could've escaped this hoodlum with both arms tied behind her back. He was gigantic and thick with muscle, but she doubted he possessed her agility and speed.

That was then. Now she didn't have a chance in hell of outrunning him, let alone his bullets.

If she got out of this in one piece, she'd throttle Rocco.

"You have thirty seconds to get down those stairs," the man growled. For the first time, she pinpointed his accent. She'd been so petrified at the man's appearance in her room she hadn't processed the fact he was Russian. As she straddled the open windowsill and put one foot on the metal fire escape that led to the building's back alley, he added, "Make it quiet. If you alert anyone in the apartments below yours, I will shoot them first, then you."

ROCCO PLUCKED an apple from the dish on Justine's kitchen counter, gave it a quick scrub against his dress shirt, then took a bite. He'd waited on Justine's sofa long enough for his stomach to rumble, the gurgling echoing over Justine's music. A second, more painful rumble reminded him he hadn't eaten since yesterday evening. He hadn't been able to stomach breakfast this morning and the desserts well-wishers offered after the graveside service didn't appeal.

He filched a napkin from an open package on top of Justine's hip-height refrigerator and swiped it across his chin before taking another huge bite. Suddenly, he needed food like a man who'd been left to starve on a barren island.

What was taking the woman so long? Was she putting on makeup? He couldn't fathom it. When they'd lived together, Justine was always ready in minutes.

A muffled scrape of wood interrupted his train of thought. Rocco paused mid-crunch, straining to hear. It sounded like the window being closed, but he'd looked up at Justine's as he'd approached her apartment building from the alley, trying to determine whether she was awake. He could swear that window was already closed, and she'd claimed it was locked.

He tossed the rest of the apple in the trash, then knocked on her bedroom door. Silence.

Irritation flared. He knocked again. "Justine?"

He waited for a count of three, then opened the door. Nothing stirred. The bathroom was empty. The window was raised about an inch, as if she'd attempted to close it from the outside. She was gone.

A four-letter word slipped from his lips. He'd grossly underestimated the level of distrust Justine had in him.

He strode through the darkened bedroom to follow her down the fire escape, but paused before opening the window as his brain registered what he'd seen in the bathroom. As he backtracked to the bathroom for confirmation, his heart chilled.

Justine's pink- and brown-striped makeup bag sat on the edge of the porcelain sink, its sides bulging and zipper pulled shut. She wouldn't have packed it and left it behind.

Covering the room in quick steps, he returned to the window and looked down without opening it. A black sedan, its headlights dimmed, idled in the alley underneath the fire escape. He couldn't see Justine, but he could hear the low clang of the metal steps as someone —no, multiple someones—descended the fire escape floor by floor.

Even as his mind screamed *no, no, no,* instinct sent him springing over Justine's bed, through the apartment, and down the stairwell that led to the street. Fear twisted his gut as he rounded each floor, using the iron railings to propel himself forward, past the apartments that occupied the floors below hers. After what seemed an eternity, he reached the front entry and released the heavy lock.

As he exited to the street and circled the building, Rocco forced himself to slow down, keeping his steps silent. If he could sneak up behind the car before it left the alley, perhaps he could surprise them. Give Justine a chance to get away, not that she had speed on her side. At the final corner, Rocco took a deep breath and waited, ears straining, hoping he could differentiate the sounds of human movement in the alley from the usual nighttime noises of the city. For a moment, all he heard was the rush of water under a nearby sewer grate and the far-off chug of a train. Finally, he was rewarded with the click of a car door opening, then the sound of feet against cobblestone. Twenty, maybe thirty feet away.

Crouching, he hazarded a look around the building. Justine was being forced to the bottom of the fire escape at gunpoint. If Rocco wasn't mistaken, the weapon was held by none other than the brutal Russian, Anton Karpovsky.

Terror iced Rocco's veins.

When he'd looked his mother in the eye a little over a year ago and noticed a yellow haze there, he'd experienced the same deep fear. He'd known instantly that her liver wasn't functioning and that she'd kept her condition a secret from him, which meant it was serious enough to kill her. Horrified as he was, he'd also known precisely what actions to take. He was able to tap the right experts, call in favors, get her the medications necessary to give her energy and meaningfully prolong her life.

This battle was more immediate, the enemy far less predictable. Years spent in design laboratories wouldn't help him. He had no weapons, no military training. Boxing done with his trainer was strictly for fitness, not fighting. Yet Justine was alone, with no idea what was happening to her or why, and no means to combat a lethal enemy.

Worse, it was *his fault*.

He pressed his back to the wall, mustering his strength. Resources or no, if he didn't save Justine, no one would.

UNABLE TO DELAY THE INEVITABLE, Justine stepped off the fire escape and moved to the side, allowing the gunman to follow her onto the street. She refused to look at the black vehicle idling in front of her. If she kept her focus on the gunman and acted as if politeness was her habit, she might convince him that she planned to cooperate fully.

The instant he dropped his guard, she'd run, leg be damned. Better to be shot here than trapped somewhere far from civilization where she had no chance at escape.

"So deferential, Mrs. Cornaro," he mocked her. "You make this easy."

"Too easy," came a voice from the other side of the sedan. "Get her in the car."

Justine swiveled her gaze toward the man standing beside the driver's door. Even in the hazy yellow light of the alley, his dark eyes shone like those of a bird of prey. A lean, curved nose added to the effect. He lacked his compatriot's breadth and muscle, but she suspected he made up for that shortcoming with his intelligence.

A taxi passed by at the corner, then slowed and flashed its turn signal as if headed to park in front of her building. The gunman put a rough hand on Justine's shoulder and shoved her toward the rear door on the sedan's passenger side at the same time the driver said, "Quickly. No witnesses."

"Please, no—"

"*Now*, you stupid bitch," the gunman snarled.

Panic set in as he opened the rear door. Justine braced her hands against the sedan's roof, ground her feet into the cobblestones despite the fiery sensation shooting through her bad leg, and shoved backward into the gunman with every ounce of her strength. "No! I'm not leaving! Shoot me here if you have to!"

She meant it. Her neighbors were out of danger. If she bled in the street, at least she had a chance of making it to a hospital. Not so if they strangled or shot her in some far-off cabin in the woods.

The man behind her muttered in Russian and tightened his grip on her shoulder as the driver snapped, "Don't let her fight. We need to get out of here."

It was the word *fight* that did it.

In the back of her mind, she once again heard the crowds that cheered her as she flew down the slopes, heading toward the finish line in a tight crouch at breakneck speed.

Flyte! Flyte! Flyte!

It was the roar—so like the playground chants spurring kids to fight—that pulled Justine out of her own head during races and sent her hurtling toward the finish line, to hell with the risk of a wipeout. All or nothing. Win or lose. Go big or go home. It was the roar that drove her to the podium at World Cup events. It made her who she was.

She sent her elbow into the man's gut with no compunction, then ducked, hoping to skirt around him while he was off balance, but the man didn't move. He was impenetrable as a wall. She tried again, aiming lower, even as his bicep curled around her throat, constricting her airway, and the cold steel of his gun pressed against her temple.

This time, she connected with soft tissue and was rewarded with a gratifying *whuumpf*. In the next second, he dragged her to the ground with him. Knowing it was her only chance, she kicked hard and shoved at his arm, then scrambled to move her body away from his. A glimpse underneath the car made her realize she had only seconds before the driver made his way around to assist. Faster than her mind could process it, a second set of feet appeared on the driver's side of the car, then there were two men on the ground.

"Justine! Go!"

Rocco. Gratitude flooded through her even as she was hit with the sickening realization he was in danger of losing his life. She yanked her ankles free of the kidnapper's grasp and yelled, "Watch out! They have guns!"

"Run, dammit!" A grunt punctuated the order.

She stumbled to the front of the car, but searing pain in her leg blackened her vision, forcing her to lean against the hood in an attempt to regain her equilibrium. Her eyesight cleared just in time to see her assailant push up off the ground. She took two steps toward him and slammed the open car door against his head, then turned and ran straight into a hard, firm body. Strong hands wrapped around her forearms. A scream formed in her throat, but died when she realized the man who grabbed her wasn't the driver, but Rocco.

She blinked at him in confusion. "Where's the—"

"Run." Blood oozed down the side of his face from a cut on his temple, but he seemed unaware of it as he propelled her down the alley. A *shoop* sounded near her ear, then a fist-sized section of wall exploded from the building beside her, sending white chunks of stucco flying through the air.

They were shooting. Why in the world would someone *shoot* her?

She tried to slow as gut instinct told her to surrender, but Rocco's firm grip on her arm kept her moving forward. He rounded the corner, then turned onto the street fronting her apartment, pulling her along beside him. She took an odd step to keep from hitting the curb. The move sent pain knifing through her leg.

He guided her across the street, then cut to another alley, one that led to an area filled with popular sidewalk cafés and restaurants. When Rocco glanced over his shoulder for signs of pursuit, he must have seen her pained expression, because his steps faltered and he released her arm.

She shook her head and waved for him to keep going. "It hurts, but better that than to get killed. They won't call it a night 'til they find us." Bravado fueled her words more than ability. If it hadn't been for Rocco's supportive hold, she might've limped back into her apartment to call the police. An idiotic proposition, given that the men had weapons and had gotten through a locked window easily enough the first time. They'd be inside her apartment again long before the police could arrive.

"I'll get us somewhere safe as soon as I can."

"That'd be ideal."

Rocco took her hand and changed direction, leading Justine away from the strip of darkened restaurants before steering her toward a familiar stone bridge. A twenty-something woman in a short skirt sat on its edge, her legs intertwined with those of a man whose nose was pressed to hers. She clung to the back of his leather jacket and smiled in the way of new lovers before she angled her head for a kiss.

"The Old City?" Justine's question emerged in a huff as Rocco hustled her onto the long, wide bridge, which led over a dry moat to Dubrovnik's famous Pila Gate.

"They can't bring their car. It's our best chance to lose them."

They hurried past the entangled couple, who didn't glance up despite the odd appearance of two panicked people sprinting across the bridge in the middle of the night, one of whom wore a flapping blue nightgown over a pair of sweatpants.

Once Rocco and Justine entered the arched gate, they found themselves on the Stradun, the neighborhood's main pedestrian street. In the daytime, tourists jammed its length and breadth to window shop, eat ice cream cones, and gawk at the medieval architecture inside the ancient city walls. At this hour, the Stradun was silent aside from the echo of their footfalls against the cobblestones. Metal grates covered shop windows, tarps blanketed kiosks, and even the stray cats that frequented the area in search of dropped tidbits had nestled away for the night. Only the soft yellow glow of street lamps hinted at life.

As one, Rocco and Justine turned down the first side street, then quickly turned onto another, twisting through the narrow maze until they entered an empty plaza and slowed to a walk. They kept to the perimeter, away from the street lights. As with the Stradun, the plaza was quiet as death. A dog lazing on the steps of a church cracked his eyes at their appearance, but closed them when he saw they posed no threat.

"Think we're all right?" Justine let go of Rocco's hand and leaned against the wall of a shuttered bakery, taking in lungfuls of air. She hadn't run—really run—since her accident. While she'd known her leg was a wreck, she hadn't realized how badly her cardiac fitness had deteriorated. Rehab sessions hadn't quite prepared her for this.

Rocco sank to a crouch, resting his back against the wall beside her and planting his forearms on his knees. His head angled back as his breathing slowed. "For now. I don't think they saw us go over the bridge. Even if they did, it would've been from their car. They would've had to find a place to ditch it."

Justine nodded. Once her breathing finally regulated, she asked, "Where to now?"

Rocco checked his watch. "Nearly two a.m. Odds of finding a hotel are nil."

"A hotel?" She gawked at him in disbelief as he pushed to stand. "I was thinking more along the lines of the nearest police station. Those guys were—"

Rocco's eyes widened and he reached for her arm to silence her. A heartbeat later, she heard it, too: a rough voice coming from one of the streets on the opposite side of the plaza, accompanied by the heavy sound of shoes slapping stone.

"Quick." He cut sideways into another tight street, past several medieval buildings and a small fenced garden. To Justine's surprise, he stopped short and tested the latch on the garden gate. When it didn't give, he interlaced his fingers to create a stirrup. "Up."

"If it's them, we'll be trapped—"

"We can't keep running. Go."

CHAPTER 4

THERE WASN'T time for further argument. Justine stepped into the pocket Rocco created and let him propel her over the fence so she landed on her good leg. He followed, pausing for a moment to untangle his pants from decorative ironwork before landing beside her. They crept to the back of the garden, tucked themselves amongst a darkened row of bushes, and braced their backs against the stone wall of the building that served as the garden's rear border. Branches scratched at Justine's face and arms, but she didn't care. All that mattered was that they survive the night.

Approaching voices made her draw in a sharp breath. She stole a sideways glance at Rocco. Shadows made his expression difficult to read, but the tense set of his shoulders as he crouched beside her in the thick foliage proved he shared her fear. As if sensing her need for reassurance, Rocco turned his head and pressed a silent kiss to her temple before he grabbed her hand and held it against his thigh.

Frozen in place, they waited. It didn't take long to realize the sounds belonged to the men who'd attempted to kidnap her. The section of the street visible through the garden fence remained empty, but the low, angry instructions hissed back and forth were unmistakable. The Russians were getting closer.

"The kids on the bridge," Rocco whispered in her ear. "I bet they told the men we went this way."

He let go of Justine's hand and pulled her body to his so she was in a tight ball against the front of his chest, making the two of them as small as possible. Her leg throbbed and her foot began to cramp, but her position prevented her from moving without making noise. Tears formed at the edges of her eyes as her body screamed with the need to shake out her foot, but she remained still. She reminded herself of her earlier statement to Rocco: better to hurt now than be killed. Because if those men heard her, she and Rocco would both die.

Bright light pierced the blackness of the garden as the narrow beam of a flashlight swept through the iron fence to illuminate a set of worn wooden benches. After a pause, it moved left of their hiding place, going stone by stone over the wall of an adjacent building. Bushes ran along the wall's base and a statue of the Virgin Mary stood at a break in the greenery. An unlit candle rested at her feet.

Rocco's stomach chose that moment to emit a loud, rolling gurgle. His arms tensed as the light jerked, then arced in their direction. Justine's breath threatened to burst from her lungs as the brilliant beam crept over the bushes, then stopped a few feet to their left. After what seemed an eternity, it moved again, passing over them and continuing to the wall forming the garden's other boundary. A fat calico cat yowled before turning away from the intruder who'd deigned to disturb its sleep. The light moved the rest of the way around the garden, then returned to a tree near the cat. The light slid up the tree, spotlighting the large branches one by one. It remained idle for a moment as the men conversed, then the garden plunged into darkness. A metallic clang rang through the night as one of the men rattled the gate and found it locked.

Rocco's fingers dug into the flesh of Justine's arm. They hadn't been spotted, but they were far from safe. The men remained near the gate. Justine couldn't understand a word they said, but the gist of their hushed discussion was clear. They'd heard Rocco and Justine fleeing the plaza and knew they were close. Both thought they'd heard the jolt of a metal gate or fence being touched. They doubted it could've been caused by the cat, but weren't sure what to make of it.

Without moving a muscle, Justine strained to see through the gloom. The scarred man who'd entered her bedroom stood with his back to the gate. Though Justine couldn't see his face, he showed no signs of having taken a hard elbow to his privates or being struck by the car door. He stood tall, shoulders squared, with his gun holstered easily at his hip. If she and Rocco were forced to run again, he'd have no trouble giving chase.

The burly man shifted, affording Justine a better view of the driver. Blood caked the area under his curved nose and streaked across his right cheek, as if he'd attempted to wipe it away. Given the dim glow of the streetlights, it was impossible to tell for sure, but his nose appeared broken. He tapped away at a cell phone screen, then angled his head toward the plaza, urging the larger man to follow.

"Keep still," Rocco murmured into her hair as the men's footsteps faded. "If they suspect we're here, they'll double back."

She nodded against Rocco's chest, unwilling to risk a spoken response. Her leg and foot ached as they hadn't since she'd awakened from the surgery following her accident. She closed her eyes and concentrated on keeping her breathing even in an effort to mitigate the pain. In and out, in and out.

All it did was make her more aware of Rocco.

The scent of his warm skin permeating the fabric of his dress shirt. The faint tinge of Scotch on his breath. More gurgling from his stomach. The rapid yet steady beat of his heart near her ear. The solid muscle of his arm at the back of her waist. His hand on the outside of her thigh, keeping her from toppling sideways out of the bushes. The strange brush of his new beard grazing her forehead.

She'd thought him intoxicated when he knocked on her door. As he held her now, she realized it was concern rather than inebriation that had caused his agitated hands-in-pockets stance as he entered her apartment and begged her to leave so she'd be safe from a danger he wouldn't name.

Questions flooded her brain. Who in the world were the Russians?

Why did they want her? Did Rocco know they were coming? How did he find her in the alley?

"I know it hurts. Another minute or two and you can change position," he whispered. "We'll leave soon."

She nodded again and continued to breathe—just breathe—two counts in, two counts out. He tightened his arms around her and lifted so he bore more of her weight, which eased the pressure on her legs.

This was the Rocco she met all those years ago. The protective, loving Rocco she married. The man who didn't give a rip about her fame, her medal count, or her endorsement deals. The man who smelled so damned amazing, despite having spent the day burying his mother and the night sprinting through the streets of Dubrovnik's Old City.

The man with so many secrets.

She exhaled in one long whoosh. If he'd brought this hell upon her, she'd kill him.

WIND RUSTLED the leaves of the lone tree in the convent's rear garden.

The stray cat nestled near its trunk stretched, yawned, then meandered to the middle of the garden. It sprang to the seat of a wooden bench and resettled, only to rise again when a discarded grocery bag blew into the fence. The cat glowered at the flapping plastic, then leapt from the bench, squeezed between the iron rails as far from the ensnared bag as possible, and disappeared into the city streets.

In front of Rocco, Justine's shoulders expanded and contracted with the measured rhythm of her breathing. He marveled that she'd held still for so long, especially given her injury. A lifetime of elite-level training had given her a mental toughness few possessed. Still, much as he wanted to wait another ten or fifteen minutes to be certain Radich and Karpovsky were gone, he suspected even Justine's stamina wasn't infinite.

With any luck, Radich had crawled into a small, dark hole to put an ice pack on his face and Karpovsky had gone with him.

"I'm going to look. If the coast is clear, I'll wave you out."

Rocco felt more than heard Justine mumble into his shirt. Taking it as assent, he released her upper body and eased away from her, then picked his way out of the bushes and crept along the grass to the fence. He saw no movement, heard nothing out of the ordinary. He leaned over the fence to ensure no one was on the street, then turned to signal for Justine only to discover she was already tiptoeing across the grass toward him. She moved awkwardly, one shoulder higher than the other, but her grimace of pain disappeared when she caught him studying her.

"Figured it was safer to make noise once instead of twice."

Since he hadn't heard her behind him, he wasn't about to tell her she should've stayed put.

Her gaze went to the gate. "Think we can unlock it from the inside instead of climbing?"

"Let's hope."

It took less than ten seconds to locate the latch and cautiously open the gate. After another check to ensure the area was empty, they stepped into the street, then turned in the direction opposite the one in which the men had gone. Keeping to the shadows, Rocco guided Justine toward the city walls while pulling his cell phone from his back pocket to call a taxi. "I'll have it meet us a few blocks outside the Old City. I hate to ask, but are you going to be able to make it that far?"

"Don't have a choice unless I plan to sleep here, and I don't."

An *I'm sorry* nearly popped out of his mouth before he thought better of it. Justine must have a million questions; apologizing to her before he could explain the night's events wouldn't serve either of them. Not that he could explain, even if he tried.

He got through to a taxi service and made arrangements for the pickup. When asked for his destination, he provided the address of a villa uphill from his own.

Justine said nothing. She remained silent for the rest of their walk through the Old City, then for the entirety of the ride. Only her eyes seemed to move, constantly checking the taxi's rearview mirror to see if anyone followed them. It wasn't until Rocco paid the driver and the vehicle's taillights disappeared that she turned to him.

He expected a demand to know the identity of their pursuers, why the men attempted to kidnap her, or why Rocco had the cab drop them off a few houses away from his own. Instead, what came out of her mouth was a flip, "When you told me I was in danger, did you have the slightest inkling I'd spend my Tuesday night running through the Old City in my pjs?"

"It's technically Wednesday."

She crossed her arms over her chest and angled her face to the stars, as if silently pleading for help from the heavens. "I'm technically going to kill you if you don't give me a full explanation, beginning with" —her look turned direct and venomous— "what...the...hell?"

"I'd love to, but I can't." Before she could make good on her promise, he held up a hand. "Not entirely. And doing so while standing in front of my neighbor's house at this hour isn't exactly wise."

"God forbid we do anything unwise tonight."

He'd earned that, he supposed. Calmly, he said, "Before we talk, I want to check out the villa to make sure it's secure and pick up a few things. Then we're both getting out of here to someplace safe."

"How about we get to the *police*?"

"We will." Eventually. Once he figured out what in the world he'd tell them...and how he'd answer their inevitable questions without blowing his entire life—and those of his siblings—to shreds.

"Now?"

"Soon."

"Of course. Soon. We've been shot at, chased, beaten—you're still *bleeding*, for Pete's sake—but hey, let's go to the villa first." Despite her anger, she kept her voice down. "I could give you a thousand other arguments, but since I'm in moccasins, sweats, and a nightgown with no money and no phone, I don't suppose I'd win any of them." She swooped a hand in the direction of his villa. "Let's go."

He wasn't going to give her a chance to reconsider. He strode through a stand of trees to approach his villa from the rear, keeping his pace slow for Justine's sake. Behind him, she continued to mutter. Finally, he swung around and asked, "What are you mumbling about?"

"I said, 'good thing I still have on my bra. Too bad it wasn't made by Nike.'"

He turned back toward the villa, refusing to rise to the bait. She had every right to be angry. She was hurt and tired and had no idea what was happening. But he was angry, too.

A man shouldn't have to bury his mother, deal with his biological father's spouse, and defend his estranged wife from gunfire all in a twenty-four hour period. And—he pressed a hand to his temple and realized that Justine was right, he was still bleeding—he shouldn't have to pound his fists into another man's face.

The stone wall surrounding his property materialized in front of them. He stopped and used his cell phone to access his surveillance system. All was in order. Nevertheless, he approached the rear gate with his senses on alert and gave the back yard a thorough scan before disengaging the locks and going in.

"You think they might come here?" Justine's question was barely audible as she slipped through the gate behind him.

"It's not out of the question." He led her through the back door, then up the wide staircase to the master bedroom without turning on the lights. They both knew the villa well enough to move through it in the dark. The bedroom, in particular.

"There's aspirin and ibuprofen in the medicine cabinet."

She ignored his offer, tracking his movements instead. "You're packing a bag."

"I told you, we're going to go somewhere safe. Then we both need to sleep." He could feel her argument coming and cut it off. "We can't deal with the police when we're this tired. Chances are your neighbors called when they heard gunfire and the police are already on it."

"In that case, chances are I could go back to my apartment and sleep in my own bed."

"Justine." Two simple syllables carried the weight of his fatigue, both physical and mental.

She slumped into the chair in the corner. It wasn't like her to give up during an argument, which solidified his decision to prioritize sleep. They were both exhausted and on edge. He strode to the bathroom to grab his shaving kit, then rummaged in a drawer to find a toiletry pack he'd received a few weeks earlier on a flight. It didn't have makeup, but it'd provide Justine with the basics. He threw in the aspirin and ibuprofen along with antibiotic ointment and a few bandages before returning to the bedroom.

Justine's eyes were closed. Long wisps of hair had fallen across her face. Before he could reach out to wake her, she asked, "Where are we going?"

"I'm thinking."

"Think faster."

"Follow me."

Sliding one backpack strap over his shoulder, he went to the study and accessed its hidden safe. He couldn't risk having anyone—the police or the Russians—go through his private materials. After stuffing the papers and memory stick in his backpack and adding his laptop computer, he remembered the cornflower blue box Queen Fabrizia had left behind. If anyone entered the study, he didn't want them to find it and question its origin. He withdrew it from his desk drawer without looking inside and added it to the backpack.

"Ready?"

She nodded, though he could see she was fighting to stay on her feet. With a glance out the window to ensure all remained quiet, Rocco turned and took the stairs down to the garage. Bypassing the cars, which he assumed Karpovsky and Radich could identify, he grabbed the old Vespa his sister Lina had asked him to store. Justine didn't argue as he slipped the backpack onto her shoulders and urged her to climb on behind him. After checking the gas gauge, he eased it out of the garage and took an indirect route to the marina, where he parked the Vespa behind a row of trash cans.

"I'm not spending the night on your yacht."

"Too dangerous," he agreed. "We're going to my stepfather's boat instead."

"That's not what I meant." She paused. "Wait…I didn't know Jack had a boat."

"My mother planned to sell it after he passed away." Of course, she'd never gotten around to it. "Kos has arranged for maintenance, so it should be in good shape."

"Rocco—"

"It's a place to sleep. We'll deal with the rest tomorrow."

She stared at him, indecision clouding her light blue eyes before she slung the backpack at his chest. "First thing in the morning, I'm going to the cops."

CHAPTER 5

ROCCO CORNARO WAS a momma's boy.

Justine hadn't known that when she met him, of course. One didn't discover such character traits during early evening conversation at a ski bar in the storybook setting of Garmisch-Partenkirchen, Germany. Or even the next day, after being tossed out of the same bar at closing time, talking for yet another hour beside the fire in her hotel lobby, then experiencing mind-blowing sex with a sensual, attractive, well-built man whose world view and manner of speaking made it clear he was no ordinary ski bum. A man who, unlike the other men who'd pursued her, wasn't the least bit interested in managing her career or stealing a piece of her spotlight. Rocco was well traveled, confident, astute, and possessed an inner calm that most men she knew lacked. Likely because he was eight years her senior, an age gap that suited her just fine.

In Rocco, she finally found a man who valued a woman with a strong sense of self. A woman who pursued her Olympic and World Cup goals with as much passion as he pursued his scientific ones, who understood his desire to make his mark on the world. A woman with whom he shared off-the-charts sexual chemistry. A woman who found his design work interesting rather than dull, and who didn't ask a lot of questions about his family.

Of course, that was the point upon which their relationship eventually splintered.

They married in Aspen between World Cup events a few short months after that first meeting. Only Justine's parents, Rocco's mother, and Rocco's siblings Enzo and Lina had attended. The Cornaros flew home after the simple mountainside ceremony. Justine's parents gifted the newlyweds a bottle of expensive champagne and the key to a ritzy hotel suite, then left with an abundance of happy tears and hugs.

Rocco and Justine proceeded to get plowed, laugh their heads off over the fact their wedding was the least-planned event in either of their highly scheduled lives, and make slow, passionate love for the next two days, until Justine had to leave for an event in Grenoble and Rocco flew to Boston for a meeting with a venture capital group interested in funding his work.

Over the next three years, they spent enough time apart to miss each other madly—Justine training and competing on the World Cup circuit, Rocco busy in various research labs or traveling to medical conferences—and enough time together in hotels around the world to fall more deeply in love without having to adjust to each other's inevitable faults.

It wasn't until she and Rocco decided to establish a home base in Croatia, where his mother had settled after Jack Cornaro retired and Rocco had recently purchased a villa and rented lab space, that the faults became apparent.

Teresa Cornaro had an inexplicable hold over her eldest child. And Rocco could not—or would not—explain why. At first, Justine attributed Teresa's odd, possessive behavior toward Rocco to the fact she'd lost her husband shortly before Rocco and Justine married. But then there were the hushed conversations when mother and son were together. The suspicious manner in which Teresa studied Justine when she thought Justine wasn't looking. Teresa's insistence that Rocco skip the most high profile of Justine's races, stating that it would keep the limelight on Justine's skiing rather than her personal life.

Justine could've understood the sentiment if it'd come from Rocco. Coming from Teresa, the edict pushed Justine's weirdness buttons.

Then there was Teresa's pointed suggestion that Justine keep her condo in Tahoe when Justine had offhandedly mentioned putting it on the market. Only after Justine explained that there was no point now that she and Rocco were married did Teresa explain with over-played sincerity that she thought it'd be a smart long-term investment.

When Teresa's liver disease became evident to Rocco, he moved his mother into the villa without telling Justine in a case of take-action-first, apologize later. Though Justine felt a deep sense of betrayal—after all, she'd left the tour only two weeks earlier to conva-lesce from her skiing injury—she let Rocco's actions slide, knowing the situation would be temporary. Teresa was dying; there was no denying it, only delaying it, and it made Rocco feel as if he had a sliver of control over the situation. And at that point, Justine had convinced herself that she'd be skiing again in no time, doctors and prognosis be damned.

But one late spring afternoon—the first following her accident where she felt healed enough to venture out alone on foot— she walked into the villa with an armload of groceries and paused on the way to the kitchen when she spotted Teresa and Rocco standing in front of an Italian entertainment news broadcast. A photo of Sarcac-cia's Prince Stefano flashed on the screen. Whatever the announcer was saying, both Rocco and Teresa appeared riveted. In a good mood from her excursion and curious about the show, given that neither Rocco nor Teresa cared a whit for celebrity gossip, Justine entered the room behind them. Justine had barely translated the wording at the bottom of the screen—*secret love child*—only to have Teresa snap off the television. Neither Teresa nor Rocco would answer Justine's ques-tion about what they'd been watching.

It should've been a little thing—an offhanded thing—but the inten-sity of their expressions told a different story. Justine changed the subject by asking about Teresa's visit to the doctor the next day. Later that night, when she privately asked Rocco what had been on television and he gruffly told her to drop it, her patience ran out. She demanded that he tell her what they'd been watching. Why a freaking gossip show about foreign royalty was secret. Why everything about his mother was such a big secret.

He refused. She left.

He asked her to return once, a few days later when he showed up at her hotel room with a bottle of wine and dinner. He told her he missed her. They made love. Romantic, passionate love. But he didn't apologize. He said it was a private concern of his mother's and that he wouldn't betray her confidence.

Justine told him she missed him, too. She meant it with her whole heart. But she wouldn't move back to the villa. Not even when she was told during a follow-up appointment for her leg injury that her career was over. She'd wanted Rocco's comfort desperately that night, but she refused to let Teresa see her laid low. She refused to allow Rocco to console her knowing he'd never ask the same of her.

She found a short-term rental not far from the rehab center and moved in.

They'd been at an impasse for nearly a year now, neither of them wanting to let the other go...but neither of them able to move forward. While Justine hadn't hoped for Teresa's death, deep down she'd known that she needed to wait for it before making any decisions about her marriage or returning to the States.

Until a need to make a decision dropped into her lap in the form of a job interview. That's when she realized—Teresa or no Teresa—she needed to move on. If Rocco couldn't be honest with Justine about his mother—because as much as he swore it was his mother's issue, Justine knew it was Rocco's, too—what other secrets did he hold? Did he truly love her?

A low groan near Justine's ear woke her. She blinked, taking in the unfamiliar surroundings. A firm body curved behind hers, generating heat under the covers. A light rocking motion indicating she was on a boat. Memories of the previous night clicked into place. Shots. A menacing man in her bedroom, his cold, flat eyes staring her down.

Fleeing through the streets. The ache in her left leg. The suit she'd left behind in her apartment.

She flipped back the coverlet and flailed for a clock, even though she knew it was too late. The sun shone too brightly against the shaded portholes of the boat's lone room for her to have a chance of making the meeting.

"It's nine-thirty." The grit of sleep laced Rocco's voice. He'd dozed beside her in the boat's narrow bed, his arm draped over her hip as he'd done when they'd slept under the same roof.

She'd been too tired to object to the fact there was only one berth on board, having used the last of her energy to convince him to let her clean his head wound after they'd boarded. Her ministrations revealed a deep gouge where the driver caught Rocco with the metal band of his watch during their scuffle…at least, that was Rocco's drowsy guess as to what happened. He also speculated that it could've occurred when he tackled the guy.

He'd drifted off as she'd dabbed at the dried blood with a wet paper towel. She'd tucked the pillow under his head, studied the wound to be sure the bleeding stopped, and remembered nothing after that.

She plucked the blood-tinged paper towel from the tiny night table. Apparently she'd fallen asleep before she could throw it away. Before she could find a clock and set an alarm.

"Mind if I use your phone?"

"Gotta plug it in first. It's out of juice." Using his elbows, he pushed to sit and watch her. Hair over his left ear was spiked sideways and pillow lines crisscrossed that side his face. The phone showed a minimal charge and only a weak signal. "You calling the police?"

"I have an appointment this morning. I need to cancel."

"You can't tell them why."

At her side-eyed glare, he corrected himself. "Please don't tell them why. At least until I have a better handle on what happened last night."

"I wasn't going to. I prefer to talk to the police before I tell anyone else."

Before Rocco could say more, Justine's call went through. She left an apologetic message with the administrative assistant who'd arranged the job interview, explaining that she'd been unavoidably detained due to a family emergency. After she promised it was a short-term issue and expressed sincere regret, she ended the call.

"That sounded important." Rocco swiped a hand over his bearded chin and swung his legs over the side of the bed. To her surprise, Justine saw they were bare. He'd kicked off his shoes and discarded his bloodied dress shirt when they'd arrived on board, but had fallen asleep in his slacks. He must've awakened at some point during the night.

Now that she thought about it, he must've covered her while he was at it. She didn't remember burrowing under the coverlet.

"I'll reschedule." If she could. Given that the team conducting the interview stopped in Croatia specifically to meet with her while on their way back to New York from an assignment in Greece, she'd have to arrange a trip to the States. Assuming they'd give her a second chance.

Rumbles from Rocco's stomach were audible as he rummaged through his backpack and withdrew a pair of jeans and a heather blue T-shirt for himself, then handed her an airline toiletry kit. She flashed back to the noise she'd heard from his stomach while they'd been hiding in the garden. "You didn't eat yesterday, did you?"

"Had an apple last night."

"Before we do anything else, let's get food. Then I need to brush my teeth and find clothes other than these." She'd rather not wear dirty sweats and a nightgown to the police station.

"Food's easy. Kos keeps a few essentials on board, though it's nothing grand. And check the storage space under the bed. Some of the clothes might fit you." He eyed the moccasins she'd kicked off next to the bed. As some point last night, the stitching had come apart on the side of one. "Can't help with shoes, though."

She bent down to open the drawer, hoping she didn't sound ungrateful as she asked, "Your mother's?"

"Lina's. When she visited last summer, she stayed here instead of at the villa so she could go island-hopping along the coast. Accidentally left a few things behind."

While Rocco checked out the mini-fridge and cabinet to see what Kos had stocked, Justine found a sundress, a pair of jeans, two T-shirts and a hooded sweatshirt. "You never sent them back to her?"

"I offered, but she said she'd pick them up next time she was in town." He located a carton of Parmalat and an unopened box of cereal. "Guess she forgot after the funeral."

Mention of the funeral cast a pall over them both. "If I haven't said it yet, I'm sorry about your mother."

"You haven't, but you didn't exactly have the opportunity. Thank you." He handed her a bowl of cereal once she'd replaced her night-gown with the jeans and a T-shirt. The jeans were a little tight on her thighs, but passable, and better than the mud-stained sweatpants.

"Why'd you come to my mother's funeral?"

Justine nearly dropped her bowl at the unexpected question, though she should've known he'd seen her hiding near the tree. "I wanted to say goodbye."

"You and my mother weren't exactly bosom buddies."

Honesty time. "I wasn't there for her so much as for you. I wanted to say goodbye to you."

His rear end hit the chair harder than it should've as he took a seat across from her. Though his, "Really?" sounded perfectly calm, it came too late to hide the bone-deep pain that flashed in Rocco's eyes before he looked down at his cereal to pour milk and shovel in a bite. That quick look grabbed Justine by the gut and twisted her inside out. She wished there was a way to make this easier.

"That phone call? I had a job interview scheduled this morning. I suspect it's out of the question now, but the opportunity excited me enough that I'll pursue others."

"A job? Doing what?"

The disbelief in his voice rankled. "I'm capable of working, Rocco. I finished my degree during the off-seasons."

"I didn't say you weren't capable—"

"Your tone of voice did." She stirred the flakes, which held no appeal despite the hunger gnawing at her belly. "It's in broadcasting. I'd cover World Cup skiing and certain events at the Winter X Games."

"No one would be better." He took a bite of his cereal and considered her as he swallowed. "You'd be traveling again."

"Mostly in the States. Colorado, Utah, Tahoe. Not like when I was competing."

"You'd move back to Tahoe?"

"Moot point now." The network probably had a dozen other former winter athletes chomping at the bit for the job.

"You didn't want to talk it over with me first?"

Tension filled the confines of the boat's cabin. A move home meant divorce, and they both knew it. It was the one word they'd never said aloud. She hadn't been willing to broach the subject with Rocco until she had to.

"Rocco, there was no guarantee I'd get the job. But I didn't know how to…I mean…with all you've had going on—"

"Bull." Rocco's spoon clattered against the table and he reached for her hand. His fingers encircled hers. "I allowed issues with my mother to come between us. That's why you didn't feel you could talk to me. Not because I was distracted."

Justine allowed her eyes to drift closed for a moment and shook her head as Rocco caressed her thumb with his stronger one. She should pull away. But her heart missed the feeling of having him hold her hand. He'd always been her sanity. Her rock. Until he kept Teresa's secrets and made her feel like the third wheel in her own marriage.

"She's gone, Justine."

"Does it matter?" Even as the words left her mouth, Justine thought better of them. She looked apologetically at Rocco. Twin lines of exhaustion creased his brow and his hair was a dark, ruffled mess, but he contemplated her with the same golden-flecked light brown eyes she'd fallen for that night when they'd met in Garmisch. The night they'd talked about everything but the competition she'd just finished and the medical conference he was in town to attend. She'd known that night he was the most interesting, intelligent man she'd ever met. If anyone would get the better of her, it'd be Rocco Cornaro. She'd welcomed the challenge.

Until now. Now it hurt.

"That didn't come out right," she said. "What I meant is, no matter what my issues with Teresa, it doesn't address the deeper issue in our relationship."

"The horrid sex?" His fingers tightened fractionally around hers.

She couldn't help but grin at his attempt to lighten the mood.

"Trust, then."

"Trust," she acknowledged. "How can I talk to you when you won't talk to me? When you won't let me see who you are on the inside? What's truly going on in your life?"

"I'm trying to do that now."

Right. Rocco talked, but without touching upon what mattered. Unable to finish her breakfast, Justine slid her fingers from Rocco's and rinsed her bowl in the sink. It bought her time to breathe. Once she shut off the water and dried her hands, she spun to face him. She had so many questions. She started with one she hoped he could answer.

"Who were those men?"

CHAPTER 6

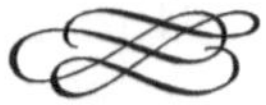

It was the question he'd been dreading since they fled down the alley, but it was easier to address than the question of their marriage.

"The skinny guy's name is Viktor Radich."

She blinked, apparently surprised that he had an answer. "The guy you took down?"

"You trying to make the point that you took down the big one?"

She shrugged, but he saw in her eyes that he'd given her ego a boost. "Maybe."

"Radich was the man I tackled. The one with the gun was Anton Karpovsky." Rocco leaned back in his chair. "He looked ready to throw up when we ran. What'd you do, knee him?"

"Elbow, but the same effect as a knee. Then I hit him with the car door." Her shoulders tensed and a dark look passed over her face. "Didn't stop him from shooting at us, though. Those were real bullets. He wanted to kill us."

"I don't think that was Plan A." It was as much comfort as he could offer under the circumstances.

"Could've fooled me. You know that guy came into my room while I was packing? Right through my locked window and pointed a gun at me as easily as you handed me that bowl of cereal. Like he'd done it so many times before, he was on autopilot."

A full-body shudder rocked Justine. Her pride at escaping such a powerful man evaporated as she spoke and the impact of the night's events settled over her. Rocco guided her to the bed. She needed to sit, to work the fear out of her system and realize she was safe, at least for the time being.

Once she settled, he put an arm around her shoulders, hoping a gentle touch would drain her tension. "Tell me exactly what happened."

She heaved out a breath. "I heard a noise by the window when I came out of the bathroom, and there he was. He let me put on my sweatpants and slippers first, but said if I made a sound on the fire escape, he'd shoot my neighbors. He would've done it, too. I don't know what those men wanted, but if he'd gotten me into that car, I might be dead now." She slid her gaze sideways. "They're Russian, aren't they? That's what the accents sounded like. The big guy, especially."

"I think they're Russian mafia. Or hired by the Russian mafia."

"Are you serious?" She fisted her hands against her thighs and turned to fully face him. He allowed his arm to slide from her shoulder and rested his hand on the bed beside her. "Wow. You are. You knew they were coming after me?"

"I didn't know if the threat was real."

"But you were warned. By whom? Them?"

"No, definitely not those two." Telling her the truth would open a can of worms he couldn't deal with at this very moment, not in addition to the threat of losing their marriage, or worse, their lives, if they didn't act quickly and sensibly right now. "But I don't know how much I trust the source."

"I'd say that source knew what they were talking about."

"On that point, apparently so." Nevertheless, he didn't trust Fabrizia. The woman's very existence had made his mother's life a living hell...at least until his mother found Jack Cornaro and the will to walk away from Carlo.

"Yet you won't tell me who."

"No."

Frustration thinned her lips. "All right, then. Why would the Russian mafia kidnap me? And why would whoever-it-is tell you instead of coming straight to me? I don't have the connections or the profile I used to, not like I did before my accident. I have a decent amount of money socked away from my endorsement deals, but it's not enough to tempt kidnappers."

"They wanted to get to me. To my newest designs." He stood, needing to pace, but the constricted cabin didn't allow for much movement. "Once they had you, they could bargain for my work. It's worth more than either of us could afford in ransom."

Her expression changed as understanding dawned. "There's too much security at the villa and your office to make you an easy target. That's why they came for me."

"Exactly." Justine had been there when he'd had the system installed. She understood that his net worth—the proceeds from his earlier medical devices and the reputation they had earned him in the medical community—made him a target for thieves.

"You know I've been working on a new pump," he told her. "As of last week, the designs are complete. I'm ready to move on to build the prototype and file the patent application. If it works—and I believe it will—it'll be a big step forward in controlling Type I diabetes. It'll be much better than current pumps in the accuracy with which it reads a patient's blood sugar levels, then self-dispenses the appropriate level of hormones. It'll also be less expensive to manufacture than current devices."

"I thought you were still months or even years away." Her eyebrows lifted. "You made a lot of progress."

"I haven't told you the best part." He couldn't keep the thrill from his voice. "It's small and it's simple. So small and simple that—if parents are given the right training in how to use it—it can work for toddlers. We've been after a reliable treatment method for toddlers for so long…I could die a happy man if this works."

"Rocco, that's incredible."

"Thank you." The look of genuine appreciation on her face—despite the fact he knew she was still angry with him—gave him hope. And, he had to admit, he wanted her to be proud of him. Of what he'd accomplished, of how many children his work could help. "Unfortunately, I'm apparently not the only one who knows its value. Radich was renting the office above mine. He's a computer guru and a surveillance expert, which means he was likely able to see or hear what I was doing, even if he couldn't get to the work itself."

"You think they'll try to break into your office?"

"If he was able to watch me, he'd know I rarely left anything of value overnight, and with my mother's funeral, I wouldn't be at my lab for several days. I kept the software and product design on a memory stick and stored it in the villa's safe. I have it in the backpack."

He could see the wheels spinning in Justine's head as she eyed the black bag in the corner of the cabin. "If they had that stick, they could copy your work and sell it."

He nodded. "There are certain countries where companies will pay dearly for medical technology without regard to the fact it's stolen. More than I'm worth. Those thieves would rather have my designs than any kidnap ransom I can afford."

"You don't think they'll stop looking for us, do you?"

"Not as things stand." He settled beside her on the bed once more, though he didn't touch her. "I've partnered with two of my professors from the Biomedical Engineering department at Johns Hopkins on the pump's development. They'll be responsible for building the prototype and starting the testing process. If we deliver the designs to them, it makes things much tougher for the Russians. First, it'll be harder to steal from the university than from me, even with all my security. Second, I can finalize the patent application. Once that's filed, the Russians' ability to command top dollar will disintegrate." He waved his hand like a magician concluding a magic trick. "Poof, the threat to us is gone."

Her gaze went to his backpack once again. "Since you have the laptop and the memory stick here, can you e-mail everything?"

"I'd never send it over e-mail. The laptop I use for design work isn't even connected to the Internet. Too vulnerable to hackers. It's possible that's why Radich was brought in on this job...to hack into my computer and steal the designs without me being aware of it." Rocco had been turning over possible solutions in his head ever since they boarded the boat, but there was only one. "We have to go to Baltimore. Deliver the designs in person."

Her eyes widened. "We?"

"It's the only way I'll know you're safe. If I were to leave without you—"

"I'd go straight to the police." This time, she put a hand on his knee. "I'll be perfectly safe."

"No."

She pulled away, disbelief clouding her gaze. "You don't even trust the police?"

"It's not about trust. Police are obliged to follow procedure, which means they'll focus first on what happened at your apartment last night. We'd spend hours being grilled about it—how I knew those men were coming, who warned me, what I know about them—and that won't decrease the risk to our safety. If anything, it'll put us in a place where it's easy for Radich and Karpovsky—and anyone else who's working with them—to find us. The minute we walk out of that station, we're sitting ducks."

"You're asking me to trust you" —her mouth pinched in anger— "yet you won't tell me how you knew I was about to be kidnapped. You don't want to go to the police—I know you're not giving me the full story there—and you still won't even tell me why you and your mother found a damned entertainment report fascinating. Yet you want me to follow you to Baltimore, without so much as my own toothbrush—"

"Not follow. Come with." He couldn't help but flash a grin. "And you can keep that toiletry kit, so you technically have your own toothbrush."

"Rocco—"

"I promise, no horrid sex."

"No sex at all!"

"Ouch." He faked a stab to the chest. "But acceptable if it means you'll come to Baltimore."

She crossed her arms. "I don't have my passport."

"It's in the backpack. You never took it to your apartment, remember? I brought both passports from the safe."

"You're too smart for your own damned good."

"Apparently, or the Russians wouldn't want my designs."

She raised her thumbs to her temples and massaged small circles, as if that would help her decide, and muttered, "I am really unhappy about this."

He kept quiet, allowing her to think. After a long moment, she dropped her hands and said, "I'll go with you to Baltimore on one condition. You tell me everything you know. About those Russians, about who warned you they were coming. About why the police make you hesitant. And about your mother."

"It's not that simple. There are other people involved. People with a lot to lose." As much as Rocco hated what Carlo had done to his mother, the king's other children didn't deserve to suffer the media storm that would occur if the truth were ever revealed. They'd done nothing wrong, and by all accounts, they were good, hardworking people. Prince Stefano even had children of his own...as Rocco learned from the entertainment report that'd spurred the argument with Justine in the first place.

"If I have to trust you, then you have to trust me enough to explain." Justine stood, then grabbed her slippers and discarded nightgown from the floor. "If you can't, I'm outta here. I'll take my chances with the police."

There was no mistaking the determination on her face. Short of tying her to the bed, he couldn't force her to stay.

He bit back an obscenity, then grabbed a hat and sunglasses so he could go above without being easily recognized. "Deal. We'll sail up to Split, then take the overnight ferry to Ancona, Italy, and travel from there. I don't want to use the Dubrovnik airport."

As he whipped open the cabin door, he turned to look at Justine over his shoulder and gauge her reaction. Her responding blue-eyed stare was intense, tenacious. It was the same look she always had in the starting gate as she dropped her goggles into place, seconds before pitching herself full-tilt down a dangerously steep slope.

She didn't know what she was asking of him. He was letting his heart rule his head by agreeing to her terms. The cost could be high, both to himself and to others, but he wouldn't risk having her harmed.

"When?"

He didn't pretend not to understand. "On the ferry. We need to get out of this marina. The sooner, the better."

CHAPTER 7

She should've left Dubrovnik months ago.

On the slopes, Justine always let her heart rule. Coaches constantly begged her to spend more time studying the courses she raced, to walk the mountain more than once so she could plan how she wanted to approach each section on race day. While she did study them, she did her best when she *felt* them. When she experienced the catch of her edges against the snow in a particular turn, when she mentally timed the proper amount of air over a jump. When she crouched low, felt her balance locked in the sweet spot, and let her skis take her to the finish line instead of trying to guide them.

With Rocco, she'd done the same. She'd let her heart steer her decisions where he was concerned, feeling her way instead of making a plan or listening to logic. Logic would've long ago told her that the relationship was over and that she should move on. If she had followed logic, they wouldn't be in this mess right now. She'd be safe in Tahoe, interviewing for jobs—or perhaps already employed—and Rocco wouldn't have been left with a vulnerability exposed for the jackasses who wanted to steal his research.

Justine stifled a late afternoon yawn as Rocco went inside the small white building at the edge of Split's marina to pay for a temporary boat slip. She hung back, keeping her head down so she wouldn't be noticed by a group of men walking toward the parking lot with their fishing gear.

"Done," Rocco said a short time later when he approached the stand of trees where Justine waited. "It's about a ten-minute walk to the ferry terminal. There are shops along the way if you'd like to stop for essentials."

"Something to sleep in, a sweatshirt, and a pair of shoes. Maybe another shirt or two. And a bag, so I don't have to cram everything into your backpack."

It took less than an hour to find what they needed and make their way to the terminal. While they waited in line, Justine organized her new purchases in her backpack, keeping back a jet-black hooded sweatshirt and zipping it over her T-shirt for warmth as the sun set. Once they made it to the ticket window, Rocco nabbed an outside cabin with two beds and a small bathroom. "We lucked out that it's a Wednesday," he told her as they showed their documentation at the control booth and boarded the massive vessel. "On weekends, the ferry sells out."

"Yep, I feel lucky."

He raised a brow at her sarcasm, but wisely said nothing until they'd located their cabin and keyed in to deposit their bags. "I let my phone go dead and left it behind on the boat, just in case the Russians have the means to trace it. I'll pick up a burner phone when we get to Italy. In the meantime, we should use the Internet on board to research flights to the States. We can also check police reports from Dubrovnik to see if anyone called about the gunfire in the alley."

The cabin was warm and cozy, its window offering a view of the darkening Adriatic from each of the two beds. Fluffy pillows and a crisp white comforter tempted Justine to burrow. "If I don't nap soon, I'll be dead on my feet."

"And if I do nap soon, I won't wake up until morning."

Justine cast a longing look at the bed, then reluctantly walked to the door. Rocco was right; if her head hit that pillow, she wouldn't move for a solid ten to twelve hours, about the time they were scheduled to dock in Ancona.

As they climbed the carpeted stairs from their cabin to the deck containing the ferry's restaurant and Internet station, Rocco put a hand on her shoulder. "Tell you what. After we find a flight, let's get dinner. We've had enough cereal today. A real meal will make both of us feel better."

"Food would be good." Much as she hated to admit it to herself, his reassurance helped, and his strong, protective touch meant as much to her as the thought of a meal.

At the Internet station, Rocco took the task of searching for flights while Justine scoured the Dubrovnik news. "I have it," she said a moment later. "They mention my street and say that residents called to complain of noise in the alley just after midnight. A husband and wife insisted that they heard a gunshot, but no one else could corroborate that. Several witnesses reported yelling just before a black sedan exited the alley, but they couldn't agree on the make or model. It says, 'Police are looking for any information, as violence of any kind is rare in the neighborhood.' It finishes by mentioning that the area is adjacent to the Old City and attracts a lot of tourists."

"Nothing on Karpovsky and Radich? No descriptions?"

"No, but I'm not surprised. The angle from the windows makes it difficult to see the area under the fire escape where the sedan was parked." Which meant no one was looking for either man. "You find tickets?"

"Looks like the best option is to fly from Rome to Washington Dulles, then rent a car or hire a driver. I don't see any direct flights to Baltimore. Philadelphia's an option, too. I'm checking on times now."

"If you're paying, get us cushy seats."

He grumbled at her request, but didn't say no. She grinned, then scanned a few other Dubrovnik news sources in case she'd missed anything. Most of the articles were about an upcoming economic summit being hosted in Zagreb or concerned government discussions on funding the restoration of Dubrovnik's many churches. Then an article on Sarcaccia's newest royal family member caught her eye.

Prince Stefano's wife, Megan Hallberg, had given birth to their second child, a boy named Dario. The photo accompanying the piece showed Stefano's older brothers, Prince Vittorio and his twin, Prince Alessandro, sitting on either side of their father, King Carlo. The king was grinning from ear to ear as he held the newborn.

"Got it," Rocco said. "There's a flight with space still available day after tomorrow from Rome to Washington. And, just for you, we can go business class. I'm holding the tickets now. Figure it'll be tougher for Radich to discover our plans if we finalize booking as close to the flight as possible. Just for good measure, I'm also going to hold a flight from Rome to New York and one from Venice to New York." He finished the ticket holds, then came to stand behind her. She knew him well enough to sense his unease when he spied the photo on her screen. "What are you reading?"

"Article about the Sarcaccian royal family in the Dubrovnik paper. I know it sounds weird, but I always thought you looked like them. The twins, especially." The more she looked at Vittorio and Alessandro, the more she saw the resemblance. Their hair was the same color and texture as Rocco's, and their eyes were the same. Not only the color, a light shade of brown that stood out against their dark olive skin, but the shape. Even the way they smiled in the photo reminded her of the way Rocco smiled when he was completely at ease.

"Don't you mean that they look like me? I'm older than they are."

"And you claim you don't keep up on celebrity gossip." She logged out of the computer, then twisted in the chair and raised an eyebrow before rising to walk with Rocco to the ferry's restaurant. "At the risk of pissing off the man who's about to buy me dinner and airline tickets, you promised to tell me more about the entertainment report you and your mother were watching the day before I moved out. The one about Stefano Barrali. What was so interesting?"

The ease she'd forced into her tone worked. Though his gaze remained guarded, his shrug was casual. "My mother's Sarcaccian, remember? She likes—liked—knowing what was happening in her home country. Besides, it's good for trivia games to know which Barrali was born first."

"You already beat everyone at trivia games."

"At science, sports, and literature, sure. Entertainment and celebrities are my weaknesses."

There was an affability in his voice she recognized, one that warned her he was trying to distract her from the original subject. She waited until they were seated with menus in the ferry's expansive restaurant before trying again. "The Barrali twins' younger brother, Prince Massimo, apparently got married at the palace late last month. Private ceremony, family only. Nothing like Prince Stefano's wedding, with all the pomp and circumstance. The country all but shut down for the ceremony."

He shot her a wry look, acknowledging her effort to turn the topic back to the royals. "You're admitting that you keep up with celebrity gossip, then."

She settled on her dinner choice and closed the menu. "I was in the Milan airport the day after Prince Stefano's wedding and it was all over the televisions in the gate area. My flight from there to the States was packed with tourists who'd gone to stand outside the cathedral and watch the procession and fireworks. I couldn't believe how many people are fascinated by the royal family. It's insane how obsessed they can be."

A muscle jumped in Rocco's cheek before he set his menu on the table and scanned the restaurant for their waiter.

She was pushing him and she knew it, but if she missed this opportunity, would he ever open up? In a low, comforting tone, she said, "Rocco, I'm not stupid. There's more to that family than trivia for you. Was your mother involved with them somehow when she lived in Sarcaccia? Is that what you're not telling me?"

He turned back to the table, his eyes locking with hers. "Yes. Intimately."

Justine gaped at Rocco's blunt, unexpected response. Before she could recover, the waiter approached their table and took their orders, with Rocco asking for a bottle of Zinfandel.

"I need to settle in for this," he explained to Justine once the waiter left. "A good Zin will make it easier, though if it gets too crowded in here, or anyone moves within earshot, the bottle's coming back to the cabin with us. What I'm telling you is for your ears only. And even then, only because you wouldn't agree to come with me otherwise."

The waiter returned a moment later to present the bottle and pour. Once Rocco and Justine were alone again, Rocco raised his glass by the stem and studied the movement of the rich red liquid as he gave it a swirl. Finally, he shifted his focus to Justine. "Before I tell you this, I want you to know that I still love you. I think I fell in love with you that first night we met, when you turned away from that tall Norwegian skier to talk to me. I was eating dinner at the bar and you asked what was on my plate."

"Jägerschnitzel. Sauerkraut. And that crazy carrot salad." She remembered it as if it were yesterday. "You were still, when everything else in the bar was loud and in motion. I think you were the only person in the room who didn't know my name."

She'd had a long day of competition, but the hollowness in her stomach drove her out of her hotel in search of dinner despite the fact she had another event the next day. The traditional German bar across the street was the closest place to find a meal, so she'd hoofed it through the snow only to discover the place was packed with raucous skiing fans. She'd almost left, but spotted an open place at the bar and sidled in to place an order. A Norwegian skier she'd met years before squeezed in by her elbow. Having finished his events that afternoon, he was well on his way to an evening spent warmed by beer, bratwurst, and buxom German women. Justine turned to the man on her other side and asked what he was eating to avoid the distraction. That simple act changed her life.

"You won the combined the next day."

She raised her glass and grinned. "You bet your schnitzel I did. Broke the course record. One of the best runs I ever had."

"Followed by one of the best nights I ever had."

Justine's face heated at his heartfelt words. The night had blown away the day's victory in terms of what it meant. She took a slow sip of her wine and smiled at him over her glass. "When I went to the bar with my coach after the combined, the patrons were was giving me high fives and cheering, crowding me. Not you. I spotted you at a corner table having dinner alone. You just smiled and gave me a nod, one that said, 'good to see you again.' Everyone else wanted to have photos taken with me so they could post them online or brag to their friends. Much as I appreciated winning and all the attention, that smile meant more to me than you could know."

Once her coach left, she'd walked to Rocco's table and asked to join him, despite the fact she didn't even know his name. It was a spur of the moment decision, one driven—as usual—by her heart instead of her head. Rocco represented an island of calm in the tumult of the bar. She'd soon discovered him to be an island of calm in the tumult of her entire World Cup tour. His mind was on saving lives rather than winning medals and accolades. She loved getting to know him... until she reached the parts he refused to share.

"My mother worked for the Barrali family." The edge of Rocco's lips quirked, though his tone remained even. "She was eighteen, just starting at university, and applied through the school's student employment office for a job as a college prep tutor. Turned out the client was none other than King Carlo. He was the crown prince then, only a year or so younger than my mother. It was her job to ensure he did well on his college entrance exams and wrote competitive application essays."

Justine suspected Teresa was brilliant. Rocco always claimed he got his intelligence from her, and Justine knew her mother-in-law had graduated at the top of her high school class and been accepted to both Harvard and Oxford, though she'd decided to remain near home and attend university in Sarcaccia on scholarship. But Justine had never heard about a position with the royal family.

"She must've been thrilled. Tutoring a future king would be an amazing credential for her resume." Working for the Barralis would've opened doors all over Sarcaccia, let alone the rest of the world. "I imagine she came to know him quite well."

"She did." Rocco paused as the waiter delivered their meals. Once the young man was out of earshot, Rocco said, "In fact, my mother fell head over heels in love with him."

"Oh, no." Obviously the relationship had been one-sided; Carlo was famously in love with his wife, Fabrizia, whom he'd married immediately following his college graduation. Though the king and queen each adhered to royal decorum and avoided public displays of affection, their devotion was evident in the way they spoke of each other and in the stolen glances they shared. "Did she lose her job?"

Rocco surprised her by laughing. "No. She stayed until Carlo finished his entrance exams and his applications. She did so well preparing him that the king and queen gave my mother a sizable bonus and wrote excellent letters of recommendation for her when she left."

"They weren't aware she'd fallen for her student?"

"No." He forked a bite of his fish, then swallowed before meeting Justine's gaze. "Not even when she got pregnant."

CHAPTER 8

Rocco had to give Justine credit. She didn't gasp, drop her fork, or utter a, "you're kidding me" when he dropped the pregnancy bomb. Instead, she looked at him for a drawn-out moment in wide-eyed shock, nodded her understanding of what he'd just conveyed, then picked up her fork and speared a green bean. She didn't need to ask the question aloud; she knew Rocco was the result of the pregnancy.

They finished the meal in relative silence, each lost in their own thoughts. What little was said concerned the quality of the meal or the logistics of boarding a train to Rome the next morning. They skipped dessert, paid the bill, then bypassed the casino—now filled with passengers from a variety of countries seeking an evening's entertainment—to retire to their cabin with the rest of the bottle of Zinfandel.

As soon as Rocco locked the door behind them, they each blew out a long breath, as if they'd been running for hours and had finally crossed a finish line.

"Well…that was startling."

"I assume you have more to say than 'startling.'" Rocco toed off his shoes and pushed them into the corner before shedding his backpack. He hadn't been willing to leave it in the room while they'd gone to the computer station and to dinner.

"I'm stunned and full of questions, if that's what you mean." She put her hands to the top of her head, elbows splayed as she turned to look at him. "It's unbelievable…but I believe you."

"Pour the wine and I'll answer what I can. Whispers, though. I suspect the walls are thin."

Justine took a seat in the corner beside a Formica-topped table to uncork the wine, which she proceeded to pour into two plastic cups. Once she'd passed a cup to Rocco, she kicked off her shoes, leaned back in the chair, and stretched so her sock feet rested on the edge of the bed.

He braced himself to explain what he knew of his mother's relationship with King Carlo, but Justine surprised him by asking, "Why'd you start by telling me that you still love me?"

Rocco walked to the bed with his wine, then sank back against the pillows. "I wanted you to know that I didn't keep this from you because of anything you did. I had days—lots of days—where I almost told you. The worst were when I skipped major World Cup events. If you hadn't gotten hurt, I'd have had to skip the Olympic Trials, too. I wanted you to understand why, for you to know how much I wanted to be there to cheer you on, but I swore to my mother long ago that I'd do whatever it took to keep my paternity a secret. Long before I met you."

Comprehension lit her gaze. "She was concerned about the television coverage."

He gave a curt nod. Skiing received far more attention in Europe than in the United States, with major events aired from start to finish. "Sports reporters like to interview family members watching in the stands. I couldn't risk having to answer questions about us. How we met is safe enough, as is my career, but anything about my background before I graduated from Johns Hopkins could lead to my mother, and then to Carlo."

"You talk to reporters at medical and engineering conferences all the time."

"For professional journals with a focused readership. Their questions center on my work, never my personal life. With the sports reporters, it's different. They have to appeal to a broad audience and personal interest stories are the way to do it."

"You really think a reporter could tie you to the Barralis?"

"My mother didn't want to take the risk. Truth be told, neither did I. First, I want nothing to do with the man or his family. Second, if it ever came to light, imagine the distraction it'd be from my work. Tabloid television would be all over it. Hell, the regular news networks would be all over it. It'd completely change my life. Both of our lives."

Justine shifted in her chair. "After all these years, I'm amazed no one knows. You'd think it would've slipped somewhere along the line." Her brows rose as another thought occurred to her. "How did she conceal the pregnancy?"

He'd asked his mother the same question. "Apparently she didn't start to show until the very end of her time with the Barralis. Then she told her friends and family she was taking a semester break from school and traveling with a friend she'd met while working at the palace, using part of her bonus money. In reality, she stayed in her apartment, started work on her undergraduate thesis, and made plans for child care."

"And the whole time she was hiding out, Carlo knew?" At Rocco's acknowledgement, Justine asked, "He didn't help her? What about his parents?"

"They didn't tell his parents. My mother apparently told Carlo that she didn't want to have a baby entering the world under a cloud of scandal and insisted I be kept secret. She also feared losing control of her decision-making ability to the king and queen…where she'd live, where I'd be educated, perhaps even custody." Rocco finished his wine, then handed the plastic cup to Justine for a refill. "Carlo's parents and their staff had tight control of his finances. At seventeen, he didn't have a lot of independence, not the way his classmates did. He gave her money when he could do so without his parents being aware, but it was hit and miss. My mother was resourceful. She wanted to handle things herself until Carlo was older and they could marry."

Justine scoffed at that. "Waiting until Carlo reached the age of majority wouldn't avoid a scandal. Marrying an unwed mother would've been taboo for royals then, especially in Carlo's case, since he was heir to the throne." She gave Rocco an obvious perusal. "Then there's you. If Carlo had married your mother, anyone who saw him with you would know he fathered you."

"Believe me, I'm well aware I look like the man." Even if King Carlo's face wasn't familiar due to the man's regular media appearances, Rocco would've known from the way his mother secretly studied him as he moved from his teen years into his twenties, as if she were seeing into her past. Her expressions vacillated between nostalgia and regret, love and pain. Much as she tried to hide it, especially once she met and married Jack Cornaro, Rocco knew her too well.

"No wonder you got twitchy when I said you look like Prince Vittorio and Prince Alessandro. They're your half brothers. You've never met them though, have you?"

"No." Given their lofty positions, he imagined they'd view him with nothing but scorn. Particularly Vittorio, who was next in line to the throne.

"Ever been curious?"

"They don't know I exist. None of the Barrali children do." He shrugged, hoping she wouldn't see the tension the very thought of Carlo's legitimate offspring wrought within him. "Besides, I already have a brother and sister."

"I thought all three of you were born before your mother married Jack Cornaro." The words weren't even out of Justine's mouth when her expression changed. "No."

"Before you ask, yes, Enzo and Lina are aware King Carlo is their father. They've also kept it secret."

"But the twins are nearly five years younger than you are. He would've—"

"Been married to Queen Fabrizia by then." Rocco set his plastic cup on the nightstand. "That's why I have no desire to meet him. My mother loved Carlo deeply. She planned her life around him. Took enormous risks for him. He claimed to love her, but he didn't fight his parents when his marriage to Fabrizia was arranged…or didn't fight them hard enough. Even after he married Fabrizia, he continued to keep my mother on a string."

"Oh, Rocco."

"My mother was pregnant with Enzo and Lina at the same time Carlo was proudly announcing the birth of his twin sons to the world." Rocco heard his voice crack and hated that the man had the power to churn up such anger. "Can you imagine, fathering two sets of twins with two different women at the same time? Yet he stood on that palace balcony, with Fabrizia beside him, holding Prince Vittorio and Prince Alessandro with such pride on his face…as if they were a perfect family. All the while, there was a pregnant woman in an apartment not ten miles away with a toddler in her lap watching him on television, believing that he was going to leave Fabrizia and marry her now that he had his heirs with a proper, aristocratic wife."

Disgust roiled Rocco's stomach. He hadn't shared this with anyone before. Even when he was with Enzo and Lina, they'd kept their thoughts on their mother's past to themselves. None of them wished to appear unsupportive of their mother, who'd sacrificed so much for them.

"It bothers you, even after all these years."

"When I let myself think about it, which is rare." Dwelling on it helped no one, so he pushed it from his mind whenever necessary. "I know my mother was wrong to believe it, but she was young and in love with the father of her children. Of course, her fairy tale ending never happened. Carlo's father died only a few weeks after Enzo and Lina were born and Carlo took the throne. You can imagine my mother's shock when Carlo called her the day after his investiture and said it needed to end. He couldn't keep seeing her. He had to think of his country first. When she said she'd wait as long as was necessary, the cold-hearted bastard informed her that he'd fallen in love with Fabrizia."

He let loose a nasty bark of laughter. "Of course, *I'm* the real bastard in all this."

"Don't say that." Justine crossed the cabin, wine bottle in hand, and deposited it beside his cup on the nightstand. "Scoot."

Nudging his hip with hers, she sat beside him on the bed and took his hand. "I'm sorry, Rocco."

He held their clasped hands in front of him, taking solace in the knowledge that Justine was on his side. Despite giving his word to her when she agreed to accompany him to Baltimore, he'd been uneasy about telling her, wondering what she'd think of him. What she'd think of his mother.

"I'm sorry, too. The thing of it is, my mother said that after she got over the initial hurt, she realized that Carlo was doing what he had to do. That he'd only told her he loved Fabrizia so she'd go live her life, rather than wait for him. From the time she told me the truth about my paternity, she insisted that Carlo is a good man. That they wouldn't have been together for so many years otherwise, and what he'd done was a great personal sacrifice." He practically spit the words. Even as a youngster, he'd been shocked at his mother's naiveté. "She told me that if I ever spent time with him, I'd understand."

"But you weren't interested."

"Not in the least, and she certainly didn't encourage it. On the other hand, the blessing of Carlo's callousness is that Jack Cornaro came into my mother's life. He's the only father I've ever had. Now *he* was a good man. Jack loved my mother unconditionally. How many men would fall for a woman with three kids under the age of ten?" Rocco glanced sideways at Justine. Her eyes were bright with unshed tears that reflected the emotion in his own voice. He squeezed her hand briefly. "I wish you could've met Jack. He would've loved you, too."

"What matters to me is that he loved you."

Rocco smiled at the memory of being introduced to Jack for the first time. The lanky, easygoing American had met Teresa while working in Sarcaccia. He'd expressed over-the-top amazement that Teresa hadn't taught her three young children about American football or baseball and had taken them to parks to teach them the basics, earning their friendship even as he cautiously courted their mother.

When he'd been reassigned to Italy, he'd persuaded Teresa to marry him and make the move. He'd ensured the three children never wanted for anything, taking them on vacations throughout Europe and the United States, encouraging their academic and extracurricular pursuits, and even contributing toward their college education, despite the fact Teresa had a solid job and insisted she could handle it alone.

"You once told me that he never missed your soccer games, even though he often had to take off work to be there. That he was the one who urged you to apply to Johns Hopkins for your undergraduate degree, even though you knew it'd be tough to get accepted."

"That's true."

"You also told me he asked your permission to marry your mother, despite the fact you were only in elementary school at the time."

"Also true." He'd forgotten about that.

"Then Jack was your father in every sense of the word. No matter that King Carlo was the man present at your conception."

He released Justine's hand, pulled her fully into his arms, then planted a kiss on top of her head. When her arms snaked around his waist, he exhaled in relief. "Thank you."

Her answer was to tighten her hold on his waist. He closed his eyes, savoring the feel of her body against his and the tangle of her legs with his on the bed. After a lifetime spent keeping that part of himself locked away, it felt good to let it out, especially with the one person with whom he'd wanted to share.

"I wish you'd told me before now," she murmured into his chest. "It explains so much. Why Teresa didn't trust me, why she was so protective of you. It wasn't protectiveness so much as fear that all your lives would be shattered if the wrong questions were asked."

"I wish I'd been able to tell you before, too." He kissed the top of her head once more, then shifted so she could straighten and look him in the eye.

"I understand why you didn't." Her gaze didn't waver. "I forgive you."

"I didn't ask for forgiveness."

Much as he wanted it, it wasn't warranted. Not knowing how Justine would react—and given that the risk in revealing the secret wasn't his alone—he wouldn't have acted differently if he had it all to do again.

"I'm giving it anyway. You were in an impossible position, one that wasn't of your own making." She placed her palm against his chest and spread her fingers, warming him. And making him want her all the more. "Despite that, you should've told me."

"I gave my word."

"Your mother's mistakes shouldn't stand in the way of your happiness. Or mine. Giving your word—even if you did it before I entered the picture—nearly ruined our marriage."

Framing Justine's face with one hand, he looked into her gentle, intelligent blue eyes. Moisture edged her dark lashes. "Nearly ruined?"

"We have a lot of fixing to do." One side of her mouth lifted into a grin. In a passable Monty Python imitation, she added, "But it's not dead yet."

He moved his mouth toward hers, so close he caught the scent of the Zinfandel on her breath and heard the hitch in its rhythm. "That's the best news I've heard in a long time. Because I've never wanted you more. I'll do whatever it takes to hang on to you. To hang on to us."

Slowly, he closed the gap between them. At the first brush of her gorgeous lips, he was completely, utterly lost.

CHAPTER 9

THE TENDER SWEEP of Rocco's lips against hers sent Justine's senses reeling. For months now, she'd fought her attraction to him, knowing that as long as he kept so much of himself hidden, he'd never be able to fully give himself to their relationship. But as he angled his head, encouraging her to open to him and deepen the kiss, a pang of need tore through her that made him impossible to resist. Her fingers moved lower down the front of his shirt, spread against the soft fabric, and found the hard-packed muscle of his abs underneath.

A low groan of satisfaction rumbled through him and she was lost.

Making love to Rocco had been off-the-charts fantastic from the first. He might be a buttoned-up, focused biomedical engineer by day, but at night, he knew exactly how to touch her and when to ease off, when to be playful and when she demanded intensity. When to murmur in her ear and when silence spoke volumes. More than what he did for her physically, however, was the emotional response he drew from her whenever they made love. Before Rocco, she'd never derived such satisfaction from making another human being happy.

Rocco might not be willing to admit the depth of his suffering out of allegiance to his mother, but his kiss told Justine everything she needed to know. He hated that he'd had to live with such a secret and he was willing to do whatever he could to make their marriage not only survive, but thrive.

If she could give him a measure of peace by forgiving him, it would make her happier than she'd been in a long time.

Justine shifted her body closer, needing to feel him fully against her. He buried his fingers in her hair to kiss her hard and deep. She brought up her knees so she could straddle him, intent on returning his kiss with equal passion as she wrapped her arms around his neck.

He pulled back, eyeing her with suspicion. "This better not be pity—"

"If that's what you think, I'm doing it wrong."

"You're incapable of doing it wrong."

His hands dropped to her waist as he kissed her, then cradled her rear to crush her lower body to his, giving her physical evidence that she was doing everything exactly right. She sighed her surrender. In one swift motion, he rolled and pinned her beneath him before giving her another fierce, fiery kiss. Every fiber of her being, from the top of her scalp to the soles of her feet, burned for him. They'd done this hundreds of times, yet there was a new, delicious, aching, facet to their lovemaking, one brought on by knowing they'd laid their emotions bare. Rocco's deepest secret was out. They'd fought danger together and—thus far—had won. They were on the same team, together in every way.

Rocco's hands slid between them, lifting the front of her shirt to expose her bra, then his hot mouth went to her stomach. She couldn't get his shirt off fast enough, needing to feel his bare skin against hers, to drag her mouth over his shoulder and neck, to savor the salty sweet taste of him. Soon her jeans and his joined their shirts somewhere on the cabin floor.

"Oh, Rocco," she whispered as he brought his body back down to hers, his hands bracketing her ribs, then sliding around to her back, arching her from the sheets so they were chest to chest. His heart pounded against hers, his warm breath electrified her as his lips found her cheeks, her throat, her collarbone. "Yes, yes."

She could sense the tension ratcheting higher and higher within

Rocco. A deep moan escaped him, then his mouth was on her breast. Her head fell back as she clutched at him. If they weren't on the ferry, with passengers in cabins on either side of theirs, she'd have screamed with the pleasure of it.

He captured her thigh, encouraging her to open more fully to him before he cupped her, stroked her, drove her mad with need.

She rewarded him with a groan as he found her most tender spot and massaged her in slow, agonizing circles. He pressed another kiss to her collarbone as she pressed kiss after kiss to the top of his head. Oh, but she missed the feel of him against her. The familiar scent of his shampoo, the texture of his thick hair. The strength of his broad, muscular back. But there were new sensations, too. The rough scratch of his beard against her skin. The security of knowing this wonderful, protective, complicated man trusted her with his darkest secrets.

"We should slow down," he murmured against her shoulder.

"Don't you dare." She'd never wanted him more desperately.

"Thank God."

A choked cry of, "now, please, now, now," erupted from her, spurring him onward as he shifted, and in one move, buried himself fully inside her, then pushed her back to the sheets and made love to her with a mixture of both heated desire and tender awe.

The energy coiling within her intensified. She wrapped her legs tighter around his sweat-slicked back, hanging on to him as if her life depended on it, and met him stroke for stroke.

"Jus…I'll explode if I—" he hissed through his teeth. "I never—"

Her muscles tightened, spasmed. In a rush, her entire body seemed to unspiral as jolt after jolt tore through her, so powerfully even her face heated with the force of it. Moments later, Rocco's muffled cry of soul-deep satisfaction accompanied the cascading wave of his own ferocious release.

As he collapsed against her, cradling her to him, her first thought was *mind-blowing*. It wasn't simply the physical euphoria, but a profound sense of intimacy, one she'd never before experienced, even with Rocco.

She knew from the poignant, lingering touch of Rocco's lips to her damp forehead that he felt it, too.

His fingers interlaced with hers. "I'm never letting you go again."

Her only response was to clutch him tighter.

MORNING ARRIVED FASTER than Justine thought possible. She stretched, anticipating the stiffness that came from sleeping in a strange bed, but found her muscles and joints warm and loose. Only her left calf ached, reminding her of her injury, but that happened no matter how she slept.

A pair of solid arms encircled her waist. A moment later, Rocco's lips danced a trail across her shoulder. Into her ear, he whispered, "How long until we disembark?"

"The horn blew and there was an announcement in Italian a few minutes ago, so we must be in the docking area. Ten to fifteen minutes at most."

"I was hoping you'd ignored the announcements. And the horn." He nuzzled against her cheek, his facial hair rasping her skin. "I can do a lot in ten minutes."

"I'm well aware. It's a tempting offer, Mr. Cornaro."

The horn sounded again, drawing a mumbled curse from Rocco before he rolled away. "You'd think the fine citizens of Ancona would protest being awakened by ferry blasts every morning."

Justine reached over the side of the bed to find Rocco's pants and fling them over her shoulder for him to catch. "The sooner we're ashore, the sooner we'll be in Rome."

"And safe in a hotel."

One where they could lounge in each other's arms for a full day before boarding their flight to the States. With that thought driving her, she kept pace with Rocco for the walk to the train station. Justine nabbed a seat at one of the station's cafés while Rocco purchased their tickets. It didn't take him long to join her.

"First class to Rome, departing in an hour," he told her after he ordered an espresso, eggs, and toast from the waitress. "We'll be at Termini before one o'clock. There's a family-owned bed and breakfast I know of located about five blocks from the station. Easy walk. We'll see if we can get a room there when we arrive."

"If you've been there before, would Radich check it?"

"I usually stay at the St. Regis Grand, which is a few blocks from the train station in a different direction." He grinned. "That's the only reason I know where this place is located. I've walked by it when sightseeing in the neighborhood around the St. Regis."

The idea of Rome tempted her. "Too bad we can't chance exploring the city. I've only been once. I had a connecting flight cancelled and was stuck for a day. Managed to see the Colosseum and Palatine Hill, but that was it. No time to see the Pantheon or other sights."

"Maybe on our return, once we know the designs are safe at Johns Hopkins." He accepted his espresso from the waitress and Justine thanked the woman for her own cinnamon-topped cappuccino. "I'm stunned you've never spent time there, given how well traveled you are."

"No slopes, no Justine." Her globetrotting revolved around her training. In Italy, that meant the Alps, far to the north of Rome.

Rocco's smile had the very devil in it. "In that case, I'll spend the next few days thinking of places we can explore together."

"The Vatican?" She'd always wanted to see St. Peter's and the Vatican museum, but number one on her list was the ceiling of the Sistine Chapel. She'd watched a public television special about the original Michelangelo work and a recent restoration project and had been fascinated ever since.

"My thoughts were headed in a less saintly direction, but we'll go wherever you like."

A flash of movement in the station caught Justine's attention. She shifted to look past Rocco, but nothing seemed out of the ordinary. The lobby was crammed with well-dressed locals about to board their trains for work, families pulling suitcases toward the platforms, and backpackers toting maps and travel guides. No one seemed to pay them any attention. Most had their eyes locked on the station's large arrival and departure board, waiting for their track announcements.

Rocco stiffened. "What is it?"

"I'm not sure." The hairs on her arms stood on end. "I felt like we're being watched, but I don't see anything unusual."

Concern hardened Rocco's amber gaze. "Keep your focus on me. Smile, act normally. We'll eat our breakfast, then go to the *tabacchi* shop across the station. I'll pick up some sunglasses, maybe some hair" —he swirled his hand around the back of his head— "thingies. Ponytail holders. Whatever you can use to change up your look once we're on the train. We'll go to our platform at the last possible moment."

"Make it tougher for anyone to see which train we're boarding?" At Rocco's nod, she told him, "You know, I'm likely being paranoid. It might've been my imagination."

He straightened as the waitress approached with their breakfast orders of eggs and toast. "And it might not have."

A moment later, he told her in a quiet voice, "I never did finish explaining everything. You wanted to know who warned me about the Russians."

She'd forgotten that in the shock of hearing about Rocco's parentage. "Who?"

"Queen Fabrizia herself."

His admonition to smile and act normally went out the window as she gaped at him.

"It surprised me as much as it surprises you. But now you know why I refused to reveal my source." He rolled his espresso cup between his palms, then took a sip before continuing. "Do you remember when one of the Barrali twins disappeared last year and there was speculation he was in Croatia?"

"Of course. It was big news."

"I was questioned at the farmer's market by a reporter who thought I looked like the missing prince. Nothing came of it, but Fabrizia learned about the incident and decided to have me followed, just in case. That led her security team to Radich, who then led them to Karpovsky. Queen Fabrizia was worried about you because she learned that Radich was watching you during your dinner nights with your friends."

Justine sat back in her chair. Her social life in Croatia had been limited to a small group of girlfriends, women she'd met over the course of her skiing career who trained in and around Zagreb for parts of the year and came to Dubrovnik when they could for dinner. It was a different group each time, but they kept a standing reservation every other Tuesday. Now that she thought about those dinners, a connection clicked in her brain. "Radich ate in our section."

"Yes. He was spying on you."

She closed her eyes for a moment and sucked in a breath. "I never would've thought it. Not in a million years. He never stood out. Never seemed to pay us any attention at all."

"He's easy to look past. It's part of what makes him lethal. It also means it's entirely possible he's here in the station. When it comes to surveillance, he's capable of anything."

Justine swallowed hard. The thought of facing the Russians again turned her stomach.

"Finish your breakfast. I promise, it'll be all right."

She forced a grin, but Rocco's calm expression rapidly drew a natural smile from her. In that moment, she believed him. She trusted him.

"You said first class, right?"

His laugh was loud enough to shake the table.

QUEEN FABRIZIA SENSED her husband's presence before she heard him enter. Carlo had charisma that seemed to precede him into a room.

She smiled at her assistant, Daniela D'Ambrosio, as they finished preparations for the trip she and Carlo had the next morning. "The soft yellow Missoni would be ideal for our afternoon audience with the Pope. Then Armani has promised to deliver the red silk gown for the state dinner directly to our hotel in Rome."

"Both are good choices, your Highness." The young woman

consulted her notes. "You last wore the Missoni eighteen months ago for a private baptism, so it will be fresh. And I've confirmed that the Armani will be waiting in your suite when you arrive. Would you like the nude Brian Atwood pumps you wore last time with the Missoni, or would you prefer an Italian brand?"

"When in Italy, we must go Italian." Fabrizia scanned the shelves of her walk-in closet. "I'll be on my feet for several hours. Let's take the beige Ferragamo flats. Then the gold Giuseppe Zanotti heels for the state dinner. They should work well with the red gown." Her feet ached as she looked at the Zanotti pair; they were elegant and stylish, and she knew the Italians would love her for wearing them, but dancing more than once or twice would be out of the question.

"Perhaps the gold Prada heels as backup?"

Fabrizia gave Daniela's shoulder a grateful squeeze. "Brilliant."

The woman assured Fabrizia that everything would be packed as requested, curtsied to the king, then left the royals alone.

"I'd love for you to model those for me," Carlo said, angling his head toward a strappy pair of sparkling silver heels. "But don't bother with the gowns. The heels alone are more than enough for me."

"Such simple tastes you have. Perhaps later tonight," she said with a soft pat to his lapel. "Wouldn't be appropriate in front of the Pope, however."

"I should say not." He captured her hand and held it to his chest. "I missed you yesterday afternoon."

For a split second, she thought he was being his usual flirtatious self. Though his subjects never saw that side of him, she saw it daily, even after forty years of marriage. This was something else. "I thought you went to the kennel yesterday to see how the new puppies are doing?"

"I did, but I didn't stay long. I noticed your calendar was clear, so I was hoping you'd be here in the apartment if I returned early."

"I'm sorry, darling."

"You were asleep when I returned from my dinner with the Royal Police. Busy day?"

Nothing escaped Carlo. He was giving her the chance to explain. "I took a quick trip out of the country yesterday afternoon."

"Interesting…my personal secretary was asked about a fuel recharge for the jet this morning. Just enough to go to Croatia and back." Crinkles of concern appeared at the edges of his golden brown eyes. "Teresa's funeral?"

"No, I wouldn't do that." She slipped her hand from her husband's and took a seat on the large ottoman that dominated the center of the closet, then crossed her ankles. "I went to see Rocco at his villa after the service."

Pain flashed across Carlo's face. "You should've told me. I'd have come."

"No you wouldn't have. You'd have forbidden it. And even if you hadn't, you know he wouldn't have seen you. Frankly, I didn't think he'd see me. He kept me waiting for some time." And had the audacity to make her leave the car outside the gate and walk, though she wouldn't mention that part to her husband.

"He didn't know you were coming, did he?" Carlo crossed the space to take a seat beside her. "Why did you go? And why yesterday, of all days?" A beat later he added, "I assume no one saw you?"

"No. I flew there with Umberto so he could act as my driver and my eyes." The man who regularly patrolled the entrance to Fabrizia and Carlo's palace apartments and headed their security staff was the most trusted person in their employ. "I gave Rocco the diamond and sapphire necklace you designed for Teresa, the one Kelly found in the antique chest when she did the remodeling work in Massimo's apartment."

"Good. He should have it." An aggrieved note in Carlo's voice made it clear he was thinking, *if he won't have me.* "I assume that's not the only reason you went or you'd have simply asked Umberto to deliver the necklace."

She angled her body so she faced Carlo. Knowing he had three children who carried his blood, yet who refused to see him, burned a hole in his heart she feared might never mend. "You asked me not to have him followed after he was questioned by that reporter in Dubrovnik."

"But you did." His lips thinned in disappointment.

"Yes. Not at first, not right after you asked me." She hated to confess this to him. "But—I'm sorry, darling—I couldn't shake the feeling that—"

"No apologies. Just tell me what you discovered."

She gave him a brief overview of what she'd learned about Karpovsky and Radich. About her suspicion that Rocco had been working on a project in his lab that attracted the Russians' attention. And about the risk to Rocco's wife. "I didn't believe Rocco would take action if I'd simply called or sent a message. He'd never trust me. I needed to know I'd be heard."

"But to go on the day of Teresa's funeral—"

"I had no choice. My eyes and ears on the ground feared that plans were in motion. Teresa's death would work in their favor. It meant Rocco would be emotionally vulnerable and more likely to capitulate to their demands, whatever those demands might be. I told him he needed to take action to protect himself and his wife immediately."

"Are you still watching him?"

"I promised him I wouldn't." Carlo's skeptical look made her roll her eyes, despite the fact it was warranted. "Believe it or not, I pulled off my men. However, after Kelly found the necklace I had Umberto hide a tracking device in the lining of the jewelry box in case the piece ever went missing again. It didn't occur to me that Rocco would take it with him if he fled with his wife, but—"

"He did. I see it all over your beautiful face."

Fabrizia smiled at her husband, realizing that she was forgiven for going against his wishes. "He's on the Adriatic. I believe his wife is with him. Judging from the location, my guess is that they're on the Split-Ancona ferry. I don't know where they're headed, but as long as the Russians haven't followed they're safer than they were in Dubrovnik."

"Good. He's a resourceful man and a wealthy one. We have to assume he can take care of himself and his wife now that he's aware of the danger." Carlo blew out a breath and propped his elbows on his knees, dropping his gaze to his shoes. "I only wish—"

"Someday, Carlo. Someday he'll know the truth, that being separated wasn't your choice."

"I don't know if the truth would be better or worse for him. I suspect worse. He's done very well in his life. It's selfish of me to want him in mine." He turned his head to look at her. The world at large saw him as a powerful man, one with a loving wife, six dynamic children, and the world at his feet thanks to the billions in his bank account and his political popularity. Only Fabrizia knew that the wrinkles emanating from the edges of his tired eyes came as much from sorrow as from his infectious smiles.

She wrapped her arms around her husband's broad shoulders. Carlo was an honorable man, despite the naive mistakes of his youth. He'd grown and changed. Most of all, he was a survivor.

"You love Rocco, even if you haven't seen him since he was a toddler. Never consider it selfish to love someone."

He gave Fabrizia a long, sweet kiss before resting his forehead against hers. "Thank you for that. Even if you lied to me about following Rocco...thank you."

"You do what is necessary for the people you love. And I love you more than life itself."

Somehow, some way, she'd do what was necessary to make things right for him.

CHAPTER 10

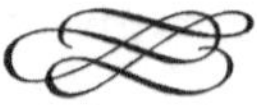

Rome fascinated Justine. From the moment she and Rocco emerged from the train station and she spied the well-preserved ruins of ancient baths standing across the street from a regal, columned building that housed modern offices above a street-level series of crowded cafés and gelaterias, she wanted to indulge in its charms. To take a day and meander into whatever alleyways and shops drew her attention, to enter one of its thousands of churches and savor the still-ness amidst the chaos of a large city. To soak in the city's millennia of history while enjoying the fashion show of its young professionals as they made their way between work and the Metro.

The crisp breeze and the bright afternoon sun that filtered through the blossoming trees only intensified her desire to explore. Unfortunately, Justine had to settle for viewing Rome from a tiny, third floor room overlooking an English-style pub. Rocco had brought them here as soon as they'd arrived at the train station, leaving no time for gawking.

"Big rugby tournament this week," Rocco observed as he followed her gaze out the window to a group of raucous men wearing kilts and Scottish jerseys who sauntered toward the pub entrance. "Anyone who's not at the stadium is finding a bar where they can watch. I imagine they'll get louder once they have a few beers under their belts."

"Not sure whether I should cheer for the Scots to win or lose. Which will make them rowdier?"

"If they traveled all the way from Scotland to see the tournament, they're primed for rowdiness either way." A smile tugged at the edges of his mouth as his attention went to the far side of the square from the pub, where a group of twenty-somethings in kelly green shirts walked. "And here come the Irish. Our odds of a peaceful night are officially zero."

He closed the lace curtain. "There's an Internet station downstairs near the front desk. How about we finalize our ticket purchase for tomorrow, then go to the mom and pop grocery on the other side of the pub to buy something for dinner?"

"It's a crime not to eat out while we're here."

"I agree. Better that we stick to the room, though. We have a good view of the square and there's a back staircase through the door next to ours. It's as safe as we can get." He ran a reassuring hand up her arm. "I'm bringing you back here. I promise."

"What if I grab takeout from the trattoria we passed just off Via Cavour? I can order while you're booking our flight. I doubt anyone would notice me between here and there."

She could see him waffling, so she punched his shoulder. "Come on, Rocco, you know you want to. I saw you eyeing the handwritten sign for homemade gnocchi as we walked by. It's only a few blocks further than the grocery store."

"Fine," he said with a laugh. "Take some cash from my wallet. It's at the top of my backpack. I'll lock up. If you beat me back, find me by the front desk."

"Gnocchi?"

"Of course. And a bottle of wine."

"Goes without saying." She pulled several Euro bills from Rocco's wallet, then took the back staircase to the street. After checking to ensure no one lurked about, she made her way to the trattoria using a circuitous route as Rocco had done when they'd walked to the bed and breakfast from the train station. The instant she stepped through the trattoria's narrow entry, she was enveloped in the scent of fresh pasta, garlic, and baking bread, then was greeted by a round, elderly gentleman wearing a pair of dark slacks and a sky blue button-down shirt. She understood enough Italian to gather that his family owned the place.

She asked for a menu, then managed to place a takeout order in passable Italian. While she waited, the owner brought the bottle of Chianti she ordered, then surprised her with a plate of cured meats on crackers and a fizzy aperitif that appeared to be made with Apertol, telling her that he loved to treat the beautiful women who entered his restaurant.

It was early and he wasn't yet busy, so she invited him to join her. She asked a few polite questions about the restaurant and was regaled with the tale of a kitchen fire his wife put out by beating it with her apron. Justine didn't understand all the details, but the gist of the story made her laugh. When the gnocchi was ready, he handed her the paper bag with a wide smile and showed her that he'd included a few cookies. She thanked him, paid, then meandered her way back to the bed and breakfast. She was about to turn the final corner when she realized she'd left the bottle of wine on the restaurant table.

"Shoot." She paused, tempted to take the bag upstairs before returning, but figured she was less likely to attract attention if she only entered the bed and breakfast once. On a sigh, she spun on her heel and took yet another route along side streets back to the trattoria. As she approached, the owner came outside with her bottle and she thanked him before turning back. This time, she walked the most direct route, taking care to blend in with the crowds of tourists and shoppers making their way along Via Cavour. She spied a sign indicating an alley cut-through to the Basilica di Santa Maria Maggiore, the Catholic church just beyond their bed and breakfast, and zigzagged through the crowd in the direction of the alley. Just before she turned the corner, she caught sight of a group of nuns in full habits standing on the opposite side of Via Cavour, laughing as if they were young girls sharing a joke. Justine paused, watching the women for a moment. Only in Rome would one see such a thing. She wished she had a camera to capture the scene: an early April evening, a boisterous group of nuns, a melting pot of tourists and locals speaking every language imaginable, all the colors of the stores' window displays. She couldn't wait to come back with Rocco to soak it in. To spend the days discovering the city's nooks and crannies, to spend the nights rediscovering each other.

Her attention snagged on a man standing outside a leather goods shop behind the nuns. While the rest of the street moved, he was still, his eyes scanning the crowd. Justine's stomach dropped in fear as she recognized him.

Karpovsky.

Dark clothing helped him blend into the display of dark leather jackets hanging along the store's doorway, but there was no mistaking his broad build or scarred face. Before he could spot her, she dodged into the alley and crossed to the shaded side, then stepped into a raised apartment entryway from which she could see him, but he couldn't see her.

How had he known to come to Rome?

Her heart thundered in her ears as she watched him pull a cell phone from his pocket. His eyes never stopped studying the crowd as he held the device to his ear and listened. After a moment, he pocketed the phone, then slid behind a group of shoppers and walked down Via Cavour in the general direction of the bed and breakfast.

Justine remained in place, waiting with her back pressed against the entryway's scarred oak door. A motorcycle turned off Via Cavour and zoomed past, followed by a taxi. Slowly, she peeled herself from the entryway and walked to the bed and breakfast, forcing herself to keep her head down and her pace steady so she wouldn't attract attention. Every sound around her seemed magnified. The scent of the food wafted up to her nose and she could feel the weight of the bottle tucked under her arm. Despite the fact her senses were on high alert, she resisted the impulse to race directly back to Rocco and safety.

She had to warn him. On the other hand, she couldn't allow herself to be seen or she'd give away the location of their accommodations... assuming Karpovsky didn't already know.

A threesome of Scottish rugby fans passed her, singing as they went. She gave them a noncommittal nod as they greeted her in drunken English, but kept her gaze beyond them, scouring the street ahead for any sign of Karpovsky.

If Karpovsky was on Via Cavour, where was Radich? Had he managed to tap into Rocco's computer usage on the ferry to see that they were coming to Rome? She couldn't imagine the skill that would take, but when it came to hackers, she supposed anything was possible.

Finally, she approached their B & B from the direction of the pub. A large contingent of Scots crowded around a television set near the entrance, while a group of men decked out in the Union Jack stood cheering alongside them. Irish and Italian fans were spread throughout the square, speaking in loud voices and using an abundance of hand gestures. Keeping to the periphery, she slipped past them, then into the back staircase of the hotel. A glance at the lobby on the way upstairs showed her Rocco had finished, so she made her way to the room.

"I can smell that through the door." Rocco's voice was cheery as he flipped the lock to admit her. "Did you remember napkins? We have glasses and silverware, but I couldn't find any paper products."

"I'm so glad you're here." She shoved the door closed, turned the lock, then set the wine on the top of the small counter that served as the room's kitchenette and made a beeline for the window, carefully edging the curtain aside. No sign of Radich or Karpovsky in the crowded square. "Karpovsky is here. He didn't see me, but I don't think we're safe anymore."

She felt Rocco behind her. "He's outside the hotel?"

"No, not that I can tell." Her heart still pounded as if the man were about to burst through the door. "He was on Via Cavour. I walked different ways to the trattoria and back—I had to go twice because I forgot the wine the first time—and I saw him about ten minutes ago on my second trip back. He was across the street from me, talking on a cell phone. I hid in a doorway in a side alley until he left. He headed this direction, so I waited a few minutes before I left the doorway, but I don't know—"

"You're certain it was Karpovsky?" Rocco's voice was low as he took the bag from her hand, then pried her death grip from the curtain. "This morning in Ancona you thought your imagination was playing tricks on you. Via Cavour is crowded this time of day. Thousands of people must be shopping there."

"Positive." She knew she sounded panicked. On an exhale, she put her hands to her stomach, attempting to settle the knot that had formed there, and made an effort to speak more slowly. "He was wearing a black shirt and gray slacks that helped him blend with the crowd, but I recognized the scars. All down here." She gestured to the side of her face. "The man is distinctive, even if he tries not to be."

Rocco's jaw worked. "I didn't see him on our train. I went through every car twice. Even waited to see who came out of the restrooms."

"I don't know how, but he's here."

"That's the question then, isn't it? How could he possibly know where we are?" Rocco set the paper bag on the counter beside the wine and reached inside for the gnocchi. "Set places and I'll open the wine. I saw a corkscrew here somewhere."

"Are you kidding?" They needed to get out of here. Get as far from Rome as fast as humanly possible.

"No, I'm not kidding, and before you ask, yes, I do believe you." He fumbled in the kitchenette's lone drawer, then came up with the corkscrew and went to work opening the Chianti. "You said he didn't see you on Via Cavour. You don't think he saw you come into the B & B, do you?"

"I doubled back and made sure no one was behind me, then was very careful when I entered the building. I doubt anyone saw me, even the drunks going in and out of the bar."

"Then for the moment, we're safe. If we go out there" —he waved the corkscrew in the direction of the window— "we have no idea what we'll face. We have nowhere to go until our flight tomorrow afternoon, and the more we wander the streets, the more we put ourselves at risk."

She watched as Rocco poured the Chianti into two glasses he'd rummaged from the small kitchenette. "I don't think I can eat. My gut is telling me to get the hell out of Dodge."

"Karpovsky would be an idiot to barge in here when there'd be dozens of witnesses. Come on. Sit. We'll think better once we eat," he assured her. "Besides, that smells too good to abandon."

After a moment's hesitation, she retrieved the two containers that held the gnocchi and set them atop the room's two-seat table. She popped the lid and couldn't stop the gasp that escaped her lips. "No wonder the bag was heavy."

"All of that came with it?" Rocco moved to her side, handing her a filled glass as he peered into each gnocchi container, then to the containers Justine continued to pull out of the bag. In addition to the gnocchi, there was warm garlic bread, steamed artichokes, and, finally, the cookies the trattoria owner had shown her.

"I didn't think so. I suspect the owner added it gratis. The cookies were definitely a bonus item." She told Rocco how she'd chatted with the man and that he'd treated her to an aperitif before showing her the cookies.

"That's Italy for you," Rocco said, raising his glass. "Here's to an unplanned night in Rome."

"With the Russians on our tail."

He pulled back and made a face. "I'm not toasting that."

"All right, fine." She raised her glass. "Here's to an unplanned night in Rome and a delicious dinner."

"Better."

He lightly clinked his glass to hers. Rich flavors of cherry, plum, and spice filled her senses as she took a sip.

"This is fantastic," Rocco said, giving the label a quick glance. "It's not one I've had before."

It was new to Justine, too, and she made a mental note of the winery. For the next half hour, she savored the meal. Never would she have pegged this as takeout food. It was the perfect blend of strong and subtle flavors. The heft of the gnocchi and the light texture of the artichokes hit the spot after a long day riding the train and walking through Rome.

A chorus of cheers rose outside the window, followed by the sound of dozens of voices raised in song.

"I recognize that one," Rocco said. "The Scots must be doing well."

"If they're in a good mood, it'll make it easier for us to slip out." She set down her fork. Now that she was done eating, her mind went back to the dilemma at hand. "You seem to think we're safe here, but I'm not so sure. If the Russians weren't on the train, how did they know we're in Rome? No way Karpovsky's appearance is coincidence."

"I've been thinking," he said as he stacked the empty containers and returned them to the takeout bag. "If one or both were in Ancona, it's possible they either saw or figured out which train we boarded. They could've come a different way—on a different train or by car—and arrived shortly after we did."

"But how would they know to come to this particular part of Rome?" It didn't make sense. "Karpovsky was only a few blocks from here. You've been very careful to cover our tracks. Private boat to Split, cash for our ferry tickets…it's like he's a homing pigeon."

An odd look crossed Rocco's face. He paused in the middle of refilling Justine's wine.

"What?"

"I bet that's exactly what it is. Damn." Rocco set down the bottle with a thump, then strode across the room to his backpack. He unzipped the sides and flipped it over on the bed, dumping clothes and toiletries across the bedspread. Several thick, legal-sized manila envelopes and a cornflower blue box that looked like a jewelry case also fell out.

"I was joking, Rocco. He couldn't have put any kind of GPS device in your bag. He hasn't been near us since you packed it in the villa."

"I carry this bag to work every day." He ran his fingers along the back of the bag, then opened a hidden zipper to reveal a padded slot perfectly sized for his computer. He withdrew the laptop and set it on the bed beside the rest of his belongings. "It's possible Radich put a tracer on here. He only would've had to brush up against me in the elevator or the kiosk line outside my office. A few seconds and presto, he has a way of tracking me. It could've been done days or weeks ago."

Justine moved to the side of the bed. "You really think so?"

"Best explanation I have." He ran his hands over the surface of the backpack as he checked it inch by inch. Angling his head toward the pile on the bed, he asked Justine to inspect the clothes. "I wasn't exactly taking my time when I packed. If there was some kind of GPS device on the surface of the bag, it could've come off and gotten stuck to them."

Justine nodded, taking the items one at a time and searching for anything out of place. As she finished each piece, she folded it and set it to the side. Other than mud on the leg of the slacks Rocco had worn the night they'd fled through the city, all appeared in order.

"Bingo."

Rocco spun the backpack to show Justine a thumbnail-sized clear sticker adhered to the lower outside edge. Only upon closer inspection, it wasn't so clear. Tiny, almost invisible wires ran through it.

"That's so small. You think that's it?" she whispered. "It blends right in."

That brought a wry grin to his face. "I doubt it can hear us. But yes, I suspect it's some type of tracking device."

"Then the Russians know exactly where we are. They've known ever since we left the villa."

"Which means they're probably within a block of us at this very moment."

CHAPTER 11

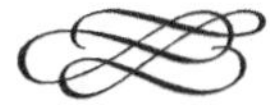

Rocco gently peeled the offending sticker from his backpack and stuck it on the edge of the nightstand, taking care not to smash any of the pin-thin wires. As Justine watched, he lifted the backpack once more, tilting it for a better view under the room's antique chandelier.

"It may not be the only one," he told her. "If I were Radich, knowing that it could fall off or be damaged, I'd have placed a backup if given the opportunity."

"Right. I'll go through the rest of the clothes."

Rocco's jaw worked as he and Justine continued their examination in silence. How could he not have suspected they were being tracked, given Fabrizia's description of Radich's skills? A man of Radich's education and resources would have access to the best in technology, and it wouldn't have taken much effort for the man to move behind Rocco and place the sticker anytime in the last few months.

Rocco ground his teeth as he finished his inspection of the backpack. Radich probably knew every time Rocco had left the house with the bag…which was every time he left the house, period, given that it contained his computer. He'd even taken the backpack to his mother's funeral, locking it in the trunk of the car so he could guarantee its security during the graveside service. The only time it hadn't been in his possession these last few months was when he'd gone to Justine's apartment to warn her, only locking the computer in the safe at the last minute when he'd decided to walk instead of drive. Now that he thought about it, that'd been a godsend. If he'd had the backpack with him that night, Karpovsky and Radich would've known he was at her apartment. He and Justine would never have escaped.

And to think that, for a brief moment, he'd believed Justine's sighting of Karpovsky might be a product of fear and imagination.

Rocco glanced at her as she held one of his T-shirts to the light, checking every square inch for signs of another sticker, then folded it and put it on the stack. If he knew anything about Justine, it was that she faced her fears without flinching. He'd seen it in the way she'd attacked ski runs in questionable weather conditions, and then in the determined set of her jaw when her orthopedic surgeon told her that regaining the strength necessary to compete at the Olympic level was a long shot, given the severity of her injury and her age. He'd witnessed it as she fought off Karpovsky in the alleyway, then felt it in the determined set of her shoulders when he'd held her in the bushes behind the convent, with the two armed Russians only feet away. Despite her pain, despite her fear, she'd remained tough, physically and mentally. He should've known the moment she'd entered the hotel room that the sighting wasn't a figment of her imagination. She wouldn't have been so intent on taking action if there was any doubt in her mind.

"Nothing," she said once she finished inspecting his shaving kit, then set it alongside his folded clothes. "What about the envelopes and this box?"

"If the exteriors are clean, then they're fine. The papers came from my safe. Mostly work-related documents or those connected to my mother's will and estate. The box I received just after her funeral. Radich wouldn't have been able to access any of it."

While he repacked his clothing, Justine scanned the outside of the envelopes and the box, then handed them to him without asking further questions. They did a quick check of her belongings, since what she'd borrowed from Lina had been stuffed in his bag, but found nothing.

Simultaneously, their gazes went to the sticker affixed to the edge of the nightstand.

"We have to assume they know where we're staying. They may even know which room," Rocco said. "Since they haven't made a move yet, I suspect they're waiting until they don't have an audience."

"Meaning we should get out of here before the bars close and the rugby fans return to their hotels." Justine flexed her fingers as she stared at the tracking device. "What do we do about that thing? Leave it?"

"If they're watching the bed and breakfast and spot us leaving without it, they'll know we've discovered it." Rocco went to the window to discreetly study the scene outside, then gestured for Justine to join him.

"It's even more crowded now." She squinted through the tiny slit Rocco had created at the edge of the curtain. "Looks like the French have arrived, but the Scots and Irish are still here."

"Pack up. We'll go down, join the crowd, and work our way inside the pub." He pointed toward a narrow alley at the back of the pub, where a man in an apron sat on an empty beer crate and smoked a cigarette. "There must be a rear exit. Let's stick the tracking device on one of the tables or under the bar, then we'll shoot out the back."

If Karpovsky and Radich believed they'd gone to the pub for dinner and to watch the rugby tournament, the pair would keep their distance until closing time at two a.m. It would buy them several hours.

"Is there enough room in your backpack for me to squeeze in my things? If we're both carrying bags and they spot us, it might look suspicious. But they're used to seeing you with yours."

"Good thinking. If it doesn't fit, I'll leave behind enough clothes to make it fit." He shifted the curtain for a better view of the square. "When we get to the pub entrance, pause to look at the menu as if we're debating whether or not to stay for dinner. We'll go inside, dump the tracker, then make our way toward the back. When we exit, let's take the alley in the direction of the cathedral. Then we'll cut toward Repubblica and take the Metro toward the river. We can cross to Trastevere and try to find another bed and breakfast there. I know of a few that are out of the way."

Justine's hand came to his shoulder. "We'll be fine."

He let go of the curtain and spun to face her. His heart soared at the trust that filled her eyes. He framed her face between his palms and ran his thumbs over the supple skin of her cheeks before giving her a brief kiss.

"I'll make sure of it."

On another day, under other circumstances, Rocco would've relished time spent in the boisterous pub. Behind the bar, a half-dozen bartenders worked nonstop, filling glasses from a long line of taps. Two waitresses edged through the crowd, serving an eclectic mix of pub-style and Italian fare to those who were lucky enough to secure a table. The stark contrast between the happy patrons cheering on their rugby teams and the solemn echo of the nearby Basilica di Santa Maria Maggiore's bells reminded him of what he loved about living in southern Europe. Rome embraced the modern while celebrating and honoring its centuries-old heritage. It enticed visitors to discover its museums and cathedrals, then linger late into the night in its restaurants and bars.

Tonight, however, Rocco had one mission in mind: getting out as quickly as possible.

Justine had played her role perfectly as they'd strolled out of the front entrance of the bed and breakfast. She'd smiled at the man working behind the front desk in the tiny lobby, then held Rocco's hand as they slowly walked around the building to the square, as if they felt secure and carefree. Conscious of any eyes that might be upon them, they paused outside the pub, looked over the menu, and debated the choices before snaking their way through the crowd. Justine even told him that dinner at the bar would be fine if they couldn't get a table. All she wanted to do was hang out, enjoy a beer, and watch sports in a laid-back atmosphere.

He feigned searching for a table, using it as an excuse to scan the patrons. There was no sign of either Radich or Karpovsky. Aiming for the back of the room, he was surprised when Justine tugged on his arm. "Here, Rocco," she said as he turned. "These men are leaving and offered us their table."

"Really?" he asked near her ear, though he kept a smile on his face. The men beside Justine were gesturing to their table and grinning at her in admiration. They sported the French team colors and, judging from the number of empty glasses on the table, had finished at least three rounds of drinks.

The man in the center, a robust blond with bright red cheeks and pale blue eyes, leaned toward Justine. "You are the American skiing champion, yes? Justine Flyte?"

"You are more beautiful in person," the man to his right said. "We're big fans. This one" —he elbowed the big blond— "is a ski instructor. He's brought us to watch ski races for years."

"You made it fun," the third man said as he pushed the glasses to the edge of the table to make space. "All that" —he put his palms together and made a swishing sound as he imitated the motion of a skier going downhill— "it is better to watch when one is so talented as you."

Justine expressed gratitude for the compliment, answered a few questions from the ski instructor about technique, then laughed with all three about a downhill race she lost by a tenth of a second to a famous French rival. As the men skirted the table to leave, the ski instructor held up his phone. Recognizing that he wanted a photo, Justine nodded and leaned in so he could snap a photo of himself and his friends with her. They thanked her, the blond man pulled out a chair so Justine could sit, then the group finally left.

"Sorry about that," Justine said once Rocco edged around the table to take a seat beside her. A few of the other patrons looked their way out of curiosity, but soon turned their attention back to the television screens. "I know it wasn't part of the plan, but I didn't want to be rude when it was obvious they recognized me."

"No problem." He shot a look at the departing Frenchmen. "You still get that much?"

"No." She didn't need to add, *not since the accident.* It was written all over her face. In that moment, Rocco was grateful the men hadn't asked about her injury or if she'd be competing again. He could see from the animated way she'd responded to their questions that her love for the sport itself hadn't dimmed. If she could get back on her skis tomorrow, she would. Yet she didn't complain, didn't wallow. His admiration for her jumped another notch.

He scooted his chair closer to hers. "You miss it?"

She considered that for a moment. "Sometimes, but not for the reasons you'd think. People outside the sport are familiar with my name, but don't necessarily know what I look like. When I'm on television, I'm usually under a helmet or wearing a hat. So the people who do recognize me are the ones who want to talk shop, like those Frenchmen. Or those who live near World Cup event sites and see the same competitors year in and year out at their hotels and restaurants."

"Guess that explains why you were surrounded whenever I stayed with you at event hotels," he mused.

"Or met me in a certain Garmisch bar." She grinned, but a beat later, her smile faded. "I know it made you uncomfortable, and not simply because you were trying to keep your paternity secret. You've never been the type to court attention."

"It's not that I mind being around large groups. I'm perfectly comfortable in a crowd." He shot a purposeful glance around the packed space. "It's hype that bothers me."

She arched one slender brow in understanding. "I can't imagine what it's like for A-list actors and actresses. Or well-known international athletes like David Beckham or Lionel Messi, who are so famous they can't grocery shop or take their kids to a playground without being stopped. It'd drive me crazy to have that lack of privacy, never mind the fact it'd get in the way of the job."

"Then there's royalty." He kept his voice low. "That's a whole different level of fame."

"It is. But to do their jobs well, they need to be known. Favorably, of course, but an unknown monarch can't get much accomplished."

He supposed that was true, assuming one wanted to spend every moment surrounded by a staff of hundreds, unable to go for an impromptu evening stroll or a night out at the movies, at least not without a cadre of security.

His train of thought was interrupted when a boisterous group of college-aged Italians entered the pub, filling what little available floor space existed near their table and blocking it from view of anyone standing near the entry.

"The Frenchmen did us a favor when they recognized you and offered us the table," Rocco noted. "Anyone who saw us enter will believe we're staying awhile, but now that we're behind this bunch, it's almost impossible for us to be seen. When there's a noisy moment in the match and everyone's distracted, let's make our move out the back."

"Sounds good. In the meantime, I'll decorate the underside of the table." Justine raised a mischievous eyebrow as she peeled the sticker from where they'd replaced it on his backpack, then stuck it to the bottom edge of their table. Less than five minutes later, a controversial call by a rugby official resulted in a steep rise in volume in the bar. Rocco nudged Justine, then hefted his backpack over both shoulders and eased around the table and past the Italians. Justine slipped her hand into his to keep them from being separated as they sidestepped their way through the crowd. Energetic cheers and the scent of freshly poured—and occasionally freshly spilled—beer permeated the space. Televisions over the bar and mounted on the walls blared the match call. A waitress balancing four steaming dinners on a tray held high over her head wiggled her way past them, then behind a knot of Irishmen to serve a packed table.

No one seemed to notice them. Everyone's focus locked on the television screens or on their compatriots as they debated the call.

Finally, Rocco spied an emergency exit sign beyond one pointing to the restrooms. He glanced back to ensure that Justine saw it, too, then guided her through the tight confines of the dimly lit hallway and past the line of patrons waiting to use the facilities. Seeing no signs warning that an alarm might sound, Rocco let go of Justine and used two hands to push the heavy metal bar on the exit door.

A blast of cool night air hit their faces as they stole outside and eased the door closed behind them. The moment it clicked into place, the pub noise lessened from a roar to a hum. Voices were still audible from the crowded square in front of the pub, but they were no louder than the sound of cars on a nearby thoroughfare or the complaint of a skinny white cat stretched across a staircase on the opposite side of the alley.

"This feels marvelous," Justine said on an exhale. "I didn't realize how loud it was inside. My ears are ringing."

"Mine, too." He took her hand once more and squeezed, glad they were free of the infernal tracking device. "Let's get out of here."

"I hope the Russians start swearing a blue streak at two a.m. when they discover we're gone."

"And not a minute before." Rocco relished the idea of Karpovsky lingering outside the bar until closing time, then realizing that he'd wasted his night and lost his prey.

Justine's answering smile kickstarted his heart. The sooner they were done with this and on with the rest of their lives, the better. He turned to lead her toward the Repubblica Metro stop when the sharp flick of a lighter and inhale of breath signaling the presence of a smoker in the alley caught his attention.

"Ah, Mr. Cornaro," came an accented voice from the shadows in front of them. "So kind of you to exit where it is quiet. And to bring your designs with you? This is added bonus."

Another voice came from behind them, "Far more convenient to simply talk business than forcing us to kidnap your wife. Safer for both of you, as well."

Karpovsky. And Radich.

CHAPTER 12

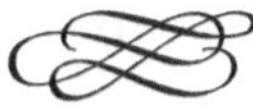

Determining that the easier path to escape was through the leaner man, Rocco slowly spun. He kept a tight grip on Justine's hand. "Viktor Radich, I presume?"

Radich moved from behind a stack of empty beer crates to the center of the cobblestoned alley. He looked different than the hunched, anonymous man Rocco had observed near his office building. Clad in slacks, casual loafers, and a light gray shirt, Radich appeared confident and perfectly comfortable in his surroundings, the type of man who could move through the streets of any world city as if it were his backyard. Other than the purple marks under each of his eyes, no doubt the result of Rocco's fist, he appeared invincible.

"I'm impressed." Radich aimed a deliberate glance at the backpack Rocco carried over his shoulders. "If you know my identity, then you should have known I possess the skill to program the GPS device so I'm alerted to tampering. But perhaps your genius applies only to the field of medical engineering?"

Two more figures moved into the alley behind Radich. Rocco's alarm must have shown on his face, because Radich laughed. "You also should've known I wouldn't allow you to escape a second time. Particularly when you've been so kind as to bring me what I really want."

"Ethics? Class?" It was a desperate move, but it was all he had. "Sorry, can't give you those. You'll have to obtain them on your own."

Beside him, Justine tensed. Not in fear, but as a prelude to action. He flexed his fingers in hers, hoping she'd take it as a warning to bide her time.

"The design plan for the artificial pancreas, Cornaro. Take five steps toward me, then set down the backpack. Once you provide me with your passwords and I check your computer to ensure it has what I need, I'll allow you to leave."

"And my wife."

Karpovsky grunted behind them. "Not your wife."

"As my partner says. Mrs. Cornaro shall remain as my insurance. Or my guest, if that's how you'd prefer to categorize it. Once I deliver a copy of your designs to those who hired me, I'll release her safe and sound." Radich's voice held none of the self-satisfaction or bullishness seen in movie-theater villains. Instead, his speech was straightforward, as if he were discussing a routine business transaction over coffee and bagels. "Five steps. Now."

As Radich's demand echoed through the confined space, a drunk stumbled into the alley a few feet behind Radich and his men. A man wearing a black hoodie was with the drunk, laughing as he tried to hold up his friend. Without needing to be signaled, one of Radich's men turned and yelled in Italian for the men to return to the square. The man in the hooded sweatshirt called back that his friend needed to throw up, adding a few choice profanities for Radich's man.

It wasn't the foul language, but the voice that made Rocco release Justine's hand and tighten the backpack straps against his shoulders.

Radich appeared unbothered by the commotion and gestured again for Rocco to drop the backpack to the cobblestones. "Five seconds, Cornaro, or your wife will not enjoy her time as my guest."

"Don't do it, Rocco," Justine spoke so softly he barely heard her. "Think of how many people need it. We have to try—"

"Quiet," Karpovsky moved within arm's reach behind them.

"It's fine," he told Justine before looking over his shoulder at Karpovsky. The man held a gun. Of course. "Can she wait over there, next to the building? If you go crazy and fire that thing, I don't want her hit."

"I hit what I aim to hit."

"Then out of the line of fire of those men." He tilted his head toward the two thugs standing behind Radich. "It's not like she can go anywhere."

"Mrs. Cornaro may stand on the opposite wall," Radich said. "Away from the bar entrance. Hands up where they're visible."

Rocco flashed a look at Justine. "Go."

"Rocco—"

"*Go.*"

Radich's eyes tracked Justine as she moved across the alley. With an inward prayer that Karpovsky was doing the same, Rocco flew backward, driving his elbow toward the man's gun.

He hoped the drunk and his friend were paying attention.

IN ONE INSTANT, Justine was backing toward the alley wall opposite the bar, her attention squared on Viktor Radich. She fumbled for the words that would convince him not to hurt Rocco, all the while hoping that someone would look down from the windows above and call the police. The designs could not fall into Radich's hands.

Before she could formulate an argument, Karpovsky grunted, Rocco yelled for her to get down, and the drunk rugby fans flew at Radich's men.

On instinct, Justine ducked. Her back slammed into the stone wall of the building, knocking the breath out of her and sending a shot of pain through her lower leg as she braced herself in a futile attempt to keep from falling. She scrabbled against the cobblestones to recover, her brain warring between the fear Radich would come for her and the need to help Rocco. He couldn't fight Karpovsky by himself, unarmed, let alone while wearing the backpack.

If she could somehow get the bag, it'd free Rocco from the weight, giving them a chance to save the designs and possibly their lives.

Radich barked out orders in Russian as he ran toward Rocco and Karpovsky. Behind him, his two men were losing their fight with the drunks...men she now realized were large, fit, and stone-cold sober. Behind them, three more men entered the alley, all armed.

Pushing to her feet despite the pain lancing her calf and shin, she raced to beat Radich across the alley. The backpack dangled from one of Rocco's shoulders as he perched on top of Karpovsky, pummeling the larger man in the face. Karpovsky seemed impervious to the blows as he gripped Rocco's throat with one hand and punched Rocco's kidneys with the other. A grimace of pain twisted Rocco's features, but he didn't relent, smashing his fists into Karpovsky's nose and cheeks.

Unmistakable clicks reverberated through the alley. Guns were being cocked. Bullets were about to fly. In such a tight space, she had no hope of escaping a shot.

"Everyone freeze!"

The command rent the night air at the very moment Justine dove for Karpovsky and Rocco. She landed beside the grappling men, knocking her shoulder into Karpovsky's head and the cobblestones. She swiveled her gaze toward the voice. The man in the black hoodie stood behind Radich, his forearm wrapped around the lean Russian's neck while he held a gun flush to the side of Radich's skull.

Shock stilled Justine. On her hands and knees, she croaked, "Kos?"

"Release Mr. Cornaro. Now." Venom filled the Croat's voice as he glared at Karpovsky, the tone so deep and threatening even Justine jerked backward at the sound.

Behind Kos, the two men who'd accompanied Radich sat with their backs against the alley wall, hands on their heads, their chests dead center in the sights of the armed men who'd entered the alley after the apparent drunks. Karpovsky turned his scarred, bloodied face enough to see his compatriots immobilized, but kept his hand at Rocco's throat, prompting Kos to add, "If you do not let go, Mr. Radich's brains will decorate the street. Yours will follow. Then your friends'. I have the authority to shoot at my own discretion and I will not ask again."

The tall, dark-haired man who'd pretended to be drunk a few minutes earlier advanced on Karpovsky, whose wild-eyed gaze went from Rocco, to the erstwhile drunk, then back to Rocco. The Russian knew he was trapped, but like an angry animal with prey in his teeth, he refused to let go.

Kos's accomplice picked up Karpovsky's gun from where it lay against one of the pub's trash barrels, handed it to Justine, then crouched to press his own angry-looking handgun to Karpovsky's head. "Remove. Your. Hands."

Slowly, Karpovsky released Rocco's throat, then raised his arms out to the sides. Rocco climbed off him, pain etching his features as he took a deep, choked breath. Kos's accomplice quickly rolled Karpovsky to his stomach, secured the huge Russian's hands with a zip tie, then searched him for more weapons while Justine moved to Rocco.

"Are you all right?" he gasped.

"I was going to ask you the same thing." The cut on his head was bleeding again, and he was holding one hand tight to his body, as if his knuckles ached. She slid a palm over his cheek. "I think you need a doctor."

"I'm fine…or I will be. I'm just glad you're okay." He stood, using his uninjured hand to help Justine. Turning to Kos, who still held his gun to Radich's temple, he said, "Thank you."

"Watch Karpovsky while Umberto secures Radich, and we'll get you and Mrs. Cornaro out of here, sir."

Rocco took Karpovsky's gun from Justine, then trained it on the soldier while the dark-haired man—the one Kos referred to as Umberto—used another zip tie to secure Radich's hands behind his back. As he was doing so, three more armed men, all dressed like the two who'd entered the alley behind Kos and Umberto, approached. They moved to the side of the alley to talk in hushed tones with Umberto, who seemed to be directing the entire group. One of the men stepped aside and spoke into a small device attached to his shoulder. Less than thirty seconds later, a windowless black van rounded the corner.

"Who are these people?" Justine asked Kos.

Kos looked at Rocco, apparently unsure how to answer. "Friends."

"Surely not your personal friends." Not running around Rome with lethal weapons. She felt her eyes go wide as the back doors of the van flew open to reveal more armed men. They leapt out, then assisted Umberto in loading Radich, Karpovsky, and their two accomplices. Another thought occurred to her and she turned to Rocco. "Are we going to have the Italian police after us for this?"

Rocco leveled a look at Kos. "They're government men, aren't they?"

Kos glanced at Justine before nodding in the affirmative to Rocco, who uttered an oath before saying, "Fabrizia. This is her doing."

For perhaps the first time in his life, the ever-stoic Kos exhibited genuine surprise. "Yes, sir. Umberto is the royal family's head of security. He called in the DIA, the Italian anti-mafia investigative forces. They're working on this as a joint mission."

Justine could see the wheels of Rocco's brain spinning. He had to wonder how Fabrizia knew what was happening in Rome…and what the king and queen revealed to the Italians in order to pull off such an operation. "How did you get involved?"

"I knew it was Queen Fabrizia who visited after your mother's funeral. Even with her hair under a scarf, she's easy to recognize." Kos hesitated, his grim expression foreshadowing bad news. "I went back to the villa yesterday morning to pick up my overcoat and found that the library and master bedroom had been ransacked. Your safe had been blown open and your desk was overturned. Queen Fabrizia's card was lying on the rug underneath the desk." Kos proffered the card, which Rocco slipped into the back pocket of his jeans without a look.

Justine put a hand on Rocco's lower back and felt the tension there at the mention of the queen's name.

"When I saw the condition of the villa, I called your cell number and got nowhere. I also tried your apartment, Mrs. Cornaro, and received no answer. I'd seen the news of possible gunfire outside your building, and combined with the break-in, I was deeply concerned.

Given the queen's unusual visit that afternoon and that she arrived with her hair and eyes covered" —Kos shrugged— "I doubted the timing was coincidental. Whoever got into the villa managed to circumvent your security. The alarms never went off, so the police weren't alerted. When I couldn't reach either of you, I decided to call the number on the card to see what I could learn before I reported the break-in. I was stunned when the queen herself answered. You know it's her private cell phone?"

At Rocco's nod, Kos continued, "She told me she knew Teresa Cornaro and had visited the villa first to offer her condolences, and second because she thought Mr. Cornaro was being pursued by people who wished to steal his work. She told me she believed you were headed to Rome, then asked me to come here to meet with Umberto. She said she would make some calls in the meantime in order to ensure your safety. I flew here this afternoon."

"On your vacation."

"I told you, sir, I don't require a vacation."

"When this is over, you're getting one whether you want it or not. If you don't go, your wife will force you to quit, and I can't have that." Rocco angled his head to study the queen's head of security more closely. Umberto was talking with the man behind the wheel of the black van. "He was the queen's driver in Dubrovnik, wasn't he?"

"Yes." Umberto saw Justine, Kos, and Rocco watching him and gave the group a curt nod before rounding the van to jump into the passenger seat. The rest of the men working with Umberto climbed in the back, keeping guard over the Russians.

"Umberto said that King Carlo and Queen Fabrizia have spoken privately with their contacts in the Italian government to ensure the men are prosecuted to the fullest extent of Italian law. The Russian government will also be notified about their activities in Italy and in Croatia. Radich is an American citizen, so the Russians may not be able to reach him, but Karpovsky is bound to be sent back there."

"Thank you," he told Kos as the van exited the alley. "I don't know what we'd do without you."

"I'm sure you'd manage, sir."

Justine smiled at Kos. "Maybe, maybe not. But we both appreciate it."

Whoops and cheers echoed from the direction of the square. "Sounds like a match just ended," she told the men. "Sooner or later, some real rugby fans will find their way back here. We should leave."

"I've been asked to assist with that, Mrs. Cornaro."

Rocco turned to Kos. "What do you mean?"

"The king and queen happen to be in Rome on a diplomatic mission. They're here for four days, meeting with the Pope and several Italian officials. King Carlo's private jet is available to take you wherever you wish to go during that time, so long as it's back here when the king and queen need to return to Sarcaccia. Queen Fabrizia suggested it'd be safer for you to leave the country until it's confirmed that no one else is after your work."

"Happen to be in Rome?" Rocco's lips thinned. "Seems awfully coincidental."

"The Barralis visit Italy several times a year. It's my understanding that the Italian and Sarcaccian governments partner on many projects, given the island's proximity to the Italian coast."

"Well, use of their plane isn't necessary." Rocco told Kos about the flight he'd already booked to the States and his plan to deliver his designs to Johns Hopkins.

Kos considered it. "You're wise to go to Baltimore, but given that it's available, I recommend taking the royal jet. It allows you to leave the country sooner and without going through public airports, which could be dangerous if the Russians have anyone else after the designs." At Rocco's hesitation, Kos added, "I hope I didn't overstep my bounds, sir, either in contacting the queen or with my recommendation."

Rocco placed a hand on Kos's broad shoulder. "I hired you for your brains and your loyalty more than your muscle, though that's come in awfully handy tonight. It was a good decision to call Queen Fabrizia when you couldn't reach me. It probably saved our lives. If it's fine with Justine, we'll go with your suggestion."

It surprised Justine that Rocco had permitted a visit from Queen Fabrizia after Teresa's funeral, but accepting the use of King Carlo's jet was even more shocking. Then again, perhaps it was a necessary step on Rocco's path to healing the wounds of his past.

She looked from Kos to Rocco. "I'll do whatever is safest. The sooner we have this behind us, the better. And the sooner patients who need it will be able to take advantage of that pump."

"The plane is fueled and waiting," Kos told them. "I'll notify the pilot. I should have you on board within the hour."

CHAPTER 13

Rocco appeared, finally, to be at peace. Justine decided it was a classic case of appearances being deceiving.

She pushed the lever to recline her chair, which was made of sumptuous leather and sported an ergonomic footrest. Across from her, Rocco dozed in his own leather chair. The lines of worry that etched his forehead from the moment he stepped foot in her Dubrovnik apartment had disappeared, replaced by the soft expression of sleep. But there was more. The cut across Rocco's forehead, once again wiped clean of blood, showed the beginnings of a fresh bruise around its circumference. On Rocco's throat, red circles the size of Karpovsky's meaty fingers marked the location of bruises to come, and more than once since they'd boarded, he'd shifted uncomfortably in response to his aching back. She suspected his knuckles didn't feel much better.

Karpovsky might be cooling his heels in an Italian jail, but he'd done plenty of damage.

Justine sighed, then stretched to nab the water bottle at her side. After muttering that Fabrizia must have spies everywhere, Rocco had been uncharacteristically quiet on the drive to the airport. He'd made small talk with the pilot after Kos dropped them off on the tarmac, but only enough for the sake of politeness until the pilot began his safety demonstration. Once the pilot showed Rocco and Justine the location of food, drinks, blankets, and pillows, and he went to the cockpit to join the copilot for the flight across the Atlantic, Rocco had lapsed into silence. There'd been a tired smile on Rocco's face as he strapped into his seat, but he was ill at ease on the aircraft, despite the fact it was the height of luxury and the two of them had it to themselves.

It didn't take the brains of a rocket scientist—or a top biomedical engineer—to figure out why. Not only did Rocco now feel indebted to a man and woman he detested, he was surrounded by the trappings of their wealth and fame. King Carlo and Queen Fabrizia had designed the interior of the jet to their personal specifications. They'd selected the carpeting, the seats, the plush towels in the larger-than-normal bathroom, perhaps even the toilet paper. The entire aircraft oozed a life lived at the height of comfort. A life Teresa had told Rocco should've been his birthright as a king's firstborn son. A life from which he'd been rejected.

It wasn't that Rocco had been raised in atrocious circumstances. On the contrary, in Teresa and in Jack Cornaro, Rocco had parents who'd taught him right from wrong, the importance of caring for his fellow man, and the value of hard work in the pursuit of his dreams. But Teresa had also driven her personal love/hate for King Carlo deep into Rocco's psyche.

Justine wished she could wipe away the loathing as easily as she'd cleaned the blood from Rocco's temple.

Straightening in her seat, Justine reached for her calf and adjusted the ice pack she'd made using a baggie and what she could gather from the airplane's ice drawer. The swelling had gone down enough that she felt comfortable stretching and flexing her toes, loosening up the muscles that'd suffered over the last few days. Her rehab docs would be stunned at how much she'd run. It'd hurt, but she'd done it.

Softly, so as not to disturb Rocco, she took the melting bag of ice and dumped it in the bathroom sink. It'd be another eight hours before they landed in Baltimore. She'd find a way to write a thank you note to Queen Fabrizia and hand it off to the pilot while Rocco slept. It was the right thing to do, though she had no idea what Rocco would think.

She exited the bathroom to see Rocco sitting upright, staring out the window at the black night.

"You're awake." Dumb, obvious statement. She wished she could take it back. It only made the atmosphere in the jet more awkward.

Rocco didn't seem to notice. After a long moment, he said, "There's a lightning storm off in the distance. Fascinating to see from the air."

Taking it as an invitation, she slid into the seat opposite his so she could watch. Spikes of electricity split the sky, illuminating the billowing clouds to their north. She sucked in a breath at the sight.

"Nature's own fireworks display."

"And thankfully far away. We're perfectly safe here." A note in his voice drew her gaze.

"Are you saying it for my benefit or yours?"

That teased a wry smile from him, and he ran a hand over the trim beard covering his cheeks and chin. She still hadn't gotten used to seeing him with it. "You always did know how to read me better than I could read myself."

"You were afraid back there."

"Damn straight. You should've been, too. I don't know if Radich had the spine to shoot us, but Karpovsky killed his wife. Probably killed his wife's sister. He would've killed us if that's what it took to get the designs."

"But he didn't." She bridged the space between them to settle her hand above his knee. Through his jeans, she could feel his quad muscles strung tight as an archer's bow. "That was brave of you back there, getting me out of the way so you could try to knock out Karpovsky and save the designs."

"It wasn't brave at all." He gave an exasperated grunt. "I wouldn't have done it if not for Kos. When he spoke, I recognized his voice and knew he was there to help."

She didn't believe that for a minute. "You know that pump is going to make a world of difference for thousands of people. Imagine if you had a two- or three-year old child with Type I diabetes. If the pump works the way you think it will, it could keep that child's hormone levels stabilized and keep them out of the hospital. It could prevent damage to their internal organs, maybe even save that child's life. If it were your child, it'd be worth any risk. You've spent your life doing this. Kos or not, you would've found a way out—"

"Sometimes there isn't a way out." At long last, he dragged his focus away from the window and faced her. The intense emotion in his dark gaze tore at Justine's soul. "Justine, I could have lost you. If it was a choice between saving you and saving the pump design, I'd have saved you. But I doubt I'd have even had a choice."

"Don't say that. You don't know—"

"I *do* know." His hand came down on hers, his strong fingers lacing through hers. "I can create another pump. It'd take time, but I could do it. If we'd been alone in that alley another minute, I'd have handed it over without blinking. I can't create another you. I wasn't being brave. I was being selfish."

She heard the truth in his voice, saw the sincerity in his gaze. He believed he would've saved her, despite the steep price. He believed wrong. If it'd come down to it, she knew he'd have done the logical thing and tried to save thousands rather than one, even if he hated it. "You call it what you want and I'll call it what I want."

His eyes flashed at that. "If anything, you were the brave one to try to save the designs, diving across the alley while Radich held a gun and Karpovsky was choking the living daylights out of me. Stupid, but brave." When she opened her mouth to argue, a flirtatious grin spread across his face. "You call it what you want and I'll call it what I want."

She felt herself returning his smile. Maybe it *was* stupid to have believed she could grab the backpack, help Rocco, and somehow escape that alley, but it warmed her to know Rocco appreciated her determination. Better still was the heated way he looked at her now, as if he imagined kissing her. And more.

Acutely aware that the pilots could step into the passenger cabin at any time, Justine closed the distance between them and gave Rocco a quick, sweet kiss, one that promised more to come when they were alone. "None of it matters now, does it? We're safe. Your work is safe. And soon there will be a group at Johns Hopkins working to develop that pump and get it through testing and on the market."

"I'll feel better when we're finished in Baltimore and on our way back home."

"Or to Rome."

"Now you're talking." He gave her hand a squeeze, then leaned back in his chair. "It'll be the honeymoon we never had. Think of what it'll be like to enjoy each other's company without the demands of your career or mine." Optimism punctuated his response. "We'll go first class all the way. Hotel, dinners, custom tours, whatever you want. You deserve some pampering after being driven from your home, shot at, and chased by those two goons. Not to mention the fact your husband fell down on the job." His tone turned serious. "I'm sorry for that, Justine. I'm sorry we lost the last year together because of my stubbornness."

She ran her thumb along the outside of his hand. "I thought you weren't apologizing."

"I am and I'm not." She saw the abrupt shift within him as he said it, the regret in the set of his shoulders and the solemnity clouding his expression. "I know you said I was forgiven without an apology, but you're owed one…at least for the way I treated you. I still believe it was right to keep my word to my mother—it was her secret, not mine —but how I handled it wasn't fair to you. I should've found another way." Deep lines formed across his brow as he spoke. "For that, and for all you went through because of me, I'm sorry. It just took me a while to realize it."

Tears burned at the back of her eyes. She'd never been a crier, but the sincerity in his words touched her heart, even if she still thought he was wrong about keeping his mother's secret.

She swallowed against the lump rising in her throat. "A day or two after your mother's funeral isn't 'a while,' especially given the nature of your relationship. But thank you." It hadn't been easy for her to forgive Rocco, but she'd known it was the best course for both of them. She suspected it was equally difficult for Rocco to ask her for forgiveness now, even partial forgiveness. In a tone meant to lighten the mood, she said, "So…Rome and a private jet to take us there. I can't wait."

They'd use the time in Rome to rediscover each other. To hold hands as they strolled the ancient streets in the moonlight, to sit side by side on the grass in the Villa Borghese gardens, stealing kisses while they people-watched. To browse the antique stores and the museums, to enjoy the lively nightlife of Trastevere. To spend the wee hours in each other's arms. Then, when she and Rocco returned to Croatia, they could talk over her employment options and what his next project might be. How they could chase their dreams together, support each other through good times and bad. To pursue everything they both wanted from their marriage in the first place.

"Unfortunately, no go on the private jet," he said, interrupting her fantasy. "I plan to send the pilots back to Rome as soon as they're ready to fly. We can go commercial on our return."

Another slash of bright lightning rent the sky outside the window, drawing a quick glance from Justine before she turned her attention back to Rocco. "The pilots have to fly back with or without us. That means doing the necessary paperwork, refueling…all of it. It's no skin off their noses to have us on board."

"I'm sure it's not, but I'd still prefer commercial. First class seats to Europe are almost as luxurious as these, and we won't have to serve as our own flight attendants." He unbuckled and strode through the cabin to a large closet near the cockpit where the pilot had indicated bedding and pillows could be found. "We can go on our schedule without worrying about inconveniencing anyone."

He handed her an expensive-looking white blanket and a pillow contoured to fit the aircraft's spacious seats. "Push the button on the side of your chair and it'll lie flat. We should be able to get a full night's sleep before we land in Baltimore. Real sleep, where we know we're not in danger." He raised a brow. "Take advantage, because it'll be the last night we sleep this far apart for a long, long time."

She bit back an argument and did as Rocco suggested while he dimmed the cabin lights. He settled himself in the chair beside hers, rather than the one across from her where he'd spent the first portion of the flight, and reclined it all the way. Once Justine had covered herself with the blanket and adjusted the pillow, she turned on her side to study him.

Rocco started to close his eyes, but intuition drove her to speak before he drifted off. "I know you didn't want to accept this flight from King Carlo. It's a big step that you did."

He lifted onto his elbow and gave the pillow a light punch, making a groove for his head. "Don't misunderstand it. I did it because it was the logical course of action to protect you and to protect what's in that bag." His eyes flicked to the backpack, which rested in the space between the two chairs, before he settled on his side and met her gaze. "My feelings for you are bigger than my disregard for that pampered egomaniac. And frankly, the" —he paused, searching for the right word— "the vitriol I feel for him doesn't extend to Queen Fabrizia. She's not my favorite person—she certainly wasn't my mother's—but she did warn me about the Russians. Without her taking the risk to come see me after my mother's funeral and then calling in the Italian authorities tonight, I might not have you now. If you want to view accepting the flight as a peace offering of sorts on my part, it was for her. Not him."

Before Justine could respond, he closed his eyes. She opened her mouth to argue, thought better of it, then rolled to her back to stare at the ceiling.

"Oh, my gosh," she muttered a breath later. "There are tiny stars over our heads." Embedded in the fabric covering the ceiling were hundreds of minuscule, pinpoint lights. Not so bright they'd keep her awake, but enough to provide the sensation she was floating through space.

Rocco flipped over to take a look. "Of course there are."

They glanced at each other, grinned, then lost themselves in laughter at the over-the-top ridiculousness of it.

Rocco had never seen Justine look more beautiful than when the two of them stepped out of the taxi that met them at the private airport just outside Baltimore. Hair disheveled, no makeup, and wearing the same clothes she'd donned before they disembarked the ferry in Ancona—it seemed like an eternity ago—and still, simply looking at her made his heart swell.

The world looked at Justine and saw an Olympic athlete. He saw the strength of her soul.

She was wrong about Carlo. He'd known the instant he mentioned flying commercial that she wanted him to reconsider, and not because the private jet was so lush. She wanted him to make peace with his biological father. Rocco disagreed, but appreciated that Justine kept that precise sentiment to herself. Her heart was in the right place. It was natural to want a reconciliation between father and son. If it weren't for the father in this case being such an ass, it'd be the stuff of Oscar-winning movies. But the father was an ass. And the father—if that's what one could even call Carlo—didn't want the son in his life. He had his own sons. Five legitimate sons and one daughter, to be exact.

Rocco had Justine. He had his brother and sister. It was all the family he needed.

He smiled at her as he fished his wallet from his back pocket.

Once he returned to Croatia, he'd find a way to repay the Barralis for use of their jet. It wouldn't be cheap, but he could afford it. He'd made plenty when, in his twenties, he'd been part of a team that developed an improved dialysis machine and sold it to a large Japanese company. A combination of good investments and improvements he'd designed for current diabetes pumps had earned him more than he ever needed by the time he was thirty-five and cemented his reputation in the medical community. It'd been enough for him to strike out on his own, to rent lab space, and to find investors willing to support his future projects.

Rocco didn't need King Carlo and his billions. Not when he was a child, not now, and especially not once this new pump went to market. He'd have more money than he and Justine could ever spend.

And unlike Carlo, he'd be improving the lives of children and their mothers. Not abandoning them.

He paid the taxi driver, then ushered Justine into the hotel. He'd asked the driver for recommendations near Johns Hopkins and the man not only provided a wealth of information, he was kind enough to call ahead to ensure Rocco and Justine could check in despite the early hour. It would allow them time to pull themselves together and have breakfast before heading to the university.

"My body clock is off," Justine said in a low voice as the front desk clerk went to his printer to retrieve a sheet for Rocco to sign. "I got plenty of sleep on the plane, but I feel like I need another four or five hours."

"If you want, we can take a quick nap before breakfast."

"No, don't let me nap. Protein and a cup of coffee will help me adjust." Given all the travel she'd done while competing, she knew how to move across time zones with the least disruption to her system. Rocco asked the clerk for suggestions for eateries nearby and he pointed them toward the diner across the street.

"It opens in half an hour and the food's outstanding. You're welcome to have a cup of coffee here while you wait." He indicated the coffee and tea station on the opposite side of the lobby. "Our business center is also open if you'd like to use the computers. The instructions are in the packet with your room key or there's wifi if you'd like to use your own."

Rocco thanked the clerk, then urged Justine to follow him across the lobby.

"I'd rather wait on the coffee until I can get food," she protested.

"Not what I intended." He paused outside the glass door to the hotel's business center. A conference table took up the center of the room while a series of desks, each with its own computer, lined the far wall. "I'm going to check my messages. Why don't you follow up on that missed job interview?"

A divot appeared between her brows. "Now? Are you sure?"

"At this point, I'm not worried about Radich or anyone else tracking us. Get online and send a note to whomever it is you need to contact. Reschedule." He couldn't help but reach for her. Skimming his fingers around the shell of her ear to tuck her hair back, he said, "You deserve to follow your dreams. If it can't be a gold medal or that fat crystal World Cup globe, then find something else. A sportscasting job. Coaching. Hell, design a ski-in, ski-out house for us in Tahoe if you want. Whatever makes you happy and fulfilled, I'm in."

"But Rocco, what about" —she shot a glance at the clerk, who was busy with paperwork but still within earshot— "your background?"

Following her dreams could put her in the public eye again, and that brought risks to him. To the Barrali family.

"One step at a time. We'll find a way to handle it."

She hesitated. Studied his face, as if assessing his sincerity. Finally, her eyes brightened. "All right. I'll do it."

He leaned forward to brush her luscious mouth with his own. It occurred to him that he was going to spend every morning this way for the rest of his life, kissing his wife first thing. It made him smile even as he kissed her.

"For the second time in the last twenty-four hours, you look teary," he whispered after he pulled back. "You welled up on the plane, too. That's not the response I want when I'm with you."

"As long as you're this wonderful, it's the response you're likely to get."

"Mmm. Maybe I should stop." He gave her one more kiss, lingering with his lips a breath from hers in spite of the presence of the front desk clerk. "Or maybe you just need to get used to wonderful."

CHAPTER 14

Justine stared at the words on her computer screen in disbelief. Within seconds, Rocco abandoned his terminal and was at her side.

"What? Something wrong?"

"It's the producer I was scheduled to meet in Croatia. She says she's sorry she missed me, but hopes we can reschedule. If I'm willing to come to the States" —she drew out the last word and shot a look at Rocco— "she'd love to meet with me. She's at the satellite office in Washington, D.C., this week, then will be back at the network's New York office next week. She says that they remain very interested in the possibility of having me join their broadcast team and hope I'll come."

"That's great!" He leaned over her shoulder and scanned the message. "Looks like she sent it last night."

"I'm just...I'm flabbergasted." She didn't think she'd get a second chance. Definitely not a second chance like this, where the producer sounded enthusiastic about the meeting.

Now that it was right in front of her, she hesitated to take it.

"Tell her you can meet her either place. That you're in the Washington area now, or you can come to New York. If she'd rather see you in New York, we can go up there when we're finished at Johns

Hopkins and take the opportunity to tour around or see a few shows. Then we'll fly back to Rome following the interview."

Justine leaned back in the springy desk chair and took a deep breath to process everything before she composed her response. "I told her I had a family emergency. If I'm available here for an interview only three days later, she's going to wonder."

"Then tell her the truth." Justine's surprise must've registered on her face, because Rocco argued, "Why not? If she wants to verify it, all she needs to do is look at the Dubrovnik newspapers to see that there was a police investigation near your apartment. Or she could call Johns Hopkins. My partners there can verify your story...at least they'll be able to by this afternoon. You can explain that you traveled with your husband to the States in order to avert a security threat to his work and that measures have been taken to prevent any future issues."

She scowled at his formal-sounding explanation. "First, like she'd believe a story about Russian mobsters, and second, *have* measures been taken?"

He answered her with a look of confidence similar to the one that enticed her when they'd talked into the wee hours their first night in Garmisch. "I think having Radich, Karpovsky, and their accomplices held by the Italians qualifies. They'll be interrogated thoroughly about who hired them and who else might want the technology." One of Rocco's broad shoulders lifted in a shrug. "In a few hours, it'll be secure at Johns Hopkins. Go ahead. Tell her you're here. If she asks for details, keep the explanation of what happened as simple as possible."

Justine scooted forward, hit reply, then wavered. "I thought we could talk about this. That I'd have more time." That they'd discuss a plan for their future *together*. Where they'd live. What they each wanted.

Being with Rocco again after over a year apart would take some adjustment, no matter how she felt about him, and he'd need to adjust to her, too. Too much had happened in the last few days. Hell, life in the last few months they'd been together hadn't been a picnic with Teresa living under the same roof. Justine needed to settle into her new reality. To decide what she really wanted, to reconsider her goals and aspirations.

"You were set to do it before and we hadn't talked."

"Things were different then." Setting up the interview had signified a new beginning for her, a life without Rocco or Teresa.

"Look, Justine, I know you well enough to know you need a challenge. This position would provide that if it's what you want." His hands came down on her shoulders and his thumbs kneaded her tired muscles. The man knew exactly what to do to calm her busy mind.

"An interview isn't a commitment." His tone was soft and reassuring. "See how it goes. Then we can talk."

Leaning back in the chair, she lifted her chin and gave Rocco a kiss of thanks before she typed a reply and hit send. He was right. An interview didn't mean she was signing away her life.

The producer's response hit Justine's inbox just before she signed off to walk across the street for breakfast, asking if she could possibly make it this afternoon. After a moment's panic and at Rocco's urging, she agreed.

"Nothing to lose," he'd assured her.

Two hours later, though, when Rocco had departed for Johns Hopkins and Justine waited at the hotel entrance for the car service that would take her first to a shop to find a suit and appropriate shoes, then to D.C. for the meeting, she couldn't shake the queasy feeling that'd settled in the pit of her stomach. It was the exact sensation that plagued her the morning of her crash, when she'd stood at the top of the run in Kitzbuhel waiting for the go-ahead to move into the starting gate and told her coach the course felt wrong. She'd flat-out told him that, for the first time in her career, her gut was telling her not to ski.

He'd put a hand to her back and reminded her that she'd tackled the course dozens of times, had mastered the toughest of its tight turns, had managed to keep her skis under her on its icy bumps and through its notoriously dangerous shadowed sections. Not only that, she'd come within two tenths of a second of winning the downhill the previous year. Out of all the competitors, she'd had the fastest training run the previous day. This was going to be her race. Her World Cup win. Her moment of glory.

She'd nodded and gone through her mental warm-up routine, determined to knock out a killer run, but couldn't shake the vibe.

She was the first racer on the course that morning. Therefore, she was the first to cross the unusual rough patch just above the third turn. The one whose ski caught, wobbled, and then finally popped off when she was forced to overcorrect, sending her flying sideways over the next jump and into the fencing at the course's edge. The one whose boot and calf somehow caught in the bright orange mesh even as her body tried to obey the laws of physics that wanted her to continue downhill at over eighty miles an hour. The one whose leg snapped with such force she heard it over the violence of the crash, the one who bled through her torn racing suit to stain the bright white snow for the 75,000 fans watching along the course and on the jumbo screen at the bottom of the slope.

The one who was airlifted out even as crews traversed the course to investigate the area where she'd caught her ski. The one forced to listen as her coach phoned Rocco to tell him to get his tail to Austria because the course medical team said she'd need to undergo emergency surgery.

She hadn't shared her coach's fury that the treacherous conditions above the turn had been missed during numerous course inspections. Nor did she share her coach's anger that his favorite racer didn't have her spouse present to cheer her on or to hold her hand in the final moments before she was wheeled into the operating room. Justine poured every ounce of her energy into enduring the surgery and the months of rehabilitation that followed so she could get back on her skis, conquer that damned course, and reign as queen of the World Cup circuit.

She'd been more sad than angry that Rocco wasn't by her side in the immediate aftermath of the wreck. He moved heaven and earth to be there when she awakened from surgery, and she'd drawn strength from that. Her anger was reserved for herself, for failing to recognize the dangerous area and, more importantly, for failing to trust her intuition. Gut instinct had enabled her to move into the top echelon of her sport, tackling runs in ways that occasionally defied conventional thinking. She should've listened to it when it told her not to ski that morning.

In a matter of weeks, she lost her career, her coach, and then her marriage. Everything that mattered to her. Everything that defined her.

As she greeted the driver and climbed into the car that would carry her to the interview, she wished she knew what, exactly, her gut was trying to tell her now.

Rocco woke to the sound of a key card sliding into the hotel room's lock. As he straightened in the chair, the draft of a research paper written by one of his partners at Johns Hopkins slid to the floor. Last thing he remembered he'd been halfway through it. His eyes must've drifted shut while waiting for Justine to return from the job interview.

The door closed behind her as she kicked off a pair of sleek black heels, then sagged against the door. A quick glance at the bedside clock told Rocco it was after eight p.m., a fact confirmed by his growling stomach, but he ignored it in favor of studying his wife. Despite what must've been a long day, she looked phenomenal. Her light brown hair was perfectly styled, she wore a close-fitting black suit and a sky blue blouse that highlighted her clear blue eyes, and best of all, despite her body language, there was a glow about her that gave him the sense the interview went well.

Her eyes widened when she got a good look at him. "You shaved!"

He grinned and ran a hand over his smooth jaw. "Figured it was time. You never did tell me what you thought of it."

"You're sexy with or without it. Different, but still sexy. What made you decide to get rid of it?"

"Wanted a fresh start." He waved his hand to encompass her suit. "So, how'd it go?"

"Uh, uh. You first, Mr. Fresh Start."

"Anti-climactic." Especially after all they'd endured to keep the designs safe. "I met with the professors, had a lunch that would bore all but the hardest of hard-core biomedical engineering geeks, then made a copy of the designs for their files. They're going over them tonight."

"That's it?"

"That's it. It's not like the movies, where Spiderman or Superman saves a piece of futuristic technology from falling into a villain's hands and suddenly the world is a better, safer place."

"The world *is* a better, safer place," she argued.

"Perhaps, but without a sweeping musical score or special effects. Only lunch with a handful of scientists and engineers."

She chuckled at that, then leaned against the entry wall and scrunched her toes into the carpet, an action he noticed she did unconsciously whenever her muscles stiffened. "So tell me the important part. What did your partners think after you talked?"

"On first glance, they think the design is brilliant." He couldn't keep the satisfaction from his voice. "They also think it'll work. We'll know more in the coming weeks and months."

The delight on her face thrilled him. "Oh, Rocco, that's wonderful. I'm so happy. And so proud of you. You should be ecstatic. It's been years of work."

"That it has." He leaned forward, resting his elbows on his thighs. "Now your turn. How'd it go? It has to be more interesting than my day."

He saw the triumph in her eyes a split second before he heard it in her voice. "Would you believe they offered me the job on the spot?"

"Of course I believe it. Who wouldn't hire you?"

She waved off the compliment even as a blush crept across her cheeks. "The producer said she'd watched me give interviews numerous times over the years and likes the way I can describe a course in layman's terms. One of her coworkers said there's been talk around their office for years that I'd be a great analyst when I retired. They also liked that my reputation is clean—no drugs, no wild partying, nothing scandalous—but have, in their words, an edge that keeps younger viewers interested. They're tired of hiring analysts and discovering ex-girlfriends with restraining orders, X-rated photos or videos, and gambling problems. I assured them I had no such issues, and voila, they made an offer."

It took him less than two seconds to cross the room and sweep her into his arms. He was rewarded with a warm, joyous hug, then felt the press of her lips against his shoulder. "Congratulations," he said into her hair. "You're going to be amazing."

"I haven't accepted yet," she said into his shirt with a laugh. "I haven't decided what I want."

Happiness flooded through him as he released her. There was a confidence and a surety about Justine he hadn't seen in a long, long time. Whether she opted to take the job or not, it was a relief to see her back to her old self.

Definitely a day for fresh starts.

"How about we discuss it over dinner? Grab those sexy shoes and I'll take you somewhere decadent."

"Wearing those shoes or any others right now would constitute torture. Mind if we do room service?"

"Not at all." They'd have as long as they wanted in Rome. While he placed an order, Justine took off her jacket and sat on the bed, settling her back against the thick pillows. He moved to her side, then slowly ran his hand up her left calf.

"Your leg's a little swollen."

"Sexy shoes will do that."

"So will all that running you did." He lifted her leg into his lap, then slowly, gently began to massage her calf. Despite the severity of her injury, she'd regained a great deal of strength, more than he'd thought possible.

"That feels great," she mumbled, leaning her head back and closing her eyes.

"So do you." When she cracked an eyelid, he said, "I didn't say that to get you into bed."

"I'm already *in* bed."

"Lucky me." He ran his thumbs along the back of her calf, easing the knots from the tense muscles. "What I really meant is that your calf feels great. Almost back to normal."

"From the outside, yes, if you can ignore the scars. The inside is a different matter. While the bones have healed, everything else feels tight. When I stretch, there's a sensation of ripping apart from the inside out."

"Have you asked the doc about it?"

The edge of her mouth twitched.

"Why not? You worried what he'll tell you?"

"I actually haven't been in a while. Rehab, yes. Doc, no." She ran a hand over her hair, pushing a few rogue strands away from her face. "I haven't been back since he told me my career was over. I didn't see much point."

"That was months ago. Longer." He ran his palms around to her shin, then up to the outside of her knee and paused. Her quads were rock solid, just as they'd been when she was competing. "You're in better shape now. Maybe you should see why you have that ripping feeling?"

"Rehab guys say it's the muscles getting used to movement. Scar tissue breaking up as I exercise and gradually extend my range of motion. Apparently it's a good thing. Painful as hell, but good." Her chest rose and fell on a deep breath. "When you came to my apartment the other night, you asked if I'd quit taking my pain meds. The answer is yes. I don't want to become reliant on them."

"You seemed sore that night, even before we went running through the streets."

"I'd had an intense session at rehab. Then I went to the cemetery and my Tuesday dinner when I probably should've gone home and rested." She flexed her foot, stretching. "I've apparently made progress, since I was able to wear heels for several hours today."

"Guess it hadn't occurred to me that you haven't worn them since before the accident."

"Not the type of thing that enters a guy's mind."

"It should've. Seeing your legs in a pair of high heels gets me going every time." He slid his hands down her calf, enjoying his rediscovery of Justine's bare, silken skin and sculpted muscle as he kneaded each tight area. When he reached her ankle, he looked up to see her studying him. She'd been watching him explore, but there was more to her gaze, an emotion she attempted to hide with a smile that didn't quite ring true.

"You want to ski again." The realization hit him with the intensity of Karpovsky's kidney punches. He stared at her in astonishment. "You think you can do it, but you're avoiding the doctor until you can prove you're strong enough for medical clearance."

"What would make you think that?" Though her voice remained steady, he saw the truth in her eyes.

"Because that's always been your dream. You wanted to finish a season with the top world ranking. You wanted an Olympic gold." He shook his head. "Perhaps I should say that in present tense. You want to be number one. You want a gold medal. Multiple golds."

"Not just one doctor, but several have told me it's impossible. And these are docs who regularly see athletes at my level. They know what's possible."

"So do you." And she wanted it. He knew it as surely as he knew Newton's laws of motion. In her heart, she hadn't quit. Not yet.

A sharp rap at the hotel door and a voice announcing the arrival of room service cut short their conversation, but not before Rocco gave Justine a long look. Rocco signed for the meal and added a generous tip as the young woman rolled in a cart, presented the food and asked if all appeared in order, then told them to call down when they were ready to have the dishes cleared.

Justine joined Rocco at the room's small table as he poured sodas for each of them. Before he could unroll his silverware from the napkin, she said, "The possibility scares you."

He snapped his attention to Justine. She hadn't touched her drink or her silverware. "Why would I be scared?"

"Of what might happen if I ski again."

"Hell yes, I'm scared." Until she said it—until *he* said it—he hadn't realized the truth of it. But the idea of having her back on skis, going downhill full bore, made his heart feel as if it were held in an icy fist that slowly squeezed the life from him. "You really are thinking about it?"

"What scares you most, Rocco, that I might get hurt?"

"That doesn't answer my question."

She pressed on, her voice gentle but firm. "Are you afraid that if I try and fail I'd be miserable? That if I succeed, we might never have the traditional married life we thought we'd have when my career ended? Or are you still, deep down, scared that your secret could be discovered?"

CHAPTER 15

SHE SEARCHED his face as her questions hung in the air, suddenly realizing that it was the one she'd sandwiched in the middle that was the most important. They'd entered into a nontraditional marriage, one where they only lived under the same roof for a month or two of her off-season. They'd expected it to be years before Justine retired, so they hadn't given their long-term living arrangement much discussion time. When her injury forced the issue, the traditional life she'd assumed they'd have never materialized. Teresa was too much a part of it.

But now she had to wonder, what did Rocco want?

Rocco rested both hands on the table. "What scares me most, Justine, is that you're scared." His voice softened as he added, "You've never been afraid of anything. Not of double black diamond slopes, not of your competition. Definitely not of us. But you were afraid to tell me you're thinking of skiing again."

"I've never been hurt before. Not like this." She angled a look at her leg.

"But?"

"But I've been told dozens of times that I couldn't accomplish things—that I wasn't fast enough, strong enough, skilled enough—

and I accomplished them anyway. Deep down, I believe it's possible."

Rocco sat back in his chair, absorbing her words. "How long have you known?"

"I didn't," she admitted. "Not until five minutes ago, when you were massaging my calf and said it out loud. But ever since I missed the job interview in Croatia, I've had an uneasy feeling in the pit of my stomach, like I was doing something wrong. Then this morning, when I read the producer's message, it intensified, almost to the point that I felt sick."

"Your inner voice had something to say."

"I suppose it did." A sigh escaped her. "But the more I think about it, the more I realize it's why I pushed myself so hard at rehab, even after the doctors told me I'd never regain the strength necessary to compete at the World Cup level. One even suggested I take the opportunity to rediscover skiing just for fun. As if competing wasn't where I found my fun." She shot him a wry look. "I can't get on skis and simply glide downhill. Even if I tried, I'd only get a few hundred yards before every cell in my body would tell me to punch the gas and smoke everyone else on the mountain."

"Nothing like telling Justine Flyte she can't do something to make her say, 'wanna bet?' is there?"

"Guess not." She took a drink of her soda and grinned. "Maybe you know me better than I know myself."

"What I know is that you have an innate drive to be the best and you've worked hard to live up to your potential. It's part of what drew me to you that first night we met."

"The pot's talking to the kettle now?"

"You bet." His smile faded to seriousness. "You're going to turn down the job, aren't you?"

She considered the question as she took a bite of the chicken parmesan Rocco had ordered for her. It wasn't what she'd find in Rome, but it wasn't half bad. "I don't know. I don't want to lose out on the opportunity. I've always planned to stay with the sport in some way after I retired from competition, and working as an analyst would keep me involved. I'd be able to find new challenges. I'd know that even if I never nabbed a gold medal or finished a season with that World Cup crystal globe in my hands, my competitive years weren't a waste. I'd be able to view them as a step along my career path." She met his gaze. "When the opportunity to take that next step is right in front of you, it's hard to turn and walk a different direction. Especially when that direction is uncertain."

"But there's more."

"There's the fact I could lose you all over again." The words came out before she could consider them. Once spoken, though, she knew them to be the truth.

"You won't—"

"I hated that you weren't with me. *Hated* it." A hard lump of emotion clogged her throat, but she barreled on. "There, I've said it. I knew you couldn't make all my events, not with work as important and time-consuming as yours, and I didn't expect it. But deep in my heart, on the big days, it killed me not to have you there."

"Like Kitzbuhel."

"Like Kitzbuhel."

She'd been the only competitor without a cadre of family members standing by holding banners and ringing cowbells. When asked about it by the media, she'd mentioned that her husband was in the medical profession and didn't have the ability to travel as much as he'd like, but that she knew he was watching and she felt him cheering her on. She finished the interview as she always did by blowing him a kiss via the camera. He'd told her that he'd captured every one of those television kisses and held them near to his heart.

It wasn't the same.

"I hated myself for not being in Kitzbuhel," he told her, though she already knew. "It ripped my guts out to know you were seriously injured and that it was your coach with you instead of me. Flying up to Austria was the longest, worst flight of my life, knowing that I probably wouldn't get there before they took you into surgery."

"It was only an hour's flight."

"Felt like a year." He scrubbed both hands over his jaw. "It won't happen again. If you decide to ski, I'll be there."

"You can't. That's what scares me." Slowly, she shook her head. "The sport has its risks no matter how well prepared I might be. If I were to get hurt again—or hell, even if I'm on a podium again—I'll wish you were with me. You'll feel guilty, even though it can't be helped, and it could drive a wedge between us we'll never be able to remove."

He was around the table before she finished speaking, framing her face with his hands. "I'll be there."

Didn't he see? "Rocco, you're still *you*. All the reasons you didn't attend before still exist. You're still the biological child of a king known for his high moral standards and his fidelity. A king who is a head of state. A king whose children don't even know you or your brother and sister exist. All it would take is for the wrong person to see you at one of my events—someone who knows the Barrali family —and questions will be asked. It's too public. Reporters would be on it like flies on cow patties. It's more likely to stay private if I'm an analyst. In that case, I won't be the story and you wouldn't appear on camera. It's too big a risk—"

He leaned down, still cradling her cheeks in his hands, so his forehead was only an inch from hers. "Cow patties, Justine? Really?"

"You're not taking this seriously."

"I'm taking it very seriously. And you're talking a million miles an hour, which is what you do when you get flustered." He dropped to his knees and buried his hands in her hair, keeping her eyes locked on his. "If you believe you can ski again, I believe it, too. When the time comes to start attending events, I'll notify Queen Fabrizia. She can decide how to handle it with her husband and children if my paternity ever comes under scrutiny….and that's a big if. It's not a problem."

How could he think that? "Everyone from legit reporters to fly-by-night paparazzi would be after you. And what about Enzo and Lina? Shouldn't they have a say in this?"

"We've always known it could come out. I'd hate for that to happen, but if it does, it does. I refuse to miss out on the best part of my life out of fear. No more. Whether you ski, you become an analyst, or you decide to run for President, I want to be by your side. Enzo and Lina will understand. If they don't, too bad." Years of internal struggle were visible in his gaze. But there was a defiance, too, one she'd never seen in Rocco before.

"I have no desire to be President." She wrapped her hands around his wrists and studied him. "Are you sure?"

"I told you when we made love on the ferry that I never want to lose you again. I meant it." His voice took on a gravelly edge. "When you said that you came to my mother's funeral to say goodbye to me… Justine, you have no idea how much that hurt. No. Idea."

Agony punctuated his words, then his mouth met hers in a gentle, searching kiss.

Never had she seen Rocco so exposed, so unguarded. She opened to him, allowing him to take what he needed. Rocco was so strong, so intelligent, so calm. He'd been her anchor during the first years of their marriage, steady in the face of the daily ups and downs that accompanied her competitions until his secrets tore them apart.

Now that he'd shared those secrets with her and risked sharing them with the world, she realized that he needed her to be his anchor, too.

She slid from the chair and pressed against him, slipping her arms around his lean waist as she deepened their kiss, and was rewarded by a groan of intense need. He explored her mouth, her jawline, her neck, his movements slow and worshipful.

When he shifted to drop kisses along her hairline, he paused with his lips at her temple. His chest rose against hers, and she closed her eyes to focus on the sensation of simply being in his arms. Oh, how she'd missed the masculine scent of him and the slow thump of his heartbeat against hers. Even the way his fingers inevitably found their way to the back hook of her bra, threatening to undo it through her clothes as his hand skirted along its edge. But this time, his hands remained around her back, holding her body flush against his.

"I want a real marriage, Justine. We made a mess of it after your injury—*I* made a mess of it—but I won't let that happen again. As long as you want to ski, I'll be there for you. If you decide not to ski, whether that's tomorrow or next year or a decade from now, I'll be there for you. We'll talk it through from now on. Where we'll live, how we'll live. Whether we spend our time on the road or holed up in a little cabin off the slopes in Colorado, or we decide to build an obnoxiously luxurious villa in Switzerland…none of that matters. As long as we keep talking, this marriage will work, traditional or not. Being married to you doesn't scare me at all. My only fear is not having you at all."

"You have me." She drew back from his embrace and saw his gaze was dark with urgency, both emotional and physical. "You have me."

He crushed her against him. "I am so damned lucky."

She smiled at the desire lacing his words, even as she freed his shirt from his pants, wanting the heat of his skin against hers. Wanting to spread her hands across the muscles of his back, to scatter kisses across his chest, to make him moan for her again. When his shirt hit the floor, the full weight of their time apart hit her. She'd missed him terribly. He belonged with her, and she with him.

He laughed as she urged him to stand, then pushed him on top of the bed. She was over him in a heartbeat, exploring the firm muscle of his abdomen with her fingertips before following the motion with her mouth.

"Justine, you make me crazy," he ground out as his hands came to her hair.

"And I love it when you twist my hair around your fingers, just like that."

She kissed her way up his torso, pausing to tease his throat with her lips, then to run her hands over his jawline and the freshly shaved skin there.

"That suit is very sexy," he murmured, "but I want you out of it."

With a grin, she rose to her knees and performed a striptease with her blouse. As hunger filled his eyes, she slowly removed her bra, one strap at a time, one cup at a time, her gaze never leaving his. Before she could shift to undo her skirt, he flipped her on the bed and did it for her, sliding it down her legs and sending it across the room. He captured one ankle in his palm and kissed the inside of her knee, then worked his way higher, until he bracketed her hips with both hands and his wondrous mouth reached her core. Arching her back in pleasure, she cried out for him as he worked magic with his tongue and his fingers, sending her closer and closer to her climax.

"Rocco, please."

"You like?"

She answered with a choked sigh as he continued, sending her over the edge. She squeezed her eyes shut against the waves of sensation as she called his name. Everything in her spiraled as she clutched at Rocco, at the sheets, at whatever she could. Then he was over her, gloriously, completely naked, though she didn't remember him removing his pants. His powerful legs nudged hers further apart as he kissed her.

"I need to be inside you," he whispered, so passionately she nearly came apart at his words alone.

"I need you, too. So much."

She'd barely responded before he was there, his muscled arms on either side of her supporting his weight. Heat rolled off him in waves as he sheathed himself fully, then slowly, gently, moved out, drawing a long sigh of satisfaction from her before he was inside her again, filling her completely, with an intensity that differed from when they made love on the ferry. Then, they'd been frantic, desperate to know each other again, to reassure themselves that they were safe. Tonight wasn't about physical abandon, but emotional. They'd shared their deepest dreams and fears and they'd come out on the other side. Together.

This was about joy, about two souls reveling in the knowledge they were forever joined.

Seeing the unconditional love in his amber eyes was the most beautiful moment of her life.

Her breath caught as he kissed her deeply, then moved with more purpose, bringing her once more to the precipice. She tried to steady her breathing, wanting the moment to last at the same time her body strove to go over the edge.

She needed him with her.

Her muscles clenched and he shuddered in response. A sheen of sweat broke out along his forehead as he pressed it to hers. "Justine—"

"Come with me."

And he did. A profoundly male cry broke from him as his entire body convulsed, shattered. His thumb went to her most sensitive spot, the pressure adding to the heady sensation of him pulsing inside her. Her entire body felt electrified as he pushed her to a dizzying peak from which she fell and fell and fell. When she finally caught her breath, he gathered her in his arms, eased her to her side, then nestled her against him. Their legs tangled and his chest pressed against her back, allowing her to feel the steady beat of his heart. For long minutes, they lay there, savoring the experience, their fingers intertwined, their world as one. A sense of peace filled her soul, as if she'd finally landed where she belonged.

With Rocco. The man she loved.

He rose on his elbow and pressed a tender kiss above her ear. When she twisted to look at him, the expression of adoration on his face brought tears to her eyes.

He brushed her hair back. "I love you, Justine. I don't think I've said it in a long time. Too long. But I mean it with my entire being. I love you more now than the day we married. I want the fairy tale with you, risks be damned. From now on, I promise to do what's best for us. Not what's best for me."

"I love you, too, Rocco." She rose to give him another kiss, smiling against his mouth as she did so. In the short time since he'd knocked on her apartment door, she'd fallen in love with him all over again.

She had nothing to fear and everything to celebrate.

CHAPTER 16

Fabrizia turned toward her husband as he removed his cufflinks and placed them on the tray near the wooden clothes butler his valet had left for the purpose. Two freshly pressed suits and dress shirts with coordinating accessories were in the armoire nearby, selected by Carlo and his valet specifically for the royal couple's final two days in Rome.

"Tired, yes, exhausted, no. I think it was a productive night."

"Thanks to you. The Italian prime minister was more open to my ideas for educational exchange programs than I expected. I suspect it's because you dazzled him in that gorgeous red gown of yours. He couldn't take his eyes off you."

"Now you're just flirting with me."

"Always." Carlo's smile made Fabrizia's heart skip as he unbuttoned his shirt. Did he realize how handsome he was?

Probably. Vulnerable, too, though, which made her next words difficult. She turned her back to Carlo to allow him to unzip her gown. Gently, he eased the pull downward, careful not to snag the delicate Armani silk, then eased the sides apart so she could remove it. As she stepped out of it, she asked, "Have you heard from Umberto?"

"I know that Rocco and his wife made it to Baltimore. The Russians remain in Italian custody. Radich is a first-time offender, but Karpovsky is apparently suspected in a killing that took place in Milan two years ago. The Russians are also working to build a case against him in the death of his sister-in-law." The king shook his head as he arranged his shirt for the valet. "I'm glad Umberto knew how to handle him. Karpovsky's about as dangerous a man as exists in this world and he had more men and firepower with him than Umberto was expecting."

"We hired Umberto specifically for his unique talents. But yes, I'm grateful he's all right. Rocco and Justine Cornaro, too." She draped the gown across the back of a plush chair beside the immense fireplace that dominated their hotel suite. Despite the seriousness of their conversation, Fabrizia noticed that Carlo watched her movements with frank appreciation. "Did Umberto tell you anything else?"

Carlo's gaze sharpened. "Such as?"

So he didn't know. "Rocco sent the plane back. It should land here in Rome in the morning."

"He decided to stay in the United States for a while?"

"I don't know. When they disembarked, he told the pilot he and Justine would make their own arrangements to fly back to Europe."

There was a brief pause before Carlo turned away to remove his slacks and socks and place them with the shirt. "He didn't wish to use my plane any longer than absolutely necessary." He took a sip of the Aberlour he'd poured himself after they'd arrived back at their suite following the state dinner. "I can't blame him. I'd have done the same in his place, knowing what he knows about me."

"It was good of you to offer the plane, Carlo. I'm sure he's thankful."

Carlo's smile didn't reach his eyes as he looked over his shoulder at her. "Perhaps, perhaps not. But I appreciate you saying so."

She extended her hand to him. "Take me to bed, then. Show me how appreciative you are of your beautiful wife."

This time, his smile did reach his eyes, but Fabrizia had little time to notice the mischief there before he corralled her about the waist and tackled her across the suite's plush bed, coming to rest with her trapped underneath him. He propped himself above her on his forearms and frowned at her in mock warning.

"You, my dear, are trying to distract me from my troubles."

She ran a fingertip along his chin. The light from the dimmed overhead chandelier made the center stone of her emerald ring shine. It had been a gift from Carlo for their fortieth wedding anniversary, a design he'd created himself. Smiling into his rich brown eyes, she savored the scent she always identified as uniquely Carlo's, a mix of his cologne, his warm olive-gold skin, and the faintest hint of whisky. "Did it work?"

"It always does." He swept his large hands up her sides, past her ribcage to cradle her breasts. "No man can resist you. I'm merely happy I'm the one with you tonight."

"Forever."

Someday, no matter what it took, she'd ensure his family was complete. If she'd managed to capture Carlo's heart when he'd been so enamored of Teresa all those years ago, she could accomplish anything.

Even find a way to reconcile Carlo with Teresa's children.

Rocco AWAKENED with a perfectly fluffed pillow under his head and a warm, rounded rear end pressed against his hips. Without opening his eyes, he inhaled deeply, savoring the blissful comfort of the bed and the light lemony-vanilla scent of Justine's favorite shampoo. She must've found a bottle at some point yesterday while shopping for interview clothing.

"Good morning."

"Mmmm…love that husky morning voice." He dragged a slow kiss across Justine's shoulder and tightened his hold on her waist. Last night had been the most amazing of his life. He'd loved Justine from the first, but the last few days brought a deeper, more powerful layer to that love, one that made his heart swell. "How'd you know I was awake?"

She shifted her backside against him. "You need to ask?"

Grinning, he pushed to all fours and captured her underneath him. Tendrils of hair lay across her face as she blinked at him. He smoothed them back, then ran his index finger along the arch of her eyebrow and down the curve of her cheek, letting it come to rest against her lush mouth. "It'd be a shame to waste."

Her eyes widened fractionally, then she snapped at his finger, catching it gently between her teeth at the last moment.

Now he was really awake. "Oh, bad girl."

She sucked. He watched. He grew harder. The woman would be the death of him, but what a way to go. Then, from the other side of the room, came the low vibration of a cell phone.

"What is that?" she asked around his finger, her brow wrinkling.

"I picked up a new phone while I was out yesterday. Sent Kos the number. He can wait." Rocco nudged against her. "This is far more pressing an issue."

She rolled her eyes and released his finger as the phone continued to buzz. "The man isn't the type to call unless it's urgent. Get on and get off."

He winked at the double entendre before reluctantly rolling away. Keeping his eyes on Justine, he crossed the room to locate the phone.

"Rocco?"

"Lina." He couldn't hide his surprise at hearing his sister's familiar voice. "What's going on?"

"Could ask you the same. I've been trying to reach you for a couple days, but Kos said you were traveling and switched phones. I didn't know you had a trip planned."

Justine gestured that she was going to get dressed for the day. Rocco shook his head no, despite knowing Lina wouldn't have called unless it was important, but Justine waved for him to continue as she eased out of the bed, turning her back toward him.

He ached to kiss and lick his way along that spine. To run his hands over the lean muscles of her arms and shoulders. To savor the spot at the base of her neck. When he kissed her there, it always made her so hot that she—

"Rocco?"

Lina's inquiry jerked him back to the present. "Sorry. Distracted."

"No kidding."

He cleared his throat and turned away from Justine so he could focus. "I had some work issues pop up and needed to make a quick visit to Johns Hopkins. Is everything okay there?"

Nothing had seemed out of the ordinary when he'd seen Lina at their mother's funeral. She'd been upset, of course, but he hadn't expected to hear from her so soon, not without reason.

"I had a call from a New York real estate agent when they couldn't contact you. There's a possible buyer for Mom's condo."

"I haven't even listed it." He found a clean pair of underwear and pulled them on, then took a seat at the head of the bed while Justine disappeared into the bathroom.

"I know. It's a neighbor. She and Mom apparently discussed it the last time Mom was in New York. Know anything about it?"

"The Metzgers," he told her. "Mom mentioned that after her diagnosis, she'd told Mrs. Metzger she was planning to put the condo on the market if none of us want it. Mrs. Metzger said she'd love to have one of us in there, but if not, she'd be willing to buy it. Probably to expand her own condo into Mom's space."

"Has Enzo said whether he wants it or not yet?"

"No. I hadn't gotten that far." Hadn't so much as unsealed the envelope with his mother's papers, let alone dealt with the condo. It was the last piece of real estate she still owned, having sold the property she and Jack owned in Croatia before moving into the villa.

"I'll put off the agent for a while, then."

Justine popped her head out of the bathroom long enough to hold up the pair of jeans she'd taken from the yacht and mouthed her thanks. Rocco nodded to her, then said, "By the way, I hope it's all right, but I was on the yacht with Justine and she didn't have a bag, so I told her she could borrow the clothes you left. She wanted me to thank you."

There was a pause on the line, during which he could've smacked himself for speaking without thinking. Then, from Lina, "Since the funeral?"

"Yes."

Another silence. "She's there with you in the States?"

"Yes."

"In that case, I hope she's not wearing the clothes right now."

He groaned. "Lina—"

"Oh, come on. The last few months have been awful for you. You bore the brunt of Mom's illness and care, and now you're having to deal with her estate. You deserve some happiness. So…you two going to reconcile?"

If Justine experienced the same powerful emotions he did last night—and he could swear she had—then they were already reconciled. Better than reconciled, in fact. But he wasn't about to share that with his sister. He glanced at the closed bathroom door. "No comment."

"In that case, you should know that I'm relying on you to provide me with nieces and nephews since it doesn't look like I'm going to have kids of my own. Tons of them, please. Athletic like their mom. It'd be preferable if they look like their mom, too."

"Lina? Shut up."

A laugh bubbled over the line, the first he'd heard from Lina since their mother confessed that her liver was failing. "Has asking me to shut up ever worked for you?"

"I've always been the persistent type."

"True." In a more serious tone, she said, "Before I let you go, have you looked through Mom's papers?"

"Not yet. I have them with me, though. Wasn't sure how long I'd be away."

"She told me that there'd be a letter for me. She wrote letters for you and Enzo, too."

His mother hadn't mentioned that to him, though he wasn't surprised. "I'll go through the packet and forward your letters as soon as I can. Today if possible. And I'll check with Enzo about the condo."

"Thanks. Call if you need help with anything while you're away."

"Will do."

"And Rocco? Take care of yourself. I worry about you."

He thanked Lina for her concern and told her he hoped to see her soon, then ended the call. He crossed the room to knock on the bathroom door and tell Justine he was done, but the sound of the shower stopped him before his knuckles connected.

So much for getting on and getting off.

Figuring there was no time like the present, he pulled on a pair of jeans, then dug through his bag to find the envelopes containing his mother's papers. At the very least, he could address anything urgent, then overnight Lina and Enzo's letters to them so he wouldn't have to deal with estate matters while he toured Rome with Justine.

That time belonged to the two of them. No interruptions, no distractions.

He settled at the room's small table with the rubber-banded stack of envelopes, each neatly labeled in his mother's hand. Knowing her death was imminent, she'd divided a good deal of her personal property over the last year, insisting that it gave her peace of mind to know it was settled. She'd told Rocco that the envelopes contained papers he'd need to close the last pieces of her estate. A separate envelope bearing a rod of Asclepius logo and a hospital return address contained copies of the death certificate from the physician who'd attended her during her final hours.

Setting aside the death certificate, he undid the rubber band on the bundle and opened the top envelope. It contained a neat stack of papers corralled by a binder clip. On top was a handwritten list of its contents: Croatian probate instructions for foreign residents, Sarcaccian birth certificate, Italian marriage certificate, list of remaining bank accounts, New York condo deed, list of all other remaining assets, list of contacts.

He frowned, surprised she'd gone so far as to include instructions for probate. He flipped past the handwritten list to the top page. As indicated, she'd made a copy of pertinent instructions for filing with the Croatian courts, highlighting a clause which read:

for foreign residents of Croatia, original birth certificates must be prop-
erly notarized and presented to the court

The next page was her birth certificate, obtained from the village where she was born in Sarcaccia and notarized. He ran a hand over the raised seal as he read the Italian-language record of a 3.4 kg live female born to Guido and Maria Fedeli.

He turned to the marriage certificate, but paused, sure he'd glimpsed a number incorrectly. He returned to the birth certificate.

"That's wrong." The inaccuracy so stunned him he'd said it aloud. His mother's birthdate was off by exactly ten years.

He went to the marriage certificate, which registered the union of Jack Cornaro and Teresa Fedeli. The dates there were accurate. He grumbled in annoyance. How could his mother, who was as detail-oriented as they came, miss that her birth certificate had a typo?

"What's wrong?"

Rocco's head whipped up. Justine stood in the doorway of the bathroom, a short white robe loosely tied at her waist. She used a white towel to rub her hair as she frowned at him. "Those are your mother's papers, right?"

He held the clipped stack aloft. "Would you believe her birth certificate has an error?"

Justine cringed. "Older or younger? If a town clerk somewhere in Sarcaccia made her older, she'll find a way to come back and throttle them."

"Ten years older. There's a digit wrong."

Her hands stilled for a moment, then she tossed the towel back into the bathroom. "That can't be right. Let me see."

"Told you," he said as she took a seat on the bed and studied the certificate with an expression of puzzlement. "It's correct on the marriage certificate. And I saw her passport when I took her to get it renewed year before last, so I know it's correct there."

Justine handed back the papers. "How could she have gotten a passport if her birth certificate is wrong? Wouldn't she have noticed? Wouldn't *someone* have noticed?"

"You'd think." It was as much a mystery to him as it was to Justine.

His mother hadn't needed her birth certificate for the passport renewal, but she would've needed it when she obtained the original. Those dates would've been checked and double-checked. "Her estate is going to hang up in probate if I can't get it rectified. It'll be a real headache."

Justine spread her hands. "It's midafternoon in Sarcaccia. Why not call the town hall where she was born and see what they say?"

He chuckled at that. "Would you believe they don't have a town hall? She was born in a town of about two hundred people. Records from the last twenty years or so are kept in Cateri, since it's the capital, but everything older than that is still held at the local church."

"Wow. That's real old country."

"You bet. She was proud of it." His mother told him dozens of stories over the years about growing up in her rural farming community, which was located on the far side of the island from Cateri, Sarcaccia's bustling cultural and political center. "I'll call and see if I can get in touch with one of the local priests. They'll be able to fix this. I wouldn't be surprised to find someone at the church who remembers her."

"She's been living abroad a long time."

He picked up his phone. "Guess we'll see how much small towns in Sarcaccia have changed, then."

A few calls later, Rocco was connected to a Father Riccardo, who greeted him warmly and promised to investigate the matter.

Rocco set the phone on top of the table and watched as Justine pulled on the jeans she'd borrowed from Lina. He'd missed watching Justine dress in the mornings. It wasn't as fun as watching her undress, but seeing her long legs slide into a pair of jeans had its own sex appeal.

"So?" she asked, eyeing him as he openly watched her. "What'd he say?"

"He's familiar with the Fedeli family. Told me he should be able to locate the information and call back within ten minutes."

"That's amazing. Who offers that kind of assistance anymore?"

He raised a brow. "Like you said, real old country."

She laughed and flung his shirt at him. "Get dressed and you can take me out for an old country breakfast after the priest calls back. I'd love to hit that diner across the street again for eggs and bacon."

"Then work it off?"

Stretching, she slid her white T-shirt over her head in slow motion, intentionally torturing him. When her face popped through the neckline, she said, "I think that can be arranged."

He moved to her side and slipped his hands under the lower edge of her shirt. "We could do a quick warm up now. We have ten minutes to kill."

"Shouldn't you look through more of her papers? Maybe there's an explanation for the birth certificate."

"Nah. It's mostly property information and bank records. Lina also said that there are letters for the three of us. But I'd much rather do this."

"Rocco, stop."

"Mmmm…too late." He buried his face in her damp hair. Amazing how a scent could do such wondrous things to him simply because that scent was hers.

"Rocco, stop. Your phone is ringing."

He heard it just as she said the words. With a groan, he released her. What he heard from the priest didn't improve his mood. After he hung up, he went to the window and stared out, trying to process the information.

Justine came up behind him and put a gentle hand to his lower back.

"Father Riccardo says it's accurate. He located their copy, which has the same date as this one. He even called the priest listed as having performed the baptism, just to be certain." Rocco's vision blurred, which turned the lights spanning the hotel's parking lot into a mass of yellow spots. He folded his arms across his chest in a futile effort to maintain his equilibrium. When it didn't work, he closed his eyes.

This can't be happening.

"You're kidding. He's still alive?"

Rocco swallowed hard as his mind raced at a million miles an hour. No matter how desperately he tried to steer his thoughts down a different road, he ran straight into the same brick wall.

"Rocco?"

He blinked. "He's in his nineties, long retired, and in typical small village fashion, his last name is Fedeli. He's one of my grandfather's cousins. He told Father Riccardo that the date is one-hundred percent accurate. He said it was easy to remember because my mother was born on my grandfather's thirty-fifth birthday."

Rocco turned to Justine, hating what he knew to be true, even as every fiber of his being rebelled against it, wanting to deny it. "I know *my* birth certificate is accurate, which means my mother was twenty-nine when she had me. Not nineteen."

Justine studied him for a moment, confusion etching her features. Then realization dawned. He saw the dread in her eyes just before she drew a sharp breath.

"Oh, Rocco. Surely she couldn't—"

"Carlo can't falsify his age. The entire world knows when he was born." Horror and disgust squeezed his chest, making it difficult to speak. "That means...that means my mother was a sexual predator. I'm the result."

CHAPTER 17

T HE SET of Rocco's jaw, the pain in his eyes…in the years she'd known him, Justine had never seen Rocco like this. Not when he'd arrived at the hospital in a panic following her accident. Not when Teresa admitted that she was terminally ill.

Not even when Justine had watched from the shadow of the trees while Rocco stood by his mother's grave and bravely delivered her eulogy, though doing so tore him apart inside.

A wave of sadness engulfed Justine, one so powerful that she stepped backward until her legs hit the bed, causing her knees to buckle so she sat.

"My mother was a predator." He said it again, lifting his gaze to the ceiling while raking his hands over his head. "He was her student. Only a teenager. She was an *adult*. She was…I just…I don't know what to think. She told us she was still in college when she took that tutoring job, but either that was a lie or the priest is lying now. *And her birth certificate is wrong. What in the world do I do with this?"

Tears burned at the back of her eyes. Her throat constricted. Instinct made her want to comfort him, to tell him it was a mistake. That Teresa never could've done what Rocco believed, what the evidence seemed to indicate. But she couldn't. She had nothing, and the scientist in Rocco would want proof to refute the evidence in front of him.

Biting her lip in an effort to hold back the tears, Justine slowly rose from the bed and went to Rocco, wrapping her arms around him.

His body tensed. For an interminable moment, she feared he'd push her away. But then his arms came down, tight around her, and he buried his face in her hair. There were no tears, no sighs. He remained still, saying nothing. She held him like that for a long time, allowing his shock to dissipate. Finally, he took a deep breath and stepped back.

"I'd ask if you're okay, but I already know the answer," she said. "Rocco, I'm so sorry. I wish I could make it better."

"You are, just by being here."

Justine said a silent prayer of thanks she and Rocco had spent such a meaningful night together, talking through their fears and ensuring that they were on the same wavelength. This morning would be even harder on him—and on her—if they hadn't.

He strode across the room to grab a bottle of water from the mini-fridge, angling a second bottle toward her. She nodded, and he brought it to her before taking a long swig from his. A frown cut across his brow as he swallowed.

"What is it?"

His dark eyes met hers. "I'm stunned you're not angry with me. And very grateful."

What? "Why in the world would I be angry?"

"I protected her. I protected her secret. You're the one who paid the price."

"So did you," Justine pointed out. "And that's assuming that you're analyzing all of this properly."

"I can't imagine another explanation."

Justine couldn't, either. She glanced at the pile of envelopes Teresa had left for Rocco, the envelopes he'd so carefully stowed in his safe, then protected on the journey to Baltimore. "Lina said she'd written letters to all of you. Maybe there's something in there that'll explain."

Exhaustion washed across Rocco's features at the idea of digging back through the pile. However, he took another drink of his water, set the bottle on the table, and scanned the envelopes, bypassing the property and bank information to unseal the manila envelope on the bottom of the stack, one that was labeled private. As Lina had predicted, it contained three smaller, white envelopes, each bearing the name of one of Teresa's children.

Rocco set Lina and Enzo's envelopes aside, then tapped his against the edge of the table several times before tossing it onto the bed. "I'm going to shower first. Give myself a few minutes before I dive in."

"Whatever you want." She'd be here when he was ready.

Justine fixed her hair and finished getting ready while his shower ran, taking it as a good sign when she heard him humming while he shaved, a habit he'd had as long as she'd known him. She doubted he even realized he did it. When he emerged, he seemed his usual self, his carriage relaxed, hair neatly combed, and jaw clean-shaven.

After packing his toiletries, he retrieved the envelope from the bed and took a seat at the table. He read in silence, without raising his eyes from the page. At the end, he exhaled and extended the single white sheet, which was covered on both sides in tight, even script. "Here."

Justine took the chair opposite Rocco's and flattened the page against the table, forcing herself not to visibly react as she read his mother's final words to him.

Dearest Rocco,

First, thank you for handling my estate. I tried to liquidate what I could and hope the remainder is straightforward so you don't have a financial mess. Unfortunately, I fear I've left you and the twins with an emotional mess, and for that I am truly sorry.

If you've sorted through the rest of these papers, I'm sure your sharp eyes found the discrepancy. You will need to use the date on the birth certificate on all court filings if you want the estate to close without raising questions.

The truth is that I am ten years older than I told you, the twins, or Jack.

I am sure you are shocked, upset, or both, but yes, that date makes me twelve years older than Carlo Barrali.

The story of how we met is as I told you. I was hired as Carlo's tutor after being referred by my university's placement office. Though I'd graduated several years before, I'd been tutoring ever since the office found a job for me during my freshman year. The affinity Carlo and I felt for each other was immediate and powerful.

You were young and innocent and the twins were on the way when Carlo's father died and he inherited the throne. When he made the decision to remain with Fabrizia, I knew there was no turning back for him. I was hurt, I was angry, but I knew he was doing what he must to protect his kingdom.

I loved Carlo with all my heart and I am convinced to this day that he loved me. However, Sarcaccian law would've labeled me a criminal for that love, despite the fact it was mutual, so all I could do was protect what remained of it...you, Enzo, and Lina.

I took an entry-level government job that enabled me to keep a low profile and told no one who'd fathered my children. Then I met Jack Cornaro. He loved me for me. Best of all, Jack loved you three children. I told him only that your biological father was out of the picture, and that was enough for him.

When Jack was transferred to Italy, he asked me to come with him and proposed marriage. It was an enormous leap of faith on his part, knowing so little about my past. I knew then that I could trust him. I also knew that leaving Sarcaccia was the best way to protect you. Each day you looked more and more like Carlo, and I feared what could happen if we stayed.

To protect you further, before we left for Italy I managed to change the birthdate on my passport. I was fortunate to find a job that enabled me to stay out of public life, raise you in a secure home, and send you to schools that both challenged you and fostered your creativity. Through it all, Jack treated you as if you were his own children. He encouraged you to study, to explore your interests, to travel. It was his idea to adopt you soon after we married, and he told me it was his great privilege.

My marriage to Jack turned out better than I ever could have dreamed. I loved him when I married him, but as the years passed, I fell in love with him. It transformed me. It made me a better person. Eventually, I told Jack about Carlo, though to my shame I couldn't bring myself to tell Jack my real age and, therefore, reveal the full nature of that relationship. I feared what

Jack would think of me. He was supportive, loving, and encouraged me to tell the three of you the identity of your biological father when you were old enough to handle it. I don't know if you remember, but he was by my side that day. He set the tone. He made it clear that no matter how you were conceived, he considered himself your true father and couldn't love you more. You, Enzo, and Lina always viewed him as such. He was the perfect male role model for you, Rocco, one who encouraged you to grow and flourish and become your own man. That, you did.

You must know how proud I am of you and of all you've accomplished. As you found success in your career, I bragged about you to everyone...waiters, my hairdresser, even the man who installed the security system at the New York condo. He's a regular at my favorite Manhattan coffee shop and has a child with Type I diabetes. He was fascinated by what you do. He told me that work like yours is what keeps his child alive.

Rocco, I can think of no higher calling.

I made grave mistakes in my life. However, I believe there was a higher purpose at work. You, Enzo, and Lina were meant to be. You were meant to accomplish all that you have and more. You were meant to make others' lives better.

Unfortunately, I could not protect you from my death and the lie I knew it would reveal. I thought about telling you after Jack died, then again when faced with my own terminal illness. In the end, I decided this way was best. You could consider the information in private.

It will be up to you, Enzo, and Lina to decide how to handle it.

I hope now you can understand why I tried so hard to encourage each of you to pursue your passions while discouraging you from a life that might attract a certain kind of public attention, the kind that invites sensationalism or international television coverage.

As I write this, you and Justine are separated. You refused to discuss the nature of your conflict with me, but I suspect it was my fault. I hope you will reach out to her and find a way to reconcile now that I'm gone. When you are with her, you stand taller, smile more often, and radiate joy. You look the way I felt when I found Jack. It is what I want for you. It is what you deserve.

For years, I know you've believed Carlo Barrali to be a villain. He is not. Nor is he a victim. Neither am I villain or victim. We are each only human and were blessed to have you, no matter the circumstance. It is because of you and the twins that I know I will reside in Heaven, where I can watch over the children I so adore. I could not ask for more, other than to wish you a life of happiness and hope that you can one day find it in your heart to forgive me.

I love you, and shall forever love you.

SLOWLY, Justine folded the letter and returned it to the envelope bearing Rocco's name. She pushed it across the table to him. He said nothing, but he asked her what she thought with a lift of his brow.

"Wow."

That drew a cold laugh from him. "A succinct summary. And an accurate one."

"Fabrizia must know. She told you none of this?"

"No." He took the envelope and shoved it back inside the larger manila one, adding Lina and Enzo's letters before he closed the flap. "Her children don't know about me or my siblings. Apparently Carlo and my mother wanted to keep it quiet in order to protect both sets of children. Guess now I know why."

"It would devastate them."

"Hell, it's devastating *me*, and my mother's the one who committed—"

She covered Rocco's hand with hers. "Your right to be upset is no less than theirs."

He closed his eyes for a heartbeat. When he looked at her again, he seemed less pained, more resigned. "I'm surprised she was able to keep the secret for so long. Jack was a smart man. At the very least, I'd think he'd suspect."

"Your mother looked incredible for her age. I wouldn't have guessed her to be ten years older."

"It's more than that." Rocco withdrew his hand and rose to pace the room the way he often did when he thought of a new angle on one of his designs and needed to work out the logistics in his head. "It's how she did it that amazes me."

"Changing a passport couldn't have been easy."

"She would've had to make the change not only on the passport itself, but in the government's computers. Otherwise, it would've come up on the system when she went through customs. I traveled with her often and she never had a problem. Her passport went right through the scanner."

A thought occurred to Justine. "You think King Carlo could've arranged it?"

Rocco paused, then shook off the idea and continued pacing. "It's more likely that my mother had access while working in her own government job. For a king to do that would've meant involving other people, and it sounds like he played his relationship with my mother so close to the vest only Queen Fabrizia knows of it. He didn't even tell his parents. If he'd been caught attempting to manipulate government records, it would've made the situation far worse."

The explanation sounded plausible. "You don't know what her government job was when you were little?"

"She only told me it was for the government. I never asked for specifics." His stretched his hands in front of him as he continued to wear a path in the hotel carpet. "Assuming she had access to change the date on the passport and in the computer system, she must've known changing the original paper certificate on file with the priests in the village where she was born was impossible. That was her Achilles heel. She knew it'd come out when she died."

"Thanks to Croatian probate law." Justine gathered up the manila envelopes Rocco had left on the table, including the one containing the private letters, and secured them with the rubber band. "I bet she wasn't even aware of it until she started dividing up her estate and realized that you'd have to produce the original birth certificate."

"Or when Jack passed away." Rocco scrubbed a hand over his chin. "She closed his estate. She would've had to present his American birth certificate to do it."

"It'd explain why she considered telling you when Jack died."

He nodded. "It also explains her stress level the last few months. Yes, she was terminally ill, but I suspected there was something else bothering her, something she didn't wish to discuss. Even Enzo noticed when he came to visit. He said she seemed troubled for reasons aside from her illness."

"Speaking of Enzo, I assume we'll fly directly to Croatia instead of going to Rome. You need to talk to Enzo and Lina. Invite them to the villa so you can do it face to face. Tell them it's about your mother's estate and they'll come."

He grimaced. "I hadn't thought that far ahead. Honestly, I'd rather go to Rome."

"Rome's not going anywhere and neither am I. The sooner this is addressed, the better. Otherwise, it'll hang over your head the entire time we're there, and what fun is that? Besides, I imagine you'll be better able to process it all once you've talked to them. They'll understand in ways I can't."

He gathered her into his arms once more. She inhaled deeply of his warm skin, fresh from the shower, and wished she could erase his mother's mistakes for him. Teresa had been right about one thing: Rocco deserved happiness.

"Croatia, then." He leaned back to meet her gaze. "When this is done, I promise you Rome."

She traced his jaw with her thumb. There'd be no Russian thugs and no secrets between them on the trip home, but in many ways, it'd be more difficult. Too difficult to expect Rocco to think beyond.

"Just promise me *you*," she said. "You're all I need. The rest will follow."

CHAPTER 18

RAIN POUNDED the windows of Rocco's villa. Justine stood alongside the thick navy draperies, her back to Rocco's desk, watching in silence as the red and yellow blooms adorning the edges of Rocco's front walkway sagged under the relentless pummeling of the early evening storm.

A week had passed since they'd returned to Croatia. She'd spent most of the time with Rocco at the villa as they waited for Enzo and Lina to arrive. The injuries he'd sustained in his fight with Karpovsky healed, and he'd made a couple trips to the office to complete work on his patent application while she'd gone to daily rehab appointments. Three days ago, she'd finally gone to see her doctor. To her shock and surprise, he'd declared her recovery one of the best he'd ever seen. Before she left, he'd told her he saw no problem if she wanted to get back on skis, but to take it slowly and cautiously, then to check in with him afterward.

She'd returned to the villa with a bounce in her step. It'd been the one bit of good news they'd had since reading Teresa's letter. Rocco had made dinner, grilling fish he'd picked up in the marketplace on the way home to celebrate. He'd raised a glass to her hard work and said all the right things, but she sensed his mind was elsewhere. Even when he mentioned hearing from his partners at Johns Hopkins that they'd reviewed his design and could start work on the prototype immediately, he hadn't displayed his usual fire.

Until he dealt with his mother's deception, Justine knew Rocco couldn't move on and couldn't truly be happy.

"They've been in there for nearly two hours," she said when Kos appeared at her side at the window. "You finish your book?"

Kos nodded. While the Cornaro siblings met in the kitchen to discuss their late mother, Justine had alternately paced and flipped through the pages of one of Rocco's science magazines. In contrast to her agitated state, Kos spent the time reclined on the sofa, deeply engrossed in a Dean Koontz novel. He and his wife planned to leave the next morning for a Mediterranean cruise, but she'd told Kos to make himself useful to Rocco—and get out of her way—while she packed. The only time Kos looked up from the book long enough to speak, he claimed his wife had given him an impossible task. He couldn't be of use to Rocco while the man was holed up in another room.

"Given what he told me about his late mother, I'm worried about him."

Justine braced her hands on the windowsill and angled a look at the burly Croat. In the years she'd known Kos, she'd never once heard him utter the word *worried*. The closest he'd ever come was using the word *concerned*, but always in regard to security protocols or the villa itself, as in, "I'm concerned about wind damage to the roof tiles." Not in a personal context.

"You and me both," she finally replied. "It's taken a few days for it to sink in, and each day, Rocco gets quieter and quieter. I'm sure having to tell Lina and Enzo what he's learned is making it all the more difficult."

Kos grunted his agreement, then turned his attention out the window, as if believing he'd said too much. Justine put a hand on his tree trunk of an arm, drawing the man's gaze back to her face. "Kos? You know you're more than an employee to him. He wouldn't have told you about his mother otherwise."

It'd been a tough decision, but Rocco explained to Justine that Kos would be better equipped to do his job if he understood the full scope of Rocco's private concerns. Justine didn't say as much to Rocco, but she thought his willingness to confide in Kos would help him come to grips with Teresa's secrets.

"I appreciate his trust."

"You've more than earned it."

A muscle leapt in his cheek as a bolt of lightning illuminated the front garden and gate, followed instantly by a thunderclap so powerful it shook the windows and the floor. "I'm glad you're here, Mrs. Cornaro. I'm less worried about him when he has you."

For the first time all day, a grin lifted the edges of her lips. "I suspect he gets into more trouble when he's with me."

"True, but you belong together." She was about to accuse Kos of harboring a secret romantic side when he added, "It's like Kirk and Spock on *Star Trek*. You've seen *Star Trek*?"

"Of course."

He nodded as if that settled it. When he saw her waiting for further explanation, he elaborated, "Kirk and Spock are both ambitious, both innovative. Captain Kirk relies on his instincts, while Spock relies on observation and data. Their approaches differ when faced with a problem, but each functions best when they have the other to question their thinking. Since you met Mr. Cornaro, I've come to believe that you are Kirk to his Spock. You believe you're getting him into trouble. I believe you're challenging his thinking. He is not the same without you, and I suspect you are not the same without him."

Justine found the comparison amusing, but kept the thought to herself. Kos's lengthy explanation and stern demeanor proved he'd given the analogy serious thought.

"I apologize, Mrs. Cornaro." He started to turn away. "I should keep such opinions to myself."

She stopped him with a gracious smile. "No, you shouldn't. I was just thinking that it's a good thing Rocco doesn't look like Spock.

Nothing against the actors who've portrayed Spock, but I find Rocco a hell of a lot sexier."

Kos paused a moment, then solemnly proclaimed, "Nor do you look like Kirk."

She caught a shockingly naughty glint in his eyes before he spun to face the door. "Sir."

Justine turned to see Rocco approach from the hallway with Lina and Enzo at his heels. She'd greeted the twins when they'd arrived at the villa earlier in the day, but hadn't had time to chat with them before Rocco whisked the pair into the kitchen. When Justine had spotted Lina at the cemetery, she'd thought Rocco's sister looked leaner than in the past. It had surprised her, given that Lina kept to a scrupulous exercise regimen and maintained a svelte figure. Now that Lina was entering the library, Justine modified her assessment. Rather than appearing fit, Lina looked gaunt, as if the weight of her mother's long illness had worn her down. Her light brown eyes, much like Rocco's—and Carlo's, Justine realized—seemed larger than ever as she gave Justine and Kos a watery smile. However, her gorgeous dark blonde hair, which she'd inherited from her late mother, was artfully arranged around her shoulders in perfect beachy waves, and her chic beige moto-style pants and white lace top made it plain she'd taken care with her appearance. Justine's heart broke for her sister-in-law. Though the mother and daughter hadn't lived near each other these last few years, Lina and Teresa had been close, speaking on the phone several times a week.

Enzo, on the other hand, appeared as robust as ever, as if he'd heard the information Rocco had to share and dismissed it as meaningless. He dropped onto the plush gray sofa and kicked out his long legs as if he owned the villa, rather than Rocco, and folded his hands behind his head. "This weather is atrocious," he declared. "Croatia should inspire visits to the beach, not a nap. Makes me want to crash for the rest of the day."

"Not there," Rocco said before taking his usual seat in the leather chair he'd inherited from Jack Cornaro. "And not now."

"Move." Lina swiped at Enzo's legs, her hand making a swapping sound as it connected with her twin brother's jeans. Enzo rolled his eyes but did as she asked, making room for her on the sofa.

"Can I bring you anything, sir?"

"No, Kos, thanks. We've been picking at food in the kitchen." He gestured toward the room's other sofa, which faced the one Enzo and Lina occupied. "Have a seat. We'd like your input. Yours, too, Justine."

As Justine moved to sit by Kos, Rocco snagged her hand, keeping her at his side. "I told Enzo and Lina everything, starting with why we had to travel to Baltimore in the first place."

"The Russian mob, Justine?" Admiration filled Enzo's voice. "And you got away. I'm impressed."

"It was Kos."

"Not when they tried to kidnap you from your apartment. Rocco said you fought like a beast then ran full bore through the streets at night in your pajamas. Good for you."

Rocco's thumb ran over Justine's. "We also read the letters. Lina's and Enzo's were similar to mine, though my mother had individual advice for us."

"Which is what caught my eye," Lina said, her gaze taking in Justine, then Kos. "In Rocco's letter, Mom mentioned that she'd discussed his accomplishments, including his work on diabetes pumps, with acquaintances. She specifically mentioned the man who installed the security system at her condo in New York."

Justine's mind made the connection even as Rocco said, "I don't know why I didn't put two and two together when I first read it, but it's possible the person she mentioned is Viktor Radich or someone who worked for him. Fabrizia said that Radich installed custom-designed security systems in the United States before he came to Croatia. I want to find out if he was working in Manhattan and, if so, if he installed the system at my mother's condo."

"She kept a lot of valuable art there," Enzo said. "Jack's entire collection. Knowing her, she'd have gotten the best security she could afford."

"It'd explain how Radich discovered where Rocco's private lab is located," Lina said. "Radich probably befriended Mom at her coffee shop. It wouldn't take much from there to get hired to install her security system."

"Which would've given him entry to her apartment and more time to pump her for information about Rocco," Enzo finished.

"I can find out for you, sir," Kos volunteered. "I may not be able to determine if Radich installed it himself, but the security firm's contact information is in my files. If it's his company, we'll know it."

"That'll be your first task when we finish." He released Justine's hand and levered himself out of the chair. "First, though, I think we should open this." He rounded his desk and withdrew the cornflower blue velvet box that'd been in his backpack during the trip to the States. Justine had been curious about it when she'd searched his belongings for GPS devices in Rome, but she'd forgotten it in the chaos of their flight to Baltimore and the revelations of Teresa's papers.

"What is that?" Enzo asked as Rocco set the box on the desktop.

"Fabrizia left this with her business card when she came to warn me about Radich and Karpovsky. All she said was that it belongs with our family, not hers, and that it was her excuse for the visit should Carlo ever discover she'd come." Rocco ran his hand over the box. "I haven't looked inside."

"You're kidding me. Why the hell not?"

Rocco glared at Enzo. "At the time I was focused on the potential threat to my wife."

"Let's see what it is." Lina rose from the sofa and took the box from Rocco. When she lifted the lid, her eyes went wide and she inhaled sharply. "Oh my gosh, Rocco. This belongs in a museum. Or on Queen Fabrizia herself."

Lina flipped the box around so everyone could see. Justine felt her jaw go slack at the same time Kos straightened and Enzo let loose a string of foul language. Pillowed on plush light blue velvet lay a necklace laden with sparkling diamonds and sapphires of the deepest blue. At the necklace's center, a giant sapphire bearing a white, crosslike star sat framed by diamonds.

"This must be worth millions," Lina breathed. "And I don't say that as an exaggeration." She turned the box so she could study the piece up close. "These diamonds are as brilliant as any I've seen, and star sapphires are rare, especially this size. Look what happens when you move it under the light." She tilted the case for Rocco. "The striations in the sapphire look like they move."

"Is that a Conti & Fancetti logo inside the lid?" Enzo asked. At Lina's nod, he explained, "They're high end jewelers based in Sarcaccia. Assuming those stones are the real deal, I'm sure it really is worth millions."

"They're the real deal," she assured him, running a finger around the circumference of the piece. "Up close there's no doubt. Every setting looks like a work of art and there must be a hundred stones here."

"Why in the world would Fabrizia give it to us?" Rocco asked, beating Justine to the question that'd been on the tip of her tongue. "It couldn't have belonged to our mother. Jack was well off, but not this well off. And before she met Jack—"

"She was sleeping with a future king worth billions," Enzo finished.

"That doesn't explain this," Rocco argued. "Carlo couldn't get much money to her without his parents knowing, remember? At least, that's what she always told us. I doubt that part of her story was false. He would've been seventeen when I was conceived and only twenty-three when his father passed away and their relationship ended. He couldn't have purchased a necklace like this during those years without it being noticed."

Everyone in the room quieted. Enzo crossed the room to study the necklace, then looked at Rocco. "This is all the more reason, you know."

At Rocco's grim expression, Justine asked, "Reason for what?"

"Lina and I want Rocco to arrange a meeting with Carlo. That's what we wanted to discuss with you and Kos. Rocco doesn't think it's a good idea."

"I think it's an awful idea." Rocco rested the heels of his palms against the desktop, his dark brows knit in warning as he scowled at

Enzo. "It's a miracle no one saw Fabrizia visit here. A second miracle no one tied the arrest in Rome to the royal family...or to us. Tempting fate a third time is foolhardy."

"I want the truth." Lina raised her eyes to Justine's, then glanced at Kos. "All we have is Mom's side of the story. Her paperwork might back up what she wrote in our letters, but until one of us speaks to Carlo and hears his side of the story, we'll always wonder. My whole life, I've believed something very different than what I learned today. And it wasn't just us. Jack believed it, too."

Enzo raised the open jewelry box. "You can return this while you're there. What the queen was thinking bringing it here, I don't know, but we have no business—" He set down the box and ran his fingertips along the plush lining of the lid, where his thumb had rested while he held up the necklace. "Wait a minute."

Kos's dark eyes narrowed. "You found something."

"There's a bump in the fabric. The necklace isn't all that's in here."

CHAPTER 19

GENTLY, Enzo lifted the edge of the lining, angled the box under the desk lamp, then shrugged. "Looks like a store security tag."

"May I?"

Enzo handed it over. After a moment's inspection, Kos set the box back on the desk. "It's not a security tag, it's a tracking device. I've seen this type used by American law enforcement."

Lina pursed her lips and stared at the box as if it contained poison. "Good thing the Russians were arrested in Italy."

"Not the Russians. Fabrizia." Rocco shot a pointed look at Kos. "That's how she knew Justine and I were in Rome, and exactly where to send her security team, you, and the police."

Justine wasn't so sure. "I can't imagine she gave you the necklace as a means of spying on you. She had no way of knowing you'd keep it with you. It was far more likely you'd stash it in your safe and leave it there."

"Agreed," Enzo said, "which brings us right back to square one. Rocco, contact Queen Fabrizia. Tell her you'd like to arrange another visit. This time with her husband."

Instead of responding to Enzo, Rocco looked to Kos. "What's your take?"

"Given the value of the piece, the tracking device could've been inserted in the lining a long time ago as a means to recover it in case of theft. It may or may not have anything to do with you."

"What about seeing King Carlo?"

Kos hesitated. "Sir, it's not for me to say. If you wish, I can secure a location here in Croatia where you can meet without being seen or disturbed. However, the king's security team would need to make the arrangements on his end."

The muscles of Rocco's jaw worked before he strode to the window. As if on cue, thunder rolled through the sky, followed by a flash of lightning so bright it illuminated the entire property, silhouetting Rocco against the glass.

Justine longed to go to him, to run her hands across his broad shoulders, to massage away the concern that appeared to visibly weigh him down, but sensed now wasn't the time.

"It's a huge risk," Rocco said without turning around. "It takes only one person to see the wrong thing or ask the wrong question and our lives are changed forever."

"I'm willing to take that risk," Enzo said.

"If it was only the matter of King Carlo being our biological father, I'd be fine," Lina rubbed her forehead and grimaced. "As to the rest, I admit I'd be horrified if it came out. I'd wonder if everyone I meet has read some tabloid article about us and is whispering behind our backs. On the other hand, I know I'd find a way to deal with that kind of scrutiny. What I can't deal with is going through life not knowing what to believe about Mom."

Rocco kept his focus on the rain-soaked view. "To talk to Carlo Barrali after all these years…we're damned if we do, damned if we don't."

Another thunderbolt cracked, this time causing the lights to blink. Kos excused himself to locate flashlights and check the generator. Enzo followed close on his heels. Lina signaled Justine and mouthed, "I'll leave you two alone," then disappeared into the hallway before Justine could respond.

"They want you to talk to me." Rocco sounded simultaneously tired and amused.

"You saw Lina's reflection in the window, didn't you?"

He gave a short laugh. "Yes. Not that it wasn't predictable."

Unable to stay away any longer, Justine covered the space between them and wrapped her arms around his waist, then rested her chin on his shoulder. In the window, she saw him close his eyes as his hands and forearms came down to cover hers.

"I'm afraid I have no wisdom to share, but I'll do this as long as you'd like," she promised.

"They won't leave us alone that long."

"You're probably right." She raised onto her toes to press a kiss in front of his ear, then said, "What's your gut telling you to do?"

"To have a stiff drink and get back to work."

She smiled at Rocco's typical workaholic response. She closed her eyes for a moment, drawing in the familiar, masculine scent of his skin and the crispness of his shirt. "You must've worked a lot while your mother was ill, given how much you accomplished in those months."

"When I wasn't caring for her, it was all I did." He turned in her embrace and his troubled gaze locked on hers. "As upset as I was by her illness, it was torture losing you."

"Work was a distraction."

He ran a hand over her hair, then palmed her shoulder. "Distraction, yes. Solution, no. I knew I needed to change the situation, but I didn't know how. There aren't manuals on how to deal with your wife leaving because you've kept a secret you believe is necessary to protect your mother and siblings. Given the information I had at the time, I felt I'd pursued the logical course."

His use of the word *logical* reminded her of Kos's observation that he was Spock to her Kirk. She raised a brow. "Work won't make this problem go away, either."

Another wave of rain lashed the windows as the wind intensified. "Work is always the path of least resistance for me. But taking my mother's word was also the path of least resistance. It was *convenient*. Meeting Carlo face-to-face would be anything but."

"No argument from me on that point."

"On the other hand, it's what they want and need," he said, referring to his siblings. "So even if my gut's telling me to ignore the situation and work, I need to handle things differently than I did when you walked out. I need to do what's best for everyone involved, not what's best—or what's most convenient—for me."

Voices came from the far end of the hall. Apparently Kos and Enzo had located the flashlights. Justine cradled Rocco's chin in her hand. "It won't be easy." At his huff of agreement, she added, "But for the record, I think it's the right thing to do. You're a good man, Rocco Cornaro. Enzo and Lina won't forget it."

"You'd better be sure, because it could affect you, too. It could affect *us*. If it were to come out—"

She drew her index finger over his lips. "Do what you need to do for everyone."

He looked at her for a long moment, as if assessing her sincerity, then pressed a lingering kiss to her fingertip before stepping out of her embrace.

"All right," he said loud enough for the group in the hallway to hear over the ferocity of the storm. "I'll do it. If we're discovered, so be it. The Barrali family can make their explanations to the press."

Lina and Enzo were back in the room before Rocco finished speaking. Kos entered a few steps behind them, then calmly placed flashlights on the end tables and desk so they were within easy reach.

"Are you sure?" Lina asked. "While we were in the hallway, Enzo said that if you agreed, he'd be willing to talk to Carlo instead."

Rocco waved off the suggestion. "Fabrizia reached out to me and I'm the one Carlo's seen before, even if I don't remember it."

"You'll ask about our mother and about the necklace?" Enzo asked.

"I will. I'll let you know what happens as soon as possible." He turned to Kos. "Make the arrangements, please. Then see what you can discover about Radich."

Kos nodded, then turned to leave the library. When he reached the threshold, Rocco called out, "Kos? When you're done, get out of here. Enjoy a glass of wine and kiss your wife on the balcony of your cabin tomorrow night while the sun sets."

The big man's eyes held a smile, though his voice remained solemn. "As you wish, sir."

After Lina and Enzo followed Kos so they could say their good-byes, Rocco frowned at Justine. "Last chance. You sure you're all right with this?"

"Of course. Make the call."

"Good evening, Your Highness."

Umberto tipped his head in deference as Fabrizia ascended the stairs to the palace apartment she shared with King Carlo. As was usual at this time of the evening, the palace's head of security stood post at the landing, earpiece in place and gun at his hip, watching the comings and goings of those permitted access to the building's most private area. When his replacement arrived for the night shift, Umberto would head to his palace office, where he'd spend another hour or two ensuring security arrangements were in place for upcoming palace events and reading reports from those he supervised. He was irreplaceable, and Fabrizia thanked her stars every day that the talented man had chosen to work for her when his options were limitless.

"Good evening, Umberto. Has everyone arrived?"

"All but Prince Bruno, though I'm told he just pulled into the underground garage."

"Wonderful. Thank you." It would be an interesting night, and likely a difficult one. She couldn't begin to predict what her children would think when it was all over.

"Your Highness?"

She paused two steps above Umberto, which put her nearly at his eye level. "Yes?"

"If I may say so, your grandson is a charmer." Umberto's eyes lit with affection. "Prince Stefano allowed me to hold him when they arrived. I'm quite certain he smiled at me."

Fabrizia couldn't stop the broad grin that came to her face, no matter how undignified it might make her appear. "Dario's wonderful. Seeing him makes my day and holding him is even better. I couldn't be happier to be his grandmother."

"Then I won't keep you from him, assuming you can convince King Carlo to relinquish his hold on the child."

"Oh, I'm very convincing." She glanced up the stairs as Sophia's distinctive laughter echoed from the direction of the apartment, then looked back to Umberto. "If you finish your shift before I see you again, have a good night."

He wished her a good night as well, then she proceeded up the final few steps to the hallway that led to her apartment and took a fortifying breath before opening the door. Inside, the atmosphere was even more cheerful than the laughter she'd heard indicated. New parents Megan and Stefano looked on as Sophia held their baby in one arm while allowing him to grasp her opposite pinkie finger. Vittorio, the crown prince, and his identical twin Alessandro were deep in conversation by the fireplace while Vittorio's fiancée, Emily, stood near the windows with Prince Massimo and Massimo's new wife, Kelly, a transplant from Texas. Carlo lingered behind the sofa where Sophia sat with Dario, looking down at his new grandson in open admiration. It was the picture of family togetherness.

Only Fabrizia noticed the tension in the set of Carlo's broad shoulders. He met her eyes as she entered, flashing her a smile that spoke of decades of love. Tonight, she knew, that love would be put to the test. Not between them—they'd worked through their own difficulties long ago—but the love and respect their children had for the two of them.

She paused in the doorway to drink in the sight of her husband, with his thick salt and pepper hair and the trim physique he worked hard to maintain in order to prolong the years he'd have with his family. The bespoke charcoal suit, cream-colored dress shirt, and elegant Penrose tie spoke to his position, and his sharp gaze hinted at his intellect. But Carlo Barrali was so much more than his appearance. He had a stalwart heart, a quick sense of humor, and an instinct—above all else—to protect both his family and his country, even to his personal detriment.

She mouthed, "I love you," before she closed the apartment door and crossed the hardwood floor to the seating area, allowing the clicking of her high heels to alert her offspring of her arrival.

"Isn't he amazing?" Sophia cooed while Dario reached for her hair. The infant managed to grab a handful of long, dark strands before Sophia extricated them from his tiny fist. "I don't know how Megan and Stefano can stand to share him."

"At three a.m., I'll gladly share," Megan said with a laugh.

"Anna's spending the night with a friend again?" Fabrizia asked the question casually, though she secretly hoped her granddaughter's plans hadn't changed. Megan and Stefano's daughter was eleven and a social butterfly when she wasn't doting on her new baby brother. While Fabrizia loved spending time with Anna whenever possible, she wanted the girl far from the conversation tonight.

"She is," Megan replied. "She'll be sorry she missed seeing her Uncle Bruno while he's in town."

"Speak of the devil," Stefano said, his eyes going to the apartment door, where Carlo and Fabrizia's youngest child entered in a rush.

"Sorry I'm late. Long trip."

"Welcome home. We're glad you could make it on such short notice," Carlo said, a broad smile lighting his face. Bruno was the one child Fabrizia wasn't sure about corralling for a family meeting. Visits were rare since he attended university out of the country.

"Now that we're all here, what's this about?" Vittorio, the eldest, asked Carlo. "I thought the logistics for Dario's christening were finalized last week. Is there a problem?"

"The christening is going forward exactly as planned," Carlo told them. "This is another topic. Why don't you all have a seat? I want everyone's full attention."

Glances were exchanged around the room at the unexpected gravity of King Carlo's tone. Bruno, Massimo, and Kelly took armchairs while Vittorio, his fiancée, Emily, and Alessandro took the sofa opposite Stefano, Megan, and Sophia. Not for the first time in recent weeks, Fabrizia marveled at how much her family had expanded in the last few years.

Yes, she thought, now that her children had reached adulthood and were starting their own families, it was high time for this conversation. She took a seat in the last remaining armchair, beside Bruno and opposite where her husband stood to address the group. If any of her children were tempted to walk out before their father finished speaking, her position blocking their path would serve as a deterrent.

"Is one of you ill?" Sophia asked, unwilling to wait for her father to speak.

Fabrizia was about to answer when Carlo spoke. "So you won't feel compelled to speculate, I'll get right to the point. When I was a teenager, I was involved in an inappropriate relationship with my tutor."

Fabrizia started. Despite his penchant for directness, she'd assumed that Carlo, consummate politician that he was, would ease into the topic. Apparently not.

No one stirred except Sophia, who openly frowned as if she thought he was joking. Her expression transformed as she realized he wasn't. "Why are you telling us this? Is it about to become public?"

Alessandro spoke over her. "Why inappropriate? Just how old was this tutor?"

"She was twenty-eight or twenty-nine, I think, when it began. I was seventeen. And no, to my knowledge, it's not about to become public, though that may change." All six of his children gaped at him in a mix of horror and astonishment. He straightened his shoulders. Fabrizia could sense the toll the revelation took on him, but he continued, "I was young and imagined myself mature, given that I was raised in the public eye, so despite our age gap I fancied myself in love with her."

"And she told you she was in love with you?" Alessandro, always the most outspoken, scoffed. "That's a felony."

"I am well aware." Carlo spared Alessandro a cursory glance. "Her name was Teresa Fedeli, though she later married and became Teresa Cornaro. She passed away recently, which is why I'm telling you about this now."

Carlo looked to Fabrizia. She nodded, letting him know he had her support before he said to the entire room, "Teresa's eldest son contacted me yesterday. He wants to meet with me."

"For heaven's sake, why? What does he want?" Vittorio's hands tensed where he'd braced them on his thighs.

"Money," came Alessandro's quick response. Though he'd said it to Vittorio, it was loud enough for the entire room to hear.

"He contacted me because he is my son."

The room silenced. Even Dario seemed to sense the shift, wrenching his tiny head to blink across the room in his grandfather's direction. Before anyone could speak, Carlo continued, "In answer to your questions, yes, I'm certain. And yes, he is older than all of you. I was eighteen when he was born."

The air in the room thickened with tension. Fabrizia watched as each of her children attempted to reconcile the man they knew as their steadfast, proper father with the irresponsible image he'd conveyed of his youthful self.

"This is all…out of the blue." Massimo, usually the quietest of the siblings, spoke first. "I can't believe you kept a secret of that magnitude, let alone for that long. You were so young. How did your parents deal with it?"

"They didn't," Carlo said simply. "I didn't tell them. Teresa Fedeli was hired as a tutor for the specific purpose of helping me with my college entrance exams and applications. By the time she started to show, she left my parents' employ. When Rocco was born, I'd just finished prep school and was less than a month from starting at university. We decided it was best to keep the pregnancy quiet. In fact, Teresa insisted upon it."

"So she wouldn't be brought up on charges, I'm sure."

Carlo acknowledged Vittorio's comment with a tip of his head. "That was part of her thinking, yes, but she also wanted to protect the child. I can't blame her for that."

He crossed the room to stand behind Fabrizia's chair. Turning, she smiled up at him, then looked back to her children. "You know my marriage to your father was arranged. We didn't love each other, not in the way married couples should. However, we got along splendidly, and I could tell there was something amiss when we were out on a walk together a few weeks before our wedding."

"I told her about Teresa and Rocco," Carlo said, picking up the story. "It was difficult, because at the time, I was still secretly involved with Teresa. Even though your grandparents had arranged a marriage for me, one I knew was necessary in order to maintain the line of succession, I couldn't bring myself to cast her aside. She was the mother of my child."

Sophia's face fell. In that split second, Fabrizia witnessed her daughter's belief in her parents' relationship crumble. "You were unfaithful during your engagement?"

Fabrizia felt rather than saw Carlo's increasing strain. "I didn't see Teresa often in those days. I was busy finishing my degree and was watched every moment I was outside the palace walls, but yes. That confession—and your mother's reaction to it—should have proved to me how immature I really was. Even now, all these years later, it's very difficult to think about. But your mother handled the information with an incredible amount of poise. She asked if I still wished to go through with the wedding. I told her I did, and that I thought we'd have a wonderful future together. What's truly awful is that I didn't mean it. I believed I was in love with Teresa. I believed—foolishly—that I could have my heirs with your mother and still carry on my relationship with Teresa. I even thought that perhaps I could marry Teresa someday."

If looks could kill, those on the faces of Carlo and Fabrizia's children would've buried Carlo six times over as they stared at him. Unwilling to let her husband suffer the torment alone, Fabrizia rose to stand beside him. Bracing her hands on the back of the armchair, she said, "He wasn't the only one being immature that day. I may have acted as if I believed him, but I didn't. Rocco was three and a half years old at the time, no longer an infant. I knew your father well enough by then to realize he'd never abandon his own child. But I believed" —she glanced at Carlo— "foolishly, to use your father's word, that he would fall in love with me."

"Not so foolish." Carlo's hand came down on top of hers.

"You were slow."

"Yes." He focused on his stunned family. "Teresa became pregnant again not long after I graduated college, about seven months after your mother and I married."

Jaws dropped. Sophia's eyes filled with tears, which instantly spilled over. Stefano's head sank into his hands, and he muttered a vile four-letter word followed by what sounded like, "This is too much."

Across from Stefano, Emily's hand went to Vittorio's knee. It was obvious the crown prince had done the math in his head.

"You were already pregnant with Alessandro and me."

CHAPTER 20

Vittorio turned to Alessandro and uttered an expletive Fabrizia had never expected to hear from his lips.

In a tone that allowed no further outbursts from her children, no matter how warranted those outbursts might be, Fabrizia said, "Yes, I was. When Teresa called your father to inform him of her pregnancy, he immediately came to me and admitted that he'd seen Teresa again. Looking back now, I understand why it was so hard for him to end the relationship. It wasn't just that he had a son with Teresa, and she was—in his mind—his first love. She was also a manipulative woman. She was older, she was wiser, and she used every trick in the book to keep your father's attention and make him feel that he owed her his allegiance." To Carlo, she said, "I hope that's not overstating. Perhaps that's your story to tell?"

"No, you're right," he told her. To their children, he explained, "Spending more and more time with your mother made me realize what Teresa was doing. Not because your mother pointed it out, but because I suddenly had a basis for comparison. Your mother epitomized grace, intelligence, and compassion. I saw it in the way she took on her role as princess and worked to improve lives of those who needed assistance, and in the way she related to my parents and siblings. Most of all, I saw it in how she treated me. What I felt for her was different than what I felt for Teresa. It became a deeper, abiding love. There was nothing dark about it, nothing sordid. I knew that I had to end it with Teresa, despite the fact she was pregnant, no matter the public consequences."

"I persuaded him to wait," Fabrizia said. "I hadn't met Teresa, but I knew enough from what your father told me to despise her with every bone in my body for what she'd done to him. Not only because she was older when she pursued him, but because I was certain she got pregnant on purpose. Both times. Still, I wished no ill upon her children, and having your father break off a relationship of so many years while Teresa was pregnant wouldn't do her health any favors."

Fabrizia looked around the room, attempting to gauge her children's reactions to the barrage of information. Stefano stared at the carpet, as if he could find answers in its intricate pattern. His wife cradled Dario in one arm, but she kept her other hand on Stefano's thigh. Alessandro rose from his seat to walk to the windows. Bruno appeared shell-shocked. Sophia cried silent tears. Vittorio looked as if he were going to be ill. Massimo and Kelly kept their focus on each other, their gazes saying as plainly as if they said it aloud that they'd discuss their thoughts later, in private.

Carlo cleared his throat. "By the time the twins were born—actually, let me step back—by the time *Teresa's* twins were born—"

"Wait. What a..." Massimo paused, then let loose with an obscene military expression for messy situations. "Two sets of twins? At the *same time*? Tell me you're joking."

"I'm not." Fabrizia heard in the bite of his response that Carlo's patience was wearing thin. As his nation's sovereign, he wasn't used to being interrupted, even by his family, and no one used foul language in his presence. Ever. "By the time Teresa's twins were born, my father was terminally ill. I couldn't so much as think about Teresa during those months, between Vittorio and Alessandro's birth, my father's illness and death, and then the preparation necessary for me to take the throne. After my investiture, when I could finally breathe, I ended it with Teresa. For good."

"She didn't threaten to go public?" Bruno asked, finally stirring to life.

Fabrizia shook her head. "As devious and controlling as she might've been, she loved her children enough not to put them through that. She also recognized what going public would mean for her from a legal standpoint. However, she refused to let your father see the children and left Cateri to take a government position on the other side of the island. Not long afterward she met another man, an American her own age. She married him and moved to Italy, then to Croatia. Your father never saw Rocco again, nor did he ever meet the twins."

To Fabrizia's surprise, Carlo put his arm around her, then leaned in to kiss her cheek. Much as he showed affection when they were alone, it was rare for him to do it in public, even in front of the family.

"Your mother," he spoke to his children, but his gaze remained squarely on Fabrizia, "deserves a better man than me. I cannot imagine my life without her. Despite everything we went through in those early days of our marriage—with your mother taking the brunt of the strain—we are happy."

Fabrizia smiled up at her husband, then looked at each of her children in turn. "We realize that this is life-changing information for each of you. We want you to be able to talk to each other about it, and then talk to us. Ask us whatever you wish, whenever you are ready. This isn't a secret we wished to keep from you, but as you can imagine, it's not a tale easily told. The ramifications if it were discovered would be momentous. Now that you're all adults and Teresa has passed away, the time is right. And given that Rocco Cornaro has reached out to your father, we feel it may also be time to heal the wounds of the past."

"So you're going to meet with him?" Sophia asked, her voice thready. "Do you expect all of us to meet him?"

Carlo took the chair Fabrizia had occupied moments earlier. He leaned forward, making sure he had the full attention of each of his children. "He offered to come here, but after discussing security arrangements, we both felt it would be easiest if I were to fly to

Croatia tonight and meet with him at a private location, where there are fewer eyes and ears than at the palace. It's only two hundred and fifty miles or so to Dubrovnik, which means I can be there and back before morning. As to meeting all of you, it wasn't mentioned. If tonight goes well and I'm confident he has no ulterior motives, then I shall leave it to each of you to decide for yourselves."

Bruno rose from his chair and strode to the fireplace. His back to the room, he said, "The older one...you said his name is Rocco."

"Yes."

"And what about the twins? I assume you know their names."

"Lina and Enzo. Fraternal twins, born a few months after Alessandro and Vittorio."

Bruno ran one hand along the mantel. "Anyone else feel the need for a glass of wine?"

"Forget wine. This calls for the hard stuff. I'll pour." Sophia stood and rounded the sofa to open an antique sideboard that housed liquor. After splashing a few fingers of Scotch into a glass for Bruno—from Carlo's favorite bottle, Fabrizia noted—Sophia looked over her shoulder to survey the room. Most were either nodding or raising a hand. "How about I just keep pouring?"

Fabrizia approached the sideboard, took the first two crystal tumblers, and handed them to Vittorio and Emily. As Fabrizia returned for another two tumblers, Sophia whispered, "You're really okay with this?"

"I've never been okay with it. What that woman did to your father is reprehensible."

"I can't believe he'd be so gullible, even at seventeen. It's not like him at all."

Fabrizia took a tumbler in each hand and walked one to Massimo, then the second to his wife, Kelly. Upon returning to Sophia's side, she replied in a voice for Sophia's ears only, "It's not like him because he *learned*. The man you know now is as strong as he is because he extricated himself from Teresa. The personal cost was very, very high."

Sophia's gaze was thoughtful as she handed Fabrizia two more tumblers, which Fabrizia delivered to Alessandro and Bruno after

Megan and Stefano declined, given that they were busy with Dario. Sophia poured a glass for herself and one for Alessandro, then carried her brother's tumbler to where he stood on the opposite side of the room while Fabrizia remained at the sideboard.

"Carlo?" She held the near-empty bottle aloft.

"Nothing, my dear, thank you." His tone indicated he wished to remain clear-headed for his trip to Croatia.

"In that case, why don't we take a walk in the garden? It'll be good to stretch your legs before your flight." Returning to her husband's side, she looped her arm through his. To the children, she said, "Stay here as long as you like," then walked out with Carlo.

The moment the door closed behind them, she let go of his arm to allow him to cross the space to the hallway's tall windows, which overlooked the palace gardens. As he stared into the falling night, it struck her that this was exactly how she'd first seen Rocco at his villa. He'd had his back to her, staring out at his own gardens, and for all the world he'd appeared like a young Carlo, deep in thought.

"I feel I've sinned against my family all over again," Carlo said at last. "Not one of them would look at me as we walked out."

"You've done no such thing, though I understand why it feels that way." She joined him at the windows, then followed his gaze to the heavens. A lone star blinked in the darkening sky, high above the palace and Cateri's city lights. "It will take them time to come to terms with it all, but I have faith in our children. At the end of the day, they know the kind of man you are."

Carlo's eyes moistened and she pretended not to notice as he blinked to clear them. His voice unusually gruff, he said, "I meant what I said in there. I don't deserve you."

"Oh, stop it. You deserve everything you have and more or you wouldn't have it. Your country trusts you. Your staff would do anything for you. And your family loves you. For *you*."

When he remained quiet, she directed her attention out the window. "I was serious about the garden. Let's walk for a while. When we're ready, we'll sit on a bench, listen to the fountain, and enjoy the scent of the early-blooming roses."

A droll expression lit his features. "You plan to sit under the stars and tell me to count my blessings."

"Perhaps. And to consider that this is a new beginning."

A slow, warm smile spread across his face. He turned it on her as he extended his elbow. "In that case, I'd be honored to accompany you to the garden, Your Highness. If you're not careful, though, I might steal a kiss."

She wrapped her hands around the crook of his arm. "You wouldn't have to steal it."

* * *

ROCCO HAD to hand it to Kos. The man knew how to arrange a meeting far from the public eye, yet within easy driving distance of Dubrovnik.

Justine stood across the room from Rocco, eyeing the screen of a small video monitor in the living room of Kos's parents' vacation home. The modest stone dwelling stood high in the hills of Croatia's scenic Konavle region, surrounded by a plethora of olive, pine, and cypress tress. Kos had set up cameras and motion sensors around the perimeter years ago, making it impossible for anyone to approach without being detected. He'd explained to Rocco and Justine that he used the home as a test site for the security measures he'd instituted for Rocco and all his previous employers. It was ideal as a meeting location because no one would tie it to Rocco, yet the controls to the security system were identical to those in Rocco's villa, making it easy for him to monitor.

Rocco and Justine had arrived a few hours earlier to ensure no one else was in the area, but once their survey was complete, the torture of waiting for King Carlo to arrive made Rocco want to crawl out of his skin.

"I forgot to ask when we were talking about Kos and his cruise on the way here...did he ever find out whether Radich installed your mother's system?"

"Looks like it," Rocco answered. "He's the sole owner of the company my mother hired. He has fifteen employees, most of whom do system installation and maintenance. Kos called my mother's neighbor, Mrs. Metzger, on the off chance she knew anything. Turns out Mrs. Metzger went over the day the system was installed because she was interested in getting an estimate for her own condo. She gave a description of the guy that sounded a lot like Viktor Radich. She remembered that my mother knew the man from her coffee shop and that he had a daughter with Type I diabetes."

"Unreal." Justine grimaced. "Of all the people for your mother to trust, it's the one who wanted to steal for the Russian mafia. I'm glad Kos got to the bottom of it."

"I am, too, though I hate to imagine Radich cozying up to my mother to learn more about me."

"I'm glad he never hurt her." Justine leaned closer to the monitor. "Looks like headlights in the trees."

By the time Rocco joined her at the screen, a nondescript black sedan had come into view. The driver wore a flat hat that obscured his features, but his build was enough to identify him as he rolled to a stop near the gate, then lowered his window to push the buzzer.

A disconcerting feeling of déjà vu washed over Rocco. It didn't take a genius to tie the sensation to the moment Fabrizia parked outside his villa, intent on waiting him out from the back of a dark sedan while Umberto planted himself at Rocco's front gate. Although in this case, as Carlo had said he would, the monarch had come alone.

"I'll let him in," Justine ran her hand over Rocco's back before heading for the panel beside the front door. "Why don't you find a comfortable place to wait while I go out front to greet him?"

He nodded, grateful she understood him so well. Carlo might be a king, and could very well be a victim of an unspeakable crime, but Rocco wanted to maintain the upper hand as long as possible during this meeting.

After Justine disappeared through the front door, Rocco strode to the television and cut the video, leaving only the audible alarm engaged. If anyone approached, he'd know it, but he didn't want to be distracted by the various visual feeds while he talked to the king. After double-checking that his shirt was neatly tucked in, Rocco went to the center of the family room, where Kos's mother had a collection of floral armchairs arranged around a large, hand-hewn coffee table made of local hardwood. It was anchored by a blush pink rug, giving the home an old world feminine feel Rocco never would've associated with Kos. Rocco imagined it was unlike any home in which Carlo spent time, either.

"Rocco?"

Rocco spun at the sound of Justine's soft voice. King Carlo stood at her side.

"King Carlo." Rocco gave a brief nod of greeting, suddenly unsure of the etiquette demanded by the situation. "You found the place easily, I hope?"

"Mr. Horvat gave excellent directions."

They lapsed into silence as each man sized up the other. For Rocco, it was like looking at an older version of himself. He'd always known he took after Carlo physically, but seeing the man in the flesh was unnerving. The king's eye color and shape were identical to Rocco's, though the lines at the edges were deeper. They shared a jawline and their noses were similarly shaped. The king's graying hair was the only difference in their coloring. Rocco was certain if they put their arms next to each other, the skin tone would be identical.

What surprised Rocco most about the king's appearance, however, was his dress. Rocco had never seen Carlo on television or photographs wearing anything but a well-tailored suit, but this evening he wore a neat pair of gray slacks and a lightweight black sweater. In his hand, he held the cap Rocco had seen on the surveillance screen. In casual dress, the king appeared less intimidating.

Rocco wasn't fooled for a moment.

Justine surprised them both by speaking first. "Why don't I go out back and throw a few logs in the fire pit? If you decide to, you can come outside and join me when you're finished talking. The moon is out and there's a beautiful view out to the sea."

Before Rocco could respond, she smiled at the king and vanished down the rear hallway, which led to a mudroom and the stone patio at the rear of the house.

Carlo watched her go with a thoughtful expression on his face. When the back door closed, he turned to Rocco. "I've been a fan of your wife's for many years. I missed seeing her race this season."

"You follow alpine skiing?"

"When possible." The king moved a few steps closer, though the tension between them remained palpable. "I saw her in person two years ago in Bulgaria. I was on a state visit and had the opportunity to watch the Super G competition at Bansko."

Rocco thought back. "She won that race, didn't she?"

"Yes. And took fourth in the alpine combined the next day."

He remembered that part well. "She was upset she'd missed being on the podium twice."

"She's a fierce competitor. It's why I became a fan." Carlo gestured to the armchair in front of him. "May I?"

"Of course." Rocco waited for the king to sit, then took the chair opposite him.

"Thank you for inviting me here. I'm sure it wasn't easy for you."

Understatement of the year. "I was hoping you could tell me about my mother."

"You're direct." Carlo's brows rose, and Rocco could swear he caught a hint of admiration in the king's voice.

"Your wife told me that you are, too."

"She would." The king leaned back in his chair and crossed his legs so his ankle rested on his opposite knee. Despite the fact he was out of his element, far from his palace lodgings or his custom-built private jet, Carlo seemed perfectly at ease. More so than Rocco, even.

After regarding Rocco for several long seconds, the king said, "What is it you wish to know?"

"All of it."

The king's shoulders lifted, then dropped. "I'm aware she told you and your siblings that I'm your father. Other than that" —he spread his hands— "I can tell you that I wanted to be in your lives, or at least give you financial support, but she steadfastly refused. Given my position and that both of us wished for you to live a life out of the spot-light, I was compelled to respect her choice."

"That's you. I want to know about *her*." Rocco rarely spoke in such curt tones, but this was his one opportunity to get answers. "How old was she when you met? How old were you? And how old when I was born?"

"She was twenty-nine and I was seventeen. You were conceived when I was seventeen. Born when I was eighteen." Carlo's gaze sharpened. "Surely you know this already?"

"No, not until a week ago when I went through her papers and saw her birth certificate. All our lives we believed her to be ten years younger."

"She lied about her age?" The king's brows knit and his counte-nance darkened. "When she informed me that she and Jack Cornaro had told you about your paternity, it didn't occur to me…" He dragged his hand along his thigh, leaving tracks in the fabric of his gray slacks. "I'm sorry, Rocco. I had no idea. The discovery must have been a shock."

"That's putting it lightly. She lied to Jack, too."

"You believed us both to be teenagers." Carlo's expression grew increasingly grim. "That certainly changes things."

"She took advantage of you. She broke the law." It turned Rocco inside out to say it, but he wanted to hear confirmation from the king's own lips.

"Perhaps."

"From where I sit, there's no perhaps about it. Yet you kept the relationship going even after you married. That, I don't begin to understand."

The king exhaled, then braced his elbows on his knees and templed his fingers. "Despite our age gap, I believed myself to be mature. Whether that is true or not, it was how I felt at the time. Your mother is—was—a compelling woman. So did she manipulate me? Perhaps. But I allowed it. It took spending time with my wife to learn what a real relationship looked like, felt like. What real love looks and feels like."

"But to father three children—"

"I cannot tell you that I regret it, because I don't." Carlo leveled his gaze at Rocco. "I regret the pain it caused my wife. I regret that I didn't know you or spend time with you, as I did my children with Fabrizia. And I regret that you have had to live with the circumstances of your birth. But how can one regret three wonderful human beings who otherwise wouldn't exist?"

"Did you use birth control?"

Rocco hadn't planned the question. Asking it of this man, who held a position respected around the world, seemed the highest breach of propriety. But now that it hung in the air, Rocco realized he needed to hear the answer.

"Yes."

"We weren't planned."

Carlo considered his answer for a moment, then said, "I did not plan to have children with Teresa, no."

The set of Carlo's jaw put Rocco on edge. "You didn't want us. You believe she got pregnant on purpose."

"What do you want from me, Rocco?"

"The truth!" Rocco shot from his chair, propelled by the anger and frustration that'd dogged him from the moment he'd opened his mother's letter. "I want the damned truth! My mother was nothing but loving to me and the twins. She protected us, she encouraged us, she spent countless hours working her fingers to the bone to give us better lives. And I never saw a moment of deception in her relationship with Jack. Not one. All I knew was that you made her promises, then reneged once you married Fabrizia and had your heirs."

"That's what you *knew* because that's what she told you. What do you know now?"

CHAPTER 21

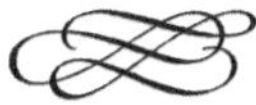

CARLO LEANED FORWARD in the floral chair, his commanding, masculine aura a stark contrast to the homey fabric, just as his steady demeanor was the polar opposite of Rocco's swirling rage.

"Did it ever occur to you that your mother lied not only to protect herself, but to protect you? What if she'd been caught? Would a trial—a very public trial, given my position as crown prince—and jail time have made things better? It wouldn't have made the situation better for me, and certainly not for the people of Sarcaccia. Would her marriage to Jack Cornaro have ever occurred? Would you have had the childhood you did?"

Carlo stood, but wisely kept his distance. "In most cases, two wrongs don't make a right. Was your mother wrong to foster a romantic relationship with her student? Yes. But once that happened, once there was a child involved, can you blame her for using every weapon in her arsenal in order to protect that child?"

"But to get pregnant again, she must've believed that you would—"

"I made Teresa no promises, Rocco." The king's words were quick, harsh. "At first, when my parents arranged my marriage to Fabrizia, I protested. But then, when I knew I had no room to argue, I thought I could have it all, the wife and the mistress. I even thought I might leave Fabrizia and marry your mother someday. But I never told Teresa that. Never. As I got to know Fabrizia, I quickly realized that what I had with your mother wasn't healthy. I only saw her twice after my wedding. I was falling in love with my wife, and I was slowly, finally maturing. I thank God every day that Fabrizia forgave me for my sins against her, including fathering twins with another woman while she was pregnant with Vittorio and Alessandro. A woman I was beginning to suspect would do whatever it took to keep her hold over me." Carlo took a step toward Rocco. "Is that what you wanted to know?"

"You're saying my mother was a conniving bitch."

"I'm saying she made mistakes, but I did, too. Terrible mistakes for which others have had to pay the price. If you need to blame me to redeem your mother's memory, so be it. In fact, if it makes you, Enzo, and Lina happier, I welcome it. It's nothing I haven't lived with my entire adult life."

"You know their names."

"Of course I know their names!" His face flushed with emotion and he put a hand to his chest. "They are my flesh and blood. Believe it or not, I've loved the three of you your entire lives. Not a day goes by I don't wish I'd raised you myself so I could know you. So I could see you change and grow and become the people you are today. But it wasn't to be. When I finally told your mother that we needed to end it —completely end it—she refused to let me see you again. I hated that. Hated what you must have thought of me." The edges of the king's mouth twitched in shock at his own outburst. He took a deep breath, then added in a calmer voice, "On the other hand, I can't fault Teresa for how she raised you. All three of you are intelligent, moral people. Good people. Over the years, I have told myself to be content with that."

Rocco grit his teeth. All his life, he'd despised this man without knowing him. Yet Carlo had loved Rocco and his siblings without knowing them. With every fiber of his being, Rocco knew the king was telling the truth about that. Both he and Carlo had been at the mercy of Teresa's filter in learning about the other.

Carefully, Rocco said, "It's a difficult thing to discover that the person you thought you knew best lied to you."

Carlo considered that. "I'm sure it weighed on her to lie to you, to your sister and brother, and to Jack, especially given what I know of her relationship with the man. But she did it to protect you. Let's give her credit for that and let her rest in peace."

Rocco closed his eyes for a beat, then turned and strode to the rear windows, which overlooked the spacious stone patio. He could see the fire pit at the far side, its flames dancing in the clear black night. As Justine had said, there was a stunning moonlit view that extended across the Adriatic. Kos's parents had trimmed just enough trees to provide a panorama of the sea while maintaining their privacy. Once his eyes adjusted to the darkness, Rocco spied Justine on one of the roughly hewn stone benches that encircled the fire pit. She sat with her back to the house and wore a light blanket over her shoulders. She'd propped her feet on the edge of the pit and her head was tipped back as she stared up at the stars.

Quietly, Carlo joined him. After taking in the view, he said, "No matter what happens after tonight, no matter how you and your siblings decide to proceed with whatever information I have given you, I am glad you contacted me. Jack Cornaro will always be the father of your heart. He earned it. But I am your father, too, and I will be here if and when you're ready."

"You're quite the diplomat."

"Years of training." Rocco cast a sideways look at the king and noticed a smile lifting the man's cheeks before he added, "Diplomatic or not, it's a sincere offer."

Rocco nodded. Before he could say anything further, the king said, "My son Stefano worked in Venezuela during his gap year. While there, he became involved with a young American woman. When the American discovered she was pregnant, she tried to reach him. Royal channels being what they are, she had difficulty. When Stefano's engagement was announced soon afterward, she decided it would be best for the child to raise her on her own. She made no further attempts at contact."

"You're talking about Stefano's wife Megan and her daughter Anna."

"Yes. They found each other again, but nearly ten years had elapsed. Ten years where Stefano didn't know his child and the child didn't know him. Watching their reunion has been both painful and rewarding. Ultimately, they have found happiness and value it."

"I'm not a preteen girl."

"No, you're not. But I value the opportunity, all the same. Perhaps more, because the entire time, I knew what I was missing."

A flurry of sparks rose from the fire. Justine reached forward and used a poker to shift the logs, sending another batch of sparks skyward before the flames settled again.

"When the queen visited, she told me that your children don't know about me. Do you plan to tell them now?"

Carlo planted his hands on the window ledge, palms down, hands wrapped around the sill so his fingers pointed back toward himself. The motion unnerved Rocco. It was exactly the way he stood and stared out the window of his villa when he needed to mull over a design problem.

"I told them early this evening, just before I flew here. Fabrizia and I thought that the time had come, given Teresa's death and your request to meet."

It wasn't the answer Rocco expected. "All of them?"

"Yes. My wife and I even called Bruno home from university. The queen let the staff believe we were discussing plans for my new grandson's christening."

Prince Stefano and his wife had a new baby, he remembered. "I imagine that was a rather interesting conversation."

"*Interesting* is an apt descriptor." The king smiled. "You're quite the diplomat."

Unbidden, a laugh erupted from deep within Rocco's chest. "Touché."

"I told them everything, then left to fly here. I don't know how they'll each react in the long run, but they're good people. Strong. Independent. I can only hope they know me well enough to...well...I don't know. If any of them feel the need to cast blame, it will be at your mother and at me. Not you or your siblings. My guess is that they'll view the three of you with curiosity and will understand that you're all in this together."

Rocco chewed on that for a moment. "Do they want to meet us?"

Carlo let out a sigh that sounded almost like a laugh. "They asked the same about you. I told them we'd take this one day at a time. The first step is for all of you to take the time to reflect on what you really want. No need to make rash decisions. I want all of you to have your questions answered first, and for each of you to come to grips with what you've learned."

"Sounds logical enough."

In front of them, Justine stood and rounded the fire pit to select another log from the bin at the side of the porch and add it to the fire.

"You married well," Carlo said. "When I heard you'd married Justine Flyte, I admit, I was surprised. From what your mother told me about you, the two of you don't seem much alike."

"She's a wild child ski champ and I'm not?"

"You're a man of science. An engineer. Your work is indoors and cerebral. Hers is outdoors and physical."

"We're both driven. Both of us want to make our mark on the world." Rocco's heart swelled as he watched Justine sit to the side of the pit, giving him a view of her profile in the golden firelight. "As for the rest, we balance each other."

"It sounds like a good match. It's the same with me and Fabrizia. I love her more than life itself." Carlo angled his body so he faced Rocco. "You two are separated, I understand?"

"We were working on things when I read my mother's papers." Since then, Rocco had been thinking about his relationship with Justine nonstop. When they'd traveled to Baltimore, he'd told her he never wanted to lose her again. He'd told her he'd be at her events, by her side whenever she wished it. He'd meant it. But when he made those promises, he'd believed the risks were all his. Namely, that his paternity would be revealed.

He never thought the risk would become Justine's. Reading his mother's papers changed that.

Carlo straightened, then folded his arms over his chest. "Judging from the way you looked at each other when I entered, it's apparent you love each other very much. I hope you find a way to reunite."

"Thank you." A weight settled in Rocco's chest as he watched Justine tuck a stray strand of hair behind her ear. "It's going to come out, isn't it? If not today or tomorrow, then eventually. It won't matter if you make it back to the palace without being seen. Now that you've told your children—which I don't begrudge you doing—too many people know."

"My family is very good at keeping their own counsel. Living in the palace, it's a necessity." His brows rose. "However, in this instance, I fear you may be right. It would only take one word uttered at the wrong time for questions to be raised," the king said. "The attention would be a lot for you and your siblings to handle."

"I can manage."

"But you worry about your siblings. You especially worry about your wife."

Rocco could only nod as he stared out at the flames. If—when—the truth were revealed in the press, it would harm Justine, perhaps irreparably.

After taking a long look at Justine, Carlo moved to the room's rustic fireplace and took a seat on its edge. "People like to talk about fame. Whether that fame is positive or negative, they say it won't change you if you resolve to stay true to yourself. But until fame happens to you, you can only look on from outside the vortex and speculate about how it affects a person who's trapped on the inside."

Rocco turned his head, curious at the pensive note in the king's voice. "Is that how you feel? Trapped?"

"At times." He shrugged. "Then again, I've been famous from the moment of my birth, so what do I know of life outside the vortex? My wife, however, wasn't famous until our engagement was announced. Fame came fast and furious then, and her learning curve was steep. Being royal isn't flash-in-the-pan fame. It's international, lifelong, and life-altering. It's the type of fame that spans both politics and entertainment. The coverage—the intrusiveness of it—can be brutal."

"How did she adjust?"

"I helped where I could. I also had to trust her to know her own limits, when she should try to reduce her exposure and under which circumstances she could allow herself to be vulnerable." He glanced toward the rear windows, then looked back at Rocco. "Fabrizia and I came to the realization that life is short, and what is most important to us is to protect those we love. Namely, our children. We've done the best we can, but they often get themselves into trouble. We've told them to raise their heads and move on and to consider fame a high-class problem, one that has its challenges, but that affords us the ability to do our jobs. Without a certain amount of fame, I wouldn't hold the cachet I do when I walk into a room with the goal of convincing a business that they should establish an office in Sarcaccia. Fabrizia wouldn't be able to raise the awareness she does for the homeless or for victims of sex crimes. Prince Stefano and his wife wouldn't have had the ability to turn our country's new conference center into the international draw that it is…which, in turn, benefits our tourism industry."

"You're saying it's all a matter of perspective."

"Most days, yes, that's what I believe."

"And today?"

He shot Rocco a wry look. "Today it's a challenge."

Rocco smiled in return, despite himself. He didn't want to like this man. The world at large adored him, but Rocco knew Carlo wasn't all the public believed him to be. As the king himself admitted, he'd made mistakes.

But, grudgingly, Rocco found himself intrigued by Carlo. He was a man who knew himself, who understood both his good and bad sides and knew how to put them into perspective. Regardless of what had happened between Carlo and Teresa, Carlo had accomplished a great deal in Sarcaccia. He'd improved the lives of his subjects, increasing both educational opportunities and the standard of living on the island while holding inflation in check and maintaining the country's strong traditions. He'd expanded tourism, yet was a staunch protector of Sarcaccia's natural beauty and fought hard to protect its wildlife and natural resources.

After taking another look outside to ensure Justine remained comfortable, Rocco crossed the room to sit beside Carlo. A heartbeat later, an antique grandfather clock in the corner chimed the hour.

"That's my cue." Carlo indicated the clock. "I'll need to leave in the next half hour to fly back to Sarcaccia if I want to enter the palace with the least chance of being seen. Before I wish your wife a good night, is there anything else you wanted to know?"

Rocco shook his head, regretting that their time had come to an end just as he'd started to understand Carlo. They stood, but as Rocco prepared to thank the king for making the trip to Croatia, he remembered. "Wait. There is something. Queen Fabrizia brought a necklace when she came to warn me about the Russians."

Carlo's eyes lit. "Ah, yes. The star sapphire. She told me she gave it to you."

"It's unbelievable. I've never seen anything like it in my life."

The king's deep laugh caught Rocco off guard. "You wouldn't because it's one of a kind. And now it's yours."

"Why?"

"It was your mother's." Still smiling, Carlo wandered back to the windows, glanced out at Justine, then spun to face Rocco. "After Lina and Enzo were born, I designed it with Conti & Fancetti and had it secretly delivered to Teresa. It was my way of saying goodbye to the relationship and of thanking her for bearing three wonderful children. I'd hoped she'd view it as a peace offering and would soften enough to allow me to see you again and to meet the twins, but she didn't. She returned the necklace immediately."

"I don't blame her."

"Neither do I," he said. "It was the misguided gift of a young man who'd suddenly become very powerful and very, very wealthy. The sapphire had been in my family for generations and I thought that by putting it into a necklace, it could be handed down to Lina someday. I wanted her to have a tangible item that would remind her for the rest of her life that she is a Barrali. I'd hoped to give something personal to you and Enzo, as well, but with Teresa's rejection of the necklace, that never happened."

Rocco moved closer to Carlo, stopping short of the windows to rest a hip against the edge of one of the upholstered chairs.

Carlo skimmed a hand over his chin and glanced up at the ceiling, remembering. "It's odd to think about it now. I did it out of a sense of loyalty and love for the three of you, but truly, where would Teresa have worn such a thing? Fabrizia warned me. She told me sending such a gift was ridiculous, but humored me. She understood the intent behind it. Later, Fabrizia rightfully pointed out that the jeweler would recognize it if it were ever worn in public and photographed, so it was for the best that Teresa returned it. I put it in a secured drawer and there it remained. As you can imagine, it's not a piece Fabrizia would choose to wear."

"It's been sitting unworn all this time?"

"My daughter-in-law Kelly wore it to a palace event recently after she found it and showed it to Massimo, but they didn't know the history of the piece."

Whatever story Rocco had expected the king to tell about the necklace, that wasn't it. He rounded the chair to retrieve Justine's handbag from where she'd left it beside the coffee table. He withdrew the velvet box and turned to Carlo. "You know I can't keep it, either. It must be worth millions."

"I doubt it's worth millions, plural. And what am I going to do with it?" The king's light brown eyes lit with humor. "Justine could find a place to wear it. Surely in your line of work you attend charity events to raise money for hospitals or scientific research?"

"Frequently, yes. But this" —he extended the box to Carlo— "belongs in a museum. Or with your family."

Carlo shook his head and kept his arms at his side. "You are my family. I want you to have it."

Rocco frowned, then slowly returned the box to Justine's handbag. "Fine. I'll hang onto it for now, though it doesn't feel right. If you can think of another use for it—maybe give it to your daughter Sophia or one of your other children—please let me know. I'll get it to you right away. I know you have Kos's contact information, but here" —Rocco reached for his wallet and withdrew one of his business cards— "this is my direct line at the villa."

Carlo took the card and read it before carefully tucking it into his pants pocket. To Rocco's surprise, the king then extended a card of his own. "Call me anytime, Rocco, for any reason. I will always take the call. And if Lina and Enzo should wish to call or meet me, I'd welcome it."

As Rocco accepted the king's card, he marveled at the depth of emotion and sincerity in the king's voice.

"I should say good night to your wife. I'll walk to my car from there." He held out a hand. "Thank you, Rocco. Coming here and seeing you again after all these years…it's my privilege."

Rocco accepted the king's outstretched hand. The simple exchange tightened Rocco's throat, but he managed to keep his tone even as he responded, "I'm glad we met, as well."

Carlo nodded, then pulled in Rocco for an embrace. A cacophony of emotions erupted within Rocco. He'd hated this man for so long, yet the quick, affectionate hug felt very much like the ones he'd received over the years from Jack Cornaro.

The king gestured to the back hall. "This way?"

At Rocco's nod, he said, "Good night, Rocco. I hope we can see each other again," then turned on his heel and disappeared, but not before Rocco saw the tears clinging to the rims of King Carlo's eyes.

CHAPTER 22

Rocco said nothing as he took a seat on the stone bench beside Justine. Sensing his need to simply think, she flipped part of the blanket over him, then scooted closer to rest her hand on his forearm.

The fire had burned down to its last embers, with only two well-blackened logs remaining, when the king had crossed the patio to wish her a good night and thank her for giving him the space to speak to Rocco. It'd been surreal, having the world-famous king grasp both her hands in his, then offer a warm, genuine smile before he departed. She'd met dozens of famous people in her career, but he had to be one of the most recognizable. She'd managed a few words of semicoherent small talk before he took his leave.

The sound of the car engine starting out front occurred at the same moment she'd heard Rocco open the back door to join her.

Once the last of the red-hot cinders disappeared, Justine eased away from Rocco to poke at the ashes. Wood smoke lingered in the air, reminding her of peaceful evenings spent at ski lodges surrounded by sky and forest and stars. "Still want to head back to the villa tonight? If not, I'll add more kindling and we can sit awhile. Otherwise, I should douse this."

"Douse it." He levered himself off the bench. "I'll go ahead and lock up, unless you'd like to use the restroom first."

She shook her head, then asked him to grab her bag from the living room. They met at the car, then buckled in for the trip back to Dubrovnik. By day, it was a gorgeous drive, with the road snaking through rural villages as it afforded glimpses of the jagged Adriatic coast. Tonight, however, even with the moonlight, Justine found it difficult to appreciate. Tension rolled off Rocco in waves.

"I liked him."

They were twenty minutes from the villa when Rocco finally spoke, his voice like sandpaper.

"I'm glad." She reached across the gearshift to touch his thigh. "I know it was difficult, but the risk was worth it for Enzo and Lina. Perhaps for you, too."

"Everything I suspected about my mother was true. I knew it in my heart before he confirmed it." Before Justine could say she was sorry, he continued, "To his credit, the king was gracious about it. He said he couldn't fault the way she raised us, and he answered my questions about the necklace. He had it made for my mother after he ended their relationship."

"After?"

Rocco glanced in the rearview mirror, then moved over to allow a car to pass. "That surprised me, too. He explained it as a misguided attempt at a combination goodbye and thank-you-for-the-children gift from a man who was still maturing and had more money than he knew what to do with. He said he'd hoped she'd take it as a peace offering and let him visit us. She sent it back." Rocco released a long breath. "Apparently, after their relationship ended, my mother wouldn't allow him to see us."

Justine wasn't sure how to take that bit of information. Rocco seemed deep in thought, though not necessarily troubled...at least not by what he'd learned about his mother from Carlo. A deeper matter gnawed at him.

"Do you think you'll see him again?"

"I suspect it's inevitable." He took his eyes off the road long enough to meet her look of curiosity. "He told his children about us. In fact, he says he told them everything right before he flew here."

"Whoa." That likely explained Rocco's distracted mood.

"That sums up my thinking on the subject." He guided the car around a series of turns that put them onto the main road into Dubrovnik. "I'm sure they were as stunned by the information as I was. More, given that they didn't even know I existed, let alone about his relationship with my mother."

"It'll be a lot for them to absorb."

"And there are a lot of them."

A note of resignation in his voice left her cold inside. "You're afraid it's going to come out."

"I can't imagine it *not* coming out, and sooner rather than later. Too much has happened since my mother died. Too many people know."

"It was hidden for over forty years, Rocco. It may stay that way forty more." At his skeptical look, she asked, "If it does come out, what's the worst that can happen? You've done nothing wrong. Neither have Enzo or Lina. The story will be shocking to those who live in Sarcaccia, but will anyone else really care?"

"Only everyone who reads about the royals while standing in line at the supermarket. Or watches the evening news."

"It all depends on the coverage, though, doesn't it? The Barralis strike me as masters of their own press. They'll find a way to spin it so it doesn't sound so bad." She gave his thigh a soft squeeze before resting her hands in her lap. "No matter what happens, I'm confident you, Enzo, and Lina will be able to manage it for as long as it's a story. After that, people will forget. Their focus will be on the next Barrali scandal, whatever it may be. Not on you."

Rocco didn't respond. His mouth remained in a thin line and he gripped the steering wheel so tight Justine suspected he'd break it between his hands if he were able. Much as she wanted him to talk, she understood he still needed time. The wounds were too raw.

When they reached the outskirts of Dubrovnik, he said, "You

received a phone call this morning. From what I heard it sounded ski-related."

"It was. My old coach."

"You told him you got the all-clear?"

She nodded. "He's fully booked, but had some recommendations for me. Good ones. He offered to put out feelers, see who might be interested in working with me. I figured you and I could talk through the options after you finished with your mother's estate."

"Where would you need to train?"

"Depending on the coach, they'd probably want to go to either Chile or New Zealand by late June or early July. I've been putting in the gym time, but I need to get on skis to see what I have. Or don't have."

"You'd need to go soon."

He knew from past years that she did most of her off-season training in the gym, working to enhance her strength, balance, and explosiveness. However, she tried to clock at least fifty of those days on skis wherever she could find fresh powder, and that meant the southern hemisphere. Given that she hadn't skied in a year, she'd need to fit in as many snow days as possible during the coming off-season if she hoped to compete.

"Within two to three weeks, I imagine. I'll talk to a few coaches first."

"Do what you need to do. Whatever's best for your career."

"I don't know how I'll ski yet. It may all come to nothing. I'm at the age where most competitors retire."

"I know you. You'll race again." He faced her after he slowed to a stop at a red light. "You turned down the television job, didn't you?"

Yesterday. It'd been one of the most difficult calls of her life, knowing the gamble she was taking. "I didn't think it was fair to keep the producer waiting. If I'm going to do this, it needs to be all or nothing."

"That's what I figured."

She frowned at his tone as the light changed and he stepped on the gas. "The way you said that…I thought you said you'd support me making another go at competing."

"I did. And I do." He turned the car onto a road that headed toward the Old City, rather than in the direction of the villa. "But I also said I'd do my best never to hurt you again."

"Oh, Rocco, no." At once his attitude became understandable. It was why he'd been pulling away from her for the last week, though he needed her more than ever. Why he'd been silent for most of the drive back from the Konavle. Why he was turning toward her apartment instead of the villa. It was all she could do not to grab the wheel and spin it toward the home they'd once shared, the home they should share again. "Don't be a martyr. There's no need."

"I'm not!" All the strain and hurt of the last week came out in those two words. "I'm being practical."

"You want to end our marriage before we've had it back for even two weeks because you think all this nonsense with your mother will be bad for my career."

"Bad? Try devastating. Think of how you'll be perceived."

"Like a woman with good taste who's married to one of the hottest, smartest men on the planet. If you call that devastating, then—"

"Stop." His knuckles went white on the steering wheel. "This isn't a joke, Justine. What my mother did…" He grit his teeth. "Maybe I've known it from the moment I read her letter. Or when we boarded the airplane to fly home and that couple in the waiting area kept sneaking peeks at you. They not only recognized you, they recognized you in a positive light. They were smiling and elbowing each other. Think of how that would change."

"It wouldn't. And if it did, I wouldn't care."

"Says the woman who assured a television producer she has no skeletons in her closet. No scandals. Nothing to detract from a long-term career in front of the camera."

"Rocco—"

"The minute you step back into your ski boots, you'll be under more scrutiny than ever. There's a reason sports broadcasters have made a trope out of the comeback kid. It makes a great story. It's the kind of story that will bring you new fans and endorsement deals. Deservedly so, because you've worked your tail off. You're a great athlete and a spectacular role model. When you do finally end your competitive career, you'll be in even higher demand than you are now, but only if you're conscious of your image."

"For being such a smart guy, you're a real idiot." How could he not see? Being with him gave her courage. He made her feel invincible.

"I promised I'd never hurt you again, but I'm stuck in a Catch-22. I hurt you if we divorce. I hurt you if we stay together." He turned onto the street where her apartment was located. She wanted to tell him to keep driving, to go to the villa, but knew her plea would fall on deaf ears. "One will be short-term pain, and one will haunt you over and over. I'm opting for the lesser of two evils."

She undid her seatbelt and twisted to face Rocco as he parked at the curb in front of her apartment. The night was as silent and dark as when they'd fled down this same street with Radich and Karpovsky on their heels. The sense of doom crushing her lungs felt as immediate now as it had then. "I'm going to chalk up everything you just said to the fact you've had a very long, emotional day. It's not normal for you. Give this time. Sleep on it. I'm happy to stay here at the apartment and give you space at the villa if that's what you need, but don't make a rash decision. We belong together. We've known it for years. I need you more than any job. And frankly, the two aren't mutually exclusive."

Taking a chance, she closed the space between them to cradle his cheek. She looked deep into his eyes, eyes filled with pain, and hoped he could see the sincerity in hers and draw strength from it. "I know you, Rocco. And I love you."

"I love you, too." He covered her hand with his, then slowly eased it away from his face to kiss her palm before lowering it to her lap. "That's why I need to let you go."

Rocco felt like a first class bastard, and not because of his birth.

Well, come to think of it, *exactly* because of his birth, and the actions his mother's choices now necessitated.

He pinched the bridge of his nose and rolled over on the library's long gray sofa, mentally replaying the night's conversations, first with Carlo, then with Justine. He'd done the right thing in both instances, but doing the right thing didn't feel right.

It felt horribly, terribly wrong. As if he'd taken a knife and plunged it deep into his own chest, and was now staring down, watching himself bleed out. Worse, he knew Justine was sitting in her apartment at this very moment, likely wide awake and staring out at the first blush of sunlight as it hit the city streets, wondering what in the world had gone wrong. What she could've said or done to change his mind.

She wouldn't believe him if he'd told her there was no going back. In Justine's mentality options always existed. A tweak to her equipment, another route down the racecourse, a subtle change that could shave an extra tenth of a second to secure a victory.

The look on her face as she'd stepped out of his car and unlocked the door to her apartment building shredded him. He'd had to force himself to put his hands on the steering wheel so he wouldn't go after her. So she wouldn't think she could hop back in the car and convince him he was making a mistake. When he'd told her he needed to let her go, she hadn't argued. Not with words. She'd stared at him as if she could make him recant with the force of her will alone.

He'd simply met her gaze until she'd finally grabbed the door handle in a huff and stepped out of the car. Those few seconds had seemed interminable.

I need you more than any job.

That was the part she failed to think through. Skiing wasn't a job for her. It *was* her. Whether she spent the rest of her life on the slopes or in front of a camera, skiing was her passion. It put sparkle in her eyes and had her talking to complete strangers as if they were lifelong friends. He wouldn't take that from her. She wouldn't be the same Justine without it.

She knew it, too, or she wouldn't have been so determined to defy her doctors, to do everything her rehab specialists asked of her and more. To push herself to the absolute limit, to toss aside the pain medication when she feared it might interfere with her long-term plans.

She'd wanted him to sleep on his decision. She was the one who needed to sleep on hers.

Rocco swiped a hand over his stubble-covered chin and pushed to sit. Unfortunately, actual sleep hadn't been in the cards. He'd tried going to bed, only to meander to the library. He'd poured a drink, but hadn't consumed it. He'd turned on the news only to mute it when a perky brunette began gushing over the irrepressible spirit of a local man who'd been injured in a motorcycle accident and was now, against all odds, learning to ride again.

That one hit a little too close to home.

His fist connected with the back of the sofa. "I love her too much for her own damned good," he muttered to himself. "And mine."

More than anyone he'd ever met, and—he knew with every cell in his body—more than anyone he'd ever meet again. Screw second acts. He had none. Justine was his first, his only chance at a happily ever after. But *she* had other chances. She was beautiful, tenacious, and had an inner light that drew people to her. The best thing he could do for Justine was let her go, though the idea of her eventually finding another man, one who'd be better for her…it turned his stomach.

He stretched and cracked his knuckles. He'd made a promise to her and he meant it. He'd do what was best for the two of them—for everyone—not what was best for him. He wouldn't put Justine through the agony of being asked again and again about her husband or her late mother-in-law. Or have Justine wonder every time she was turned down for a job if it was her marriage that ultimately decided her fate, or if she'd somehow missed the mark when judged on her own hard work and talent.

The world needed to see her for who she was. Not for the man she'd married. If it did, the possibilities for her future were endless.

A muffled hum came from his desk. He crossed the room with a curse, expecting to see Justine's number on the phone's display. He wouldn't answer it. Not yet. He needed more time and so did she. But when he glanced at the screen and noted the private number, he answered immediately.

"I apologize for waking you. I didn't intend to use your card so soon, but there's been a development."

King Carlo's voice was as clear as it'd been when they'd spoken less than six hours earlier, making Rocco wonder if the monarch had slept at all.

"What is it?"

"I was spotted disembarking the jet at three in the morning. I imagine it'll be mentioned on the morning news here in Sarcaccia. I'm attending a planning meeting for the restoration of Cateri's central library later today. The press will be there."

"Which means you'll be asked about it."

"Yes." There was a pause. "I'm sorry, Rocco. I can put off questions easily enough today. Perhaps for three or four days. But the longer I defer, the more convinced reporters will be that there's a story to uncover."

"I understand." Rocco took a deep breath. "Do what you need to do. I'll call Lina and Enzo to warn them."

"You'll have reporters at your doorstep."

"Then I won't be here."

Once he ended the call, Rocco sank into his desk chair and stared at the framed wedding photo on the corner, the one Fabrizia had studied the day she'd come to warn him. Jack and his mother looked so happy. Too bad Jack hadn't known his wife was lying to him about her past. Or maybe it was for the best. Jack had lived a robust life, one filled with love from his wife and three adopted children.

"What would you do in my shoes, Jack, knowing what I know now?" Rocco stared at the photo awhile longer, let out a long breath, then clicked his phone to pull up the list of contacts. With the right words to the right people, he could ensure Justine was far, far away from the coming fracas.

He owed her that.

FABRIZIA STRAIGHTENED her husband's collar and tidied his hair, though both were already perfectly in place. They stood in a small antechamber off the palace's famed green parlor. Because of its intimate atmosphere, the parlor was used for high level talks, press conferences, and even—rumor had it—clandestine romantic encounters during the palace's early days.

"I'll be fine," Carlo assured her. He stood as straight and tall as ever, but she could feel trepidation rolling off him in waves. "Better to do it this way so we can control the story."

She doubted the story could be controlled, but he was right. Should the paparazzi discover the Cornaros and reveal their connection to the Barrali family, the media would be vicious, playing the cover-up in a way that would make the entire family seem untrustworthy. That wouldn't do if they were to continue to successfully lead the country.

Beside them, Fabrizia's assistant, Daniela, peeked around the door that separated them from the parlor. "They're all assembled. Ready when you are."

Carlo nodded, then gave Fabrizia a soft kiss on the cheek. "No matter how this turns out, I love you."

"I know you do."

He turned to enter the parlor, where approximately a dozen reporters sat waiting for the impromptu press conference to start, but Fabrizia put a hand on his arm. "I'm coming in with you."

He frowned, then pulled Fabrizia off to the side so Daniela and the other staff members couldn't hear them. "No man wants to make the admission I'm about to make, let alone make it while knowing his wife is standing behind him being stared at and speculated about. They'll wonder what you knew and when. They'll wonder how you can stand me. They'll believe I was a fool and a cad and will question my judgment." He looked at the ceiling, getting his bearings, then back at her. "Fabrizia, it'll be—"

"My honor." She put her hands on her husband's lapel and smiled up at him. He was her heart, her soul. Hearing the torrent of objections from him only solidified her resolve. He needed her for this. "We've been together a long time, Carlo. I know all the good and all the bad. I know you're concerned about how you'll be viewed after you walk into that room and say what you need to say. It's a valid concern. But if I'm by your side, our countrymen will see in my eyes and my body language how I feel about you. It will give them confidence. If I'm not there, that also speaks volumes."

He curled his hands around hers. "Fabrizia, I can't ask that of you."

"Then don't. Simply allow it."

He studied her for a long moment. Beneath her hands, his chest rose and fell, and she felt the slow, steady beat of his heart. His nod, when it finally came, was barely perceptible.

She smiled, gave his hands a final squeeze, then followed him into the green parlor, head held high and love filling her entire being.

She was married to the most resilient, wonderful man in the world. She wanted the world to know it.

After being introduced by his press secretary, Carlo strode to the podium. Fabrizia moved to his side, standing a pace behind his right shoulder. He offered the reporters his usual greetings, welcoming several by name and wishing one of the local television personalities a happy birthday. As always, he had the room in the palm of his hand, even those reporters whose job was to pick apart Carlo's policies and endlessly second-guess his decisions.

"I appreciate all of you visiting with me today. I'm sure you had other priorities, like shopping for Marcello's birthday." A smattering of laughter echoed through the room. "However, I invited you here to discuss a personal matter. Given my position as a hereditary monarch, the line between my public life and my private life is often thin. On occasion, it's a challenge to find the balance between what the public rightfully deserves to know so Sarcaccia's citizens remain confident in my ability to govern, and in keeping personal matters to myself in order to protect my wife and children, who are" —he smiled at Fabrizia over his shoulder— "the loves of my life. Part of being a good steward of this country is keeping myself in good physical and mental health, and keeping my private life private helps me do that."

Fabrizia sensed Carlo corralling his energy. Before he could say more, the door at the rear of the green parlor opened and Princess Sophia slipped through. Though she was silent as she entered, her hot pink dress made her hard to miss. She caught Fabrizia's eye, then fingered the delicate gold chain around her throat. A small, golden rose dangled from the end. Carlo had given Sophia the necklace on her tenth birthday, then walked her out to the palace garden to show her a new variant of pink rose that had been named the Princess Sophia in her honor.

In that moment, as a smile blossomed on Sophia's face, Fabrizia knew all would be well.

"As I said when I entered the room, today's discussion revolves around a personal matter," Carlo's voice strengthened as he, too, noticed Sophia and realized that she was there to support him. "It is not a matter I wished to share. However, circumstances have changed in recent weeks."

The parlor door opened once again, this time as Vittorio, Emily, and Alessandro entered. Several reporters turned around in surprise. One snapped a photo, apparently sensing the presence of three royal children at a press conference meant a momentous announcement was forthcoming.

"Many years ago, when I was a teenager, I was involved in an inappropriate relationship with one of my tutors. She recently passed away, which is why the time has come to bring this matter to light."

As one, the reporters who'd turned toward the back of the room swiveled to face the front. Carlo continued, "Her name was Teresa Fedeli. I was seventeen and she was twelve years my senior. The relationship occurred unbeknownst to my parents. In fact, it went on unbeknownst to anyone until I told my wife shortly before our marriage."

No one stirred in the room other than Carlo, who again looked over his shoulder at Fabrizia. She briefly put a hand to his arm and smiled, then stepped away to allow him to finish.

"It was not merely improper due to the age difference, which, I know—and knew at the time—was wrong. It was also improper because I saw Teresa on two separate occasions in the year following my marriage to Queen Fabrizia." As eyes widened around the room, Carlo said, "I am the most fortunate man in the world in that my wife forgave me. Since then, the queen and I have built a strong, loving marriage, one that is founded upon trust. I have not broken that trust since."

Fabrizia looked to the back of the parlor to gauge her children's reaction and saw that Stefano, Megan, Massimo, and Kelly had joined the others. She gave them a smile at the same time the door opened once more to admit Bruno. A camera flashed in the front row, capturing what she knew had to be an expression of profound gratitude and surprise on her face as she saw that her youngest child had flown home once more to back his father. Then dozens of cameras flashed, memorializing Carlo's reaction as he gazed at his children. At that moment, two figures entered from the antechamber and remained on the opposite side of the room from the royal siblings. Fabrizia's breath seized as she recognized that Umberto had brought in Rocco Cornaro. Though the reporters paid Rocco no attention, Fabrizia knew that would change. Judging from the lopsided grin on Rocco's face as he moved further from the room's main entrance, ensuring he was well out of the view of the photographers' lenses, Rocco knew it, too.

Despite the surprise entrance of his eldest son, Carlo's voice remained firm. "With Teresa Fedeli's passing, I now have the opportunity to address what has been the great challenge of my personal life. That challenge involves the three children Teresa bore during our relationship."

Whispers throughout the room grew to outright gasps and murmurs of, "did he say three children?" and one whispered into his phone, "find all you can on Teresa Fedeli, a former tutor for the royal family," as Carlo paused to take a sip of water from a glass hidden behind the podium. Discussion ceased when the king adjusted the microphone to continue.

"Several reporters noted my three a.m. arrival at the airport a few days ago. I can now tell you that I was visiting the eldest of those children, a brilliant man named Rocco Cornaro. Rocco has known about his paternity since he was young, as have Rocco's siblings, Lina and Enzo, who are fraternal twins. In answer your questions, yes, my wife has also known about Rocco, Lina, and Enzo throughout our marriage. Our children are also aware of their half-siblings. Long ago, Teresa Fedeli and I decided to keep their existence quiet. Though doing so kept my personal failings from the public eye, it was not done for that purpose, but to protect their upbringing. They are private citizens, raised outside Sarcaccia by their mother, and wish to remain private citizens. However, it is my desire to get to know them now in a way I could not during Teresa's lifetime. I hope that you will honor my wishes and respect their need for privacy. They each have vibrant careers and personal relationships that I do not wish to see harmed because of their connection to me. That being said, I will now take five minutes of questions."

Fabrizia nodded to the reporters, then skirted the room to join her children as Carlo patiently listened to the barrage of questions and gave to-the-point answers. Most of the inquiries centered on Teresa— did he know this was a crime? Yes. Was this the reason Queen

Fabrizia dedicated herself to so many charities for victims of abuse? No, the issue transcends my own experience. Had the two sets of children met? No. Where did they live? Outside Sarcaccia.

"Thank you." Fabrizia said the words in a voice intended for Sophia's ears only, though Vittorio, who stood on Sophia's other side, also heard.

"We weren't going to let him face the firing squad alone," Sophia responded. "We didn't know you planned to join him."

Fabrizia fought to keep from smiling, given how the press might interpret it in light of the serious nature of the press conference. "I couldn't leave him up there alone, either."

Vittorio leaned closer to Fabrizia and Sophia. "Don't look across the room…but that's him, isn't it? With Umberto."

"Also a surprise. I had no idea."

Vittorio's eyes widened fractionally. "Good for him."

Sophia allowed herself a subtle perusal of the room, keeping her features calm as she got her first glimpse of Rocco. When she met Fabrizia's gaze again, she said, "He's handsome."

"He looks like *me*," Vittorio said under his breath.

"I'm going to leave before your father finishes," Fabrizia told them. "I'll be in the library if you care to join me. No more talk here."

Both Sophia and Vittorio signaled with their eyes that they'd be there. Within ten minutes, all the Barrali siblings had found seats in the palace's secluded library. Fabrizia chose her favorite chair. Its back was to the windows that overlooked the entirety of the palace gardens, instead affording her a view of the colorful Impressionist paintings that filled the spaces between the room's floor-to-ceiling bookshelves. One in particular, depicting a mother and child reading on the seashore, always imbued her with a sense of peace.

Footsteps at the far end of the library caught her attention. She tore her gaze from the painting to see Carlo entering from the main hallway.

"You did wonderfully, dear," she told him as he strode to the seat beside her.

He took in the sight of the six children scattered about the room. "I don't know about how I did, but I know how I feel. Thank you."

"Tell me that was Rocco Cornaro who came in near the end with Umberto," Alessandro said. "If not, I want a DNA test run on that guy."

"He looks like you two," Bruno said to Alessandro and Vittorio. "It's eerie."

"That was Rocco," Carlo confirmed. "He must've called Umberto after I told him I planned to hold a press conference today. I never expected to see him here."

"You invited him?" Sophia asked.

The king shook his head, then looked at Fabrizia. She held one hand palm out. "I didn't, either."

"Grandma! I have a surprise for you!"

Anna, Stefano and Megan's daughter, entered the library carrying a large tray. The dark-haired girl beamed from ear-to-ear as she tilted the tray far enough for Fabrizia to see a batch of brightly decorated cookies. Shaped like hearts, each had a unique design crafted from pink, white, red, and silver frosting.

"You made these?"

"Made them and decorated them. The new chef gave me all the ingredients and an entire countertop to work on." Anna set the tray on a nearby table and pointed to one of the cookies, which was edged in silver punctuated by pink rosettes. "See the pink? Chef Fournier bought this frosting tip last week and let me test it. Doesn't it make beautiful roses?"

"I'd say you make beautiful roses. Anna, I'm truly impressed. These cookies look professionally done."

"I hope the fact you brought them here means they're for us," Stefano said as he leaned over his daughter's shoulder to take a look. Anna spent a great deal of her free time in the palace kitchen, often making desserts as surprise gifts for the staff or to share with the neighbors at her parents' apartment near the marina.

"They are," Anna told him. "But I wanted Grandma to see them before you took a bunch."

A knock at the library's secret door caused everyone to turn. Hidden behind a curtain between two bookshelves at the far end of the room, the door led to a service hallway and was used by only select members of the staff. A beat later, Umberto appeared from behind the curtain and addressed Carlo. "Your Highness? I apologize for the interruption, but I have a guest in my office. I thought I should check with you before he departed."

"Thank you, Umberto." Carlo's gaze swept his family before he said, "Please invite him to join us."

A moment later, Rocco entered the room from behind the curtain. Umberto dipped his head in regard to the king and queen, then left, closing the secret door behind him.

Fabrizia rose from her chair to greet Rocco, but to Vittorio's credit, he spoke before Fabrizia could. He introduced himself, then said, "I imagine it's rather awkward being introduced to one's half-siblings. I'll get the most annoying out of the way first." He gestured to his left. "My twin brother, Alessandro."

Rocco shook Alessandro's hand. The introspective biomedical engineer might be out of his element in the busy palace, but Fabrizia doubted any outsider witnessing the scene in the library would know it. Rocco stood tall and looked every bit as confident as Carlo had at the same age as he circled the room, meeting each of the Barrali children and their significant others.

"You must be Anna," Rocco said to Stefano and Megan's daughter. "Umberto tells me you're a talented cook. He claims you made spinach and salmon appetizers last week that were good enough to be served at a palace party."

"Chef Fournier helped me with them," she admitted. "But I'm learning. I think I could make them on my own next time."

"That's impressive. I'm afraid my cooking is limited to a few pasta dishes my mother taught me to make."

"Pasta's my favorite," Anna said, grinning up at Rocco. "Well, pasta and pizza. My mom says that you're my half-uncle. Is that true?"

Rocco didn't miss a beat. His eyes crinkled into a smile. "Well, your father is my half-brother. I'm not sure there's such a thing as a half-uncle, but if there is, then yes, I suppose I am."

"So do I call you Uncle Rocco?"

He leaned forward. In a conspiratorial whisper meant to be heard by Stefano and Megan, who stood nearby, he said, "It's fine with me. In fact, I'd really like it. You and your brother Dario are my only niece and nephew. But let's go with whatever your parents think is best, all right? You can ask them about it later."

Anna's responding grin stole Fabrizia's breath. Rocco couldn't have given a more perfect answer.

Sophia approached and took Rocco's hand. "I'm so sorry for your loss. My father told us that Teresa was a wonderful mother to you. I'm sure you miss her very much."

Emotion swirled in Rocco's eyes at the unexpected sentiment, but it vanished as quickly as it had appeared. "Thank you, Princess Sophia."

"Oh, please. Call me Sophia. It's nicer than what they often call me." She let go of Rocco's hand and shot fiery looks at each of her five brothers. "I'm desperately hoping to discover that you're better mannered than they are."

"I do my best."

"I understand you're married to Justine Flyte," Massimo interjected. "She's amazing. My father—our father—is a big fan. He watches a lot of alpine skiing."

Fabrizia didn't miss the uneasiness that flitted across Rocco's face before he responded to Massimo with a grin. Whether it was at the mention of his wife's name or at hearing Massimo refer to Carlo as "our father," she wasn't certain, though if she had to bet on the source of discomfort, she'd choose the wife.

"He and Justine met a few days ago when he visited Croatia. I believe Justine is just as big a fan of your father's."

"We're planning a family dinner in our private apartment tonight," Carlo said, stepping into the knot surrounding Rocco. "If you're available, we'd love to have you join us. In the meantime, I'm happy to give you a tour of the less-seen areas of the palace and its grounds."

"I'd appreciate that."

"We get the hint," Stefano said to his father as he pulled his wife's arm through his. He turned to Rocco. "It's good to meet you. We'll try not to overwhelm you tonight, though if you confuse those two" —he inclined his head toward Vittorio and Alessandro— "we won't hold it against you. In fact, the rest of us consider it good for their egos when they're mistaken for each other."

"I'm the better-looking one," Alessandro retorted as Vittorio and Emily guided him out of the library with Massimo and Kelly at their heels.

"Remember what I said about their egos," Stefano muttered before leaving with his wife and daughter.

Before Sophia departed, Carlo touched her arm to stop her. Fabrizia didn't miss the meaningful look on his face. "Thank you, sweetheart, for leading the pack. It meant the world to me."

"Good. It was supposed to." She stood on tiptoe to kiss her father on the cheek. "I'll see you at dinner."

"I won't, unfortunately," Bruno said. He clapped a hand on Rocco's shoulder. "I have an exam in the morning and need to get back, but I look forward to getting to know you over the coming years. I hope to meet Enzo and Lina, as well."

"I read that you're planning a medical career?" At Bruno's nod, Rocco said, "I'm sure we'll have plenty to talk about."

"Rocco might enjoy a tour of the kennel," Fabrizia said once she was alone with Carlo and Rocco. To Rocco, she explained, "It's Carlo's favorite spot in the entire palace complex. We have a new litter of Sarcaccian Shepherds. They're beautiful, loyal dogs."

"Umberto mentioned that Massimo has one. We saw it in the garden, playing fetch with one of your staff."

"No doubt someone trying to keep the beast out of the fountain. Gaspare loves the water." She offered Rocco what she hoped was a reassuring smile. "I've matters to attend to, but thank you so much for coming. I'll see you again at dinner."

She gave her husband a quick pat on the arm as she passed by, then kept her pace brisk as she exited the library and made her way to the apartment. She had nothing on her agenda for the rest of the day—she'd assumed she'd be holed up watching news reports of the press conference, with Carlo ducking in for updates when he needed a break from reading the large pile of government documents in his office—but perhaps viewing the aftermath by herself would be better.

If it exploded as she anticipated, it'd distract her from wondering what was so important Carlo wished to speak to Rocco alone.

CHAPTER 24

The local news blathered in the background as Justine ate her lunch of grilled fish, roasted beets, and spinach salad. It was her go-to meal when she was in training. No wine, no gnocchi, no cheesy calzones. Not that she felt deprived. Nothing she ate registered on her palate since Rocco called it quits on their marriage night before last.

I need to let you go.

She rolled her eyes as she remembered their last moments together. What a stupid phrase, especially since Rocco needed her now more than ever. But given the determination she'd seen in his eyes alongside the hurt, she'd decided to get out of the car rather than point out the obvious. She told herself she'd give him seventy-two hours—three days and three nights—to absorb his conversation with Carlo, to reassess what he wanted, and to think through what was best for both of them.

He loved her and wanted her. That much was clear in the way he physically held himself back from touching her. But self-sacrificing, valiant male that he was, he obviously hadn't realized that *she* was better with him than without.

He was a man of science. He'd figure it out.

"I hope," she grumbled to herself as she forked through her salad to spear the last tomato. Teresa had nearly ruined their relationship once before. Justine would be damned if she'd allow Teresa to do so again from the grave.

Rocco should recognize that, too. Justine Flyte didn't go down without a fight.

She picked up her cell phone to reread the message from the ski coach who'd contacted her late last night saying he'd heard she'd successfully completed rehabbing her leg and was hoping to compete next season. He was currently working out of a training center in Switzerland and wanted to set up a time to talk on the phone. The man was well-known in the sport and had coached several of her friends and competitors over the years. Justine knew his style would be a good fit for hers, but she hadn't answered yet. Rocco had a few more hours before the mental timer she'd set for his response ran out.

Not that she had a plan if the hour ticked by with no contact. Should she call? Show up at his doorstep? All she knew was that she didn't want to leave Croatia without talking to him again.

She was about to set down the phone when another message appeared, this from a Norwegian coach she'd interviewed and nearly hired years ago. As with the first coach, this one wrote to say she'd heard through the rumor mill that Justine was ready to ski again and in the market for a new coach. She said she'd love another chance to discuss working together. As Justine closed the message, yet another appeared. Another world-class coach and a message nearly identical to the first two.

Her former coach must've meant what he'd said about putting out feelers for her. It was gratifying to see top-flight coaches show interest, especially after they'd witnessed her gruesome wreck, but until Rocco reasoned his way through their relationship, Justine was trapped in limbo.

She tossed back the last of her iced tea and carried her plate to the sink, only to stop short when she noticed the image on the television. She couldn't hear the newscaster's exact words, but the photo of King

Carlo in the upper corner of the screen sent her scrambling for the remote so she could turn up the volume. Before it was loud enough for Justine to hear, video feed from inside the palace panned from where the Barrali siblings stood against a lush green wall, past a doorway, to land on two figures in the corner of the room.

Her heart clenched as she recognized Rocco as the man on the right, looking larger than life. He wore a dark jacket over an open white shirt that emphasized the richness of his olive skin and the bright amber of his eyes. He'd allowed his beard to grow over the last three days, but rather than making him appear scruffy, even that short growth gave him the dark, dangerous air he'd had when he'd entered her apartment the night Karpovsky had come for her. The overall effect was one of power, as if Rocco belonged with the Barrali family, in their palace, standing next to Umberto and taking stock of the room.

But, of course, he would look that powerful. Rocco carried the Barrali genes. He was as intelligent as any of them, Carlo included, and was self-made, having reached the pinnacle of success in a challenging field without having had the benefits of being raised a Barrali.

Perhaps that was a reason for the beard, though it may have been a subconscious one. It differentiated him from Vittorio and Alessandro.

"…stood in the back of the room during the press conference, away from the king's legitimate children," the woman identified as an expert on the royal family was saying. "Though he was not introduced, based on photographs taken at Johns Hopkins, this does appear to be Rocco Cornaro, the man the king named as one of his illegitimate children with Teresa Fedeli. Two other children, Enzo Cornaro and Lina Cornaro, did not appear to be at today's press conference. The palace has neither confirmed nor denied any of the Cornaro siblings' presence at the palace today, nor commented on the nature of the relationship between the Cornaros and the royal family."

"What does this mean for the line of succession?" the news anchor asked as the camera flashed back to the news desk. "Since Rocco Cornaro is older than the crown prince, can he make any claim to the throne?"

"None whatsoever," the woman responded. "Sarcaccian law is quite clear that only legitimate children of the monarch may inherit. However, it's astounding that such a secret has been kept for over forty years. You can bet that in the coming days, political observers throughout Europe will ask what other secrets the Barrali family has hidden. It will also be interesting to see whether this impacts the family's high approval rating. Sarcaccia is rare in that the monarch is a true head of state. A slide in the Barrali family's popularity may open debate in the country about whether they should remain a monarchy or move to a more democratic system of government."

"The country does have an elected parliament, but the king holds the true power. Has there been any indication that could change with this revelation, Maria?"

"It's too soon to tell. Right now, the media is scrambling to learn all they can about these illegitimate children, all of whom are well into adulthood. I think the long-term question will be about their late mother. The king danced around the fact that a crime was committed here. He used words like 'inappropriate' and 'improper' to describe his relationship with Teresa Fedeli. Even if the king was a willing participant, this was a violation of Sarcaccia's strict laws in this area, given that he was under the legal age of consent at the time it began."

"Much more to come on this story as it evolves," the anchor said before he segued to report on a fire that gutted a warehouse near the town of Split.

Justine moved closer to the television, flipping through channels to catch what tidbits she could from other news reports. When the lunch hour ended and afternoon programming began, she switched to her computer, bringing up story after story until she found video of the entire press conference. King Carlo's statement had been brief, centering on the bare facts and asking for privacy for the Cornaro siblings.

She doubted it'd do much good, either for the king or for Rocco, let alone for Enzo and Lina.

It certainly wouldn't help her. Rocco had backed up his determination with action. He'd never call her now, not to reunite, not if he knew the press was watching his every move.

I need to let you go.

"It's not true," she said to the empty room. He needed her. He wanted her. He loved her. Maybe, at the height of emotion following his discussion with Carlo, he'd been able to pull away from her, but only because he'd wrapped his hands around the steering wheel to prevent it. And because she'd finally gotten out of the car.

But did *she* want a man willing to walk away from her based on principle?

Yes. Hell, yes. She wanted him more. Because she knew he was doing it because he thought it was best for her.

Not because it was the easy way. The *convenient* way. Or because it was for Teresa.

A slow, wicked smile crept across Justine's face. He had to come back, if only to retrieve what he'd left in her handbag. Well, now he'd probably have to travel halfway around the world for it.

Deep in her heart, she knew he'd make the right decision when he saw her face-to-face.

She picked up her phone and began tapping out messages to the coaches.

"You said you wouldn't be home when the news broke," Carlo said once Queen Fabrizia left the library. "I didn't interpret that to mean you'd be here."

Rocco smiled at the king's tone. "Seemed the rational place. Reporters won't camp out at my villa to hunt for me or question whether or not we're acquainted."

Carlo regarded him for a beat, then said, "I suppose that's true. Walk with me."

They passed through a half-dozen rooms filled with ornate furniture and antique rugs. Paintings Rocco assumed to be priceless covered the walls. Many featured past kings and queens, while others depicted Sarcaccia's gorgeous waterfront in years gone by. One painting in particular caught Rocco's eye.

"You like that one?"

Rocco paused, studying the Impressionist rendering of a grassy field at sunrise. A horse stood near a fence to one side of the painting, its head raised in anticipation as if a beloved owner stood just out of the picture. "It looks like a Degas, but it's lighter and cheerier than what he usually paints."

"You have a good eye. Degas is known for his depictions of ballerinas and dance schools, but he also painted several scenes in Paris cafés and of racehorses. This one was done for my great-grandfather after he visited France and saw one of the Impressionist exhibitions. He was taken with Degas's style and asked Degas if he'd consider memorializing a favorite horse."

"That's…stunning." Rocco couldn't imagine what an original Degas would fetch, especially one as beautiful and unique as this. There was a quality to the way the painting captured the light, making the field appear to sparkle with morning dew. It was the type of painting that invited one to linger and appreciate its nuances.

"What's stunning is that Degas said no, then presented my great-grandfather with this painting as a gift six months later. It was a complete surprise. Years later, when Degas started to lose his eyesight, my great-grandfather offered the services of his personal physician. Degas refused. Said the king had become too reform-minded and that it wouldn't be appropriate to accept help from such a person."

Rocco looked at the painting in awe. It amazed him that Carlo's great-grandfather—actually, his *own* great-great-grandfather—had known Edgar Degas and tried to help him in his later years.

Carlo ran his hand down the edge of the gilt frame. "Of course, it wasn't a political or moral issue at all. Degas intentionally isolated himself from his friends as he grew older, using whatever excuse he could. Now it would likely be diagnosed as depression, but in those days it was chalked up to the vagaries of an aging artistic temperament."

The king stepped back from the painting and smiled. "It was

because of this painting I passed my art history course in college. My great-grandfather's stories about Degas turning into a stubborn grouch who refused to accept kindnesses helped me remember which paintings he completed near the end of his life." Carlo cocked his head. "I was a terrible art history student, but my parents insisted I take the class, given the nature of our family's collection."

"You seem to appreciate it now."

"I appreciate the stories more than the art. My wife appreciates the works themselves." He gestured for Rocco to continue walking with him. "I didn't ask you to stay to discuss art, though even for me, art is an easier topic than anything of a personal nature."

"The press conference."

"The press conference." The king nodded to a guard, who bowed before she pushed open a heavy wooden door for the king and Rocco to pass through. They emerged onto a set of stone steps. At the bottom, a gravel path wended its way through the palace gardens.

"How are Lina and Enzo?"

"They left their homes yesterday to avoid the coverage. I did the same, then told them I was considering coming here."

The king folded his hands behind his back as he walked. "What did they think?"

"They didn't say and I didn't ask." He wasn't going to tell Carlo that mending fences with the twins would be an uphill battle. Not that Rocco had completely mended fences with the king himself. However, the fact that the king could've used the press conference to cast Teresa as a villain and protect his own reputation, yet chose not to do so, was a point in the monarch's favor.

"The coverage will be brutal. I doubt they'll escape it."

"They can handle it."

"Commentators will soon note that I've committed a crime." When Rocco opened his mouth to argue that the crime was his mother's, the king held up a hand to stay him. "I failed to report a felony and took steps to cover its existence for decades. Despite being the so-called victim, I'm also a head of state and held to that standard. There will be calls by the usual malcontents to censure me for hiding what happened. I have no doubt of it."

He slowed as they approached a bed of hot pink roses, most of which were still in bud. "The press may ask you, Lina, and Enzo whether you believe I should be prosecuted. Or they may interrogate you about your mother and what you knew about her relationship with me. I'll do whatever I can to draw the attention from the three of you, but I can't stop it entirely. For that, I apologize. None of you should be put in a position where you must defend your mother. Or me."

Rocco glanced down at the label identifying the roses as a variety called the Princess Sophia. "You've thought about this a great deal."

"I've had many years to do so. Years with a loving wife by my side with whom I could discuss the issue."

"You say that in a rather parental tone. I assume it's because you're making a point?"

Carlo bent to smell one of the newly opened blooms, then turned his head to smile at Rocco. "You think I didn't notice the look on your face when Massimo mentioned Justine? It spoke volumes."

"I wasn't aware of any look."

"Nor was Massimo, but your response to him confirmed my suspicion. You didn't say, 'I'll be sure to tell her' or give any other indication that you plan to see Justine in the near future."

Rocco's spine stiffened at the king's insight, but he managed to sound casual. "Was I supposed to?"

"If a prince told me my wife was amazing, yes, I'd say thank you and tell him that I'd pass the message along. So would you if you and Justine were together." He released the rose and continued on the path. Rocco joined him. "I take it you're not?"

He saw no point in denial. "It's for the best."

"Is that what she told you?"

Irritation flared at the king's directness. "I realize that you're a monarch and used to having your queries answered by those in your orbit, but I'm not—"

"That's all right. You need only listen." The king waved a hand, cutting off Rocco's argument. To Rocco's surprise, Carlo didn't seem the least bit bothered. "Being in love necessarily means letting go of one's pride. No one wishes to admit that when it comes to certain people, they'll always allow their heart to rule their head. But that's what love is, and I believe you and Justine love each other."

The king angled a look at Rocco. "How much of your separation is because you wish to protect her—because I suspect that's what your head tells you is right—and how much is a matter of pride?"

Pride? "I don't follow."

"What do you love about Justine? If it is her strength, you must let go of your own pride and trust that strength rather than your own." They rounded a corner, taking them on a path parallel to an iron fence. A dense evergreen hedge rose ten feet high on the opposite side. "I'm keenly aware of my faults and the harm they've caused to those I love, especially Fabrizia. She loves me despite my faults, and I love her despite her personality quirks."

He smiled at Rocco. "With her, they are never faults."

"Of course not."

Carlo paused beside a narrow break in the hedge. A gate, one so well-designed it was nearly impossible to differentiate from the rest of the fence, opened to Carlo's touch. The king stepped off the gravel path and onto the grass, leading Rocco through the tight opening before closing the gate behind them.

The scene spread out before Rocco's eyes drew a low whistle. "This is impressive."

"Our own secret garden."

"It's nothing like the rest."

The garden wasn't large, maybe eighty feet by twenty feet. The evergreen hedge surrounding the space was trimmed low enough to allow the sun to reach the center, yet shielded all within from view. The innermost section of the garden sported a riot of colorful blooms in the style of a wild English garden, while the outer edges, where the hedge cast its shadow, were filled with a variety of shade-loving plants in tones of green, pink, and burgundy. No formal paths appeared to exist. Instead, narrow belts of grass and moss gave visitors just enough room to meander.

"The rest of the palace gardens were professionally designed centuries ago to be used for state events. They're meant as a show-place, especially during the day. Perfect for postcards. This is only for the family. Few on the staff even know it exists."

He led Rocco toward the heart of the garden along a well-trod strip of grass. "I brought Fabrizia here a few weeks before we wed. I told her about Teresa and about you. I gave her the chance to back out of the wedding gracefully…offered to take the blame myself with the media and with our parents. She asked if I still wished to go through with the wedding. I told her that I did. However, I was still in love with Teresa, or at least thought I was. It wasn't long after my wedding to Fabrizia that I realized how wrong I was. True love was never possible between me and your mother. She had a hold over me, but it wasn't love."

The king approached a pair of stone benches nestled in the very center, where a small fountain shaped like a vase bubbled away. He waited until Rocco was seated opposite him before he spoke again. "I brought the queen here again when I found out Teresa was pregnant with Enzo and Lina. It was—bar none—the worst moment of my life. I knew how deeply it would hurt Fabrizia. I told her I wanted to end the marriage. She refused. She looked me in the eye, just as I am looking at you now, and asked if I loved Teresa. I told her I didn't, but that I had felt a sense of obligation to her after you were born. I was wracked with guilt over leaving Teresa in a small one-bedroom apart-ment to raise a child alone while I had such a luxurious life here in the palace. Then the queen asked if I loved her. I couldn't lie. I was deeply in love with her, but I knew that to continue the marriage would only bring her harm."

The king closed his eyes for a moment. Rocco was sure Carlo could picture the conversation as if it had happened yesterday. "I told Fabrizia that if the news of my infidelity ever broke, let alone the fact that I'd been involved with Teresa while Teresa was my tutor, it would be terrible for all of us, but that she would be the one harmed the most, despite the fact that Teresa and I were the ones to blame. I told her that it would be easier if the marriage ended before it all came to light. That she'd be better able to protect herself and the twins she carried."

When Carlo opened his eyes once more, his gaze turned steely. "She leaned toward me, held my jaw in her hand so I couldn't look away, and uttered three words that forever changed my life. She said, 'respect my strength.'"

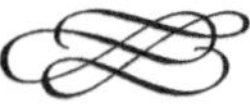

CHAPTER 25

Rocco regarded the king. He appeared so powerful, so in control. It was difficult to imagine the man who wore the crown and led a population of hundreds of thousands being so vulnerable.

"That's why you said I need to trust in Justine's strength."

"I understand the instinct to protect those you love from your failings. It's a virtuous one. But your situation is different than mine. First," —the king held up his thumb— "the failings in this case are not yours, but mine and your mother's. And second," —he extended his index finger— "in cutting Justine out of your decision, you failed to show respect for her strength."

"I never said I cut Justine out of the decision." Though he had. He'd flat-out told Justine that he needed to let her go, then refused to say another word until she was out of the car.

Carlo's raised brow showed he knew it, too, and that Rocco's slip of the tongue was an admission that there had, in fact, been a decision.

"When you talked it through, you both agreed that ending your marriage was the best course of action?" Carlo didn't wait for Rocco's response before adding, "I thought not."

"I promised her I'd do anything to protect her. Her career is a big part of who she is in here." Rocco put a hand to his heart. "I can't take that from her by making her marriage the topic of conversation when she's on the slopes. It'll hurt her chances for endorsements and sponsorships, let alone any future in broadcasting or other public roles."

She'd said as much herself when they were in Baltimore. The network was tired of hiring analysts only to discover they had scandals in their past.

"Shouldn't that be for Justine to decide?" the king pressed. "Haven't you ever had an argument where you promised that, in the future, you'd talk through your issues? Surely you've been married long enough to have had such a conversation."

"Once or twice." That very same night in Baltimore, on the heels of her job offer. They'd told each other that as long as they kept talking, their marriage would work. But he'd also promised to be by her side and support her in her career. He'd made the promise believing that the risk of doing so was in having his connection to Carlo exposed. Not in unmasking his mother as an adult who had abused her position of trust with a minor.

He couldn't both be by Justine's side and support her career. Not anymore.

"I can't have the world look at Justine and think of my mother and imagine the disgusting things she…" He flailed for the right way to finish, but there wasn't one. "I'm sorry, Your Highness. That was offensive, and you've been nothing but kind to me. I didn't mean—"

"It's perfectly all right. You're not saying anything I haven't thought about myself a thousand times over the years. Especially when I look at my wife and my children. *All* my children."

Carlo leaned forward and put a hand on Rocco's shoulder. "By the way, when we're out of the public eye, there's no need to address me as Your Highness. Carlo will do. Or whatever makes you comfortable."

Before Rocco could respond, the king stood and allowed his hand to fall away. "I have a meeting with the Minister of Education in an hour and I promised you a tour of the palace. There's much more to the place than this garden, though it's my favorite part."

"I thought the queen said that the kennel is your favorite."

He rolling laugh boomed from his chest. "Here, I'm not a king or a statesman. I'm only Carlo Barrali. I can think without the world intruding. Chew gum, blow bubbles, walk barefoot. Lie on my back and look at the stars. Even sing if the mood strikes. However, allowing my wife to believe the kennel is my favorite is far more masculine than admitting that it's this garden."

He couldn't imagine this man blowing bubbles. "Your secret is safe with me."

When they were back through the gap in the hedge, the king surveyed the gardens and cut to the far side of the palace, away from the wing containing the library. For the next forty-five minutes, they explored the kennel, where the king stopped to greet two trainers and a breeder by name, and cut back to the palace to stroll through several rooms filled with antiques and paintings, with Carlo sharing stories about several of the pieces as he had for the Degas painting they'd seen earlier. Finally, the king paused beside a thick wooden door that stood in the center of a high-ceilinged hallway that connected two wings of the palace.

"I'm afraid this is where I leave you," he said. "Umberto's office is through here. He'll ensure you're given proper access so you can join us for dinner tonight."

"You keep a very busy schedule."

"I'm in a position to help a lot of people. It makes the schedule very rewarding." A sparkle lit his eyes. "Given the nature of your own work, I'm sure you can relate."

He could. "Thank you for taking the time to give me a tour, Your Highness…Carlo."

The man had such gravitas, it seemed wrong to address him by his first name. Then again, he wasn't Mr. Barrali. Nor would Rocco call the king anything having to do with being his father. In Rocco's mind, that term was reserved for Jack Cornaro. Though as the king smiled in response to the self-correction, Rocco wondered if they'd find a middle ground someday.

More and more, he was coming to admire this man.

"I do want you to consider something." The king's voice was low. "I know you believe you are protecting Justine and her career, but put that aside for a moment to think about your own future. What do *you* have to lose if you don't trust her? If I hadn't trusted in Fabrizia's inner fortitude all those years ago, I'd still be lost. It was Fabrizia who got me through the years without you, Enzo, and Lina. It was Fabrizia who helped me maintain as normal a relationship with Teresa as was possible. It was Fabrizia who showed me love and gave me children and now grandchildren. If I didn't have Anna and Dario now...I couldn't imagine."

The king's brow furrowed and his voice took on a note of urgency. "Everything I have in life—*everything*—I have because I allowed Fabrizia in. I was certain it would be to her detriment, but it wasn't. It took me a long time to believe it, but I know that she's as happy in the marriage as I am. It's made both of us who we are today. I'm a better head of state for her love and she's better at her projects because she has mine. Neither of us would forsake it, even knowing what we'll face in the press in the coming weeks and months. I'm telling you, you have no idea what you're throwing away...for you, for Justine, and for all the others who benefit when each of you live up to your potential."

Behind Rocco, a throat cleared. Carlo looked past Rocco to a uniformed man who stood at the far end of the hallway. "Thank you, Roderick. Please inform the minister that I am on my way."

The king met Rocco's gaze and once again, Rocco had the sensation he was looking at an older version of himself...and that the older version found the younger version lacking. It was simultaneously unsettling and irritating.

"Anything is possible if you get your damned pride out of the way," Carlo said. "I'll see you at dinner."

***

"YOU READY FOR THIS?"

Justine gave her new coach the thumbs-up signal. After seeing Rocco on television at King Carlo's press conference, Justine interviewed four coaches and ended up going with Marit Brekken, a former Olympian from Norway. She'd nearly hired Marit the last time she'd looked for a coach, and in the two hours they'd been working together on the slopes this morning, Justine knew she'd made the right choice. Marit was only ten years older than Justine and had competed with a go-for-broke, ski-from-the-gut style similar to Justine's. On the other hand, Marit was known for the rigorous training regimen she'd pursued during her competitive years. The days she wasn't racing, Marit had planned every workout and every training run in order to obtain the maximum payoff for the hours she invested. Better still, Marit had raced until she was nearly forty. She understood the vagaries of training at an age when most others had retired.

If Justine was to nab a spot on the podium at the end of this year's World Cup season, she'd need to train the way Marit had, which explained why they were standing on the side of a mountain high above the village of Hemsedal, Norway, facing Justine's first expert level run in over a year, and on the very first day she'd stepped into her ski boots.

Marit raised one of her poles and pointed downhill, indicating a fork on the lefthand side of the run. Orange signs indicated that the trail was closed for training. "We have it to ourselves for the next hour, so you won't have to worry about other skiers. We should be able to get in two full runs before they open it to the public. Take this first one easy. Get to know the feel of the course. Tomorrow you can open it up and see what you have."

"Got it." Justine tightened her right glove and adjusted her grip on the pole. Her first runs this morning had been on much easier terrain, allowing her to pick up only enough speed to crave more. She wanted to fly. To feel the wind on her face, hear the light scrape of her skis carving the snow, and thrill to the adrenaline rush that came whenever she got air on a jump.

"You're not going to listen to me and take it easy, are you?"

Justine laughed. "I'm going to try."

"Remember that your shin isn't used to the pressure you'll need to control the turns on this run. Stay in control and work up to full speed, even if that's not your natural tendency. Another injury would set you back weeks or months. Right now, you're going for efficiency…getting the most you can out of each run so you'll be able to compete when the season opens. The point of today's workout is to get your legs accustomed to your equipment. Not to break records." Marit grinned. "That'll come."

Justine pressed a hand to the base of her throat, rubbed the necklace she wore under her training jacket for luck, and nodded.

On a deep breath, she set off along the course with Marit close behind. Conditions were perfect. Early May sunshine filtered through the evergreens lining the slope, affording her good visibility, and the cold winter followed by a burst of late season snow provided a solid base under the fresh powder, creating unusually good skiing for the last two official weeks of the season in Hemsedal. As Justine picked up speed, a warm spring breeze lifted her braids so they flew behind her ski helmet.

It should've felt wonderful. She should be freaking *ecstatic*. She felt hollow.

It'll come.

Once she made it to the bottom of the slope. Once she knew she could do it.

An image of Rocco filled her mind; how she wished he could see her take this first real run. Much as she wanted to deny it, it meant more to her than when he'd missed watching her in competition. Or even the day of her accident.

Eventually he'd realize that he needed to track her down and he'd find her. He had to. Until then, she needed to keep her head up and stay focused on the task at hand.

Muscle memory took over and she leaned forward, grounding her shins to the front of her boots, allowing her weight and gravity to pull her down the mountain. She rounded a turn that changed the angle of the sun, putting it directly into her eyes. At the last second, she spotted the flash of gray against the white snow. A skier, one whose cautious stance showed he didn't belong on such a steep slope, shuffled down sideways. Behind Justine, Marit yelled to cut right at the same time instinct took Justine the same way.

The skier looked up, his surprise evident as his mouth dropped open before he used his poles to shove himself forward in an attempt to avoid the collision.

Justine missed him. Marit missed him. They stopped just in time to see the man lose his balance, tilt on one ski, then tip over sideways and slide headfirst down the steep slope, a mess of arms, legs and poles. One of his skis caught in the snow and released, then the other, then he lost a pole, leaving a trail of gear on the side of the mountain.

"He must've gotten lost," Marit said as they took off after the man. He began to slow about fifty yards downhill as his outstretched arms carried the loose powder in front of him like a snowplow.

"You get his skis, I'll check on him," Justine said.

Marit crossed the slope to gather the man's equipment while Justine cruised downhill, then slowed to a stop and turned sideways in front of the man to prevent him from sliding further. He spun around so his feet were aimed downhill instead of his head, then dug his heels into the slope. The guy appeared tall and plenty athletic, but his awkward movement as he'd tried to get out of their way made it clear he wasn't much of a skier. Justine cursed herself for sending Marit after the skis instead of going herself, since she didn't know a word of Norwegian. Hoping the guy spoke English, she asked, "Are you all right?"

"I'm fine. Embarrassed as hell, but fine. I came all this way to see you, and here I am—"

Justine did a double take, staring down at the snow-covered man in gray. She recognized that voice. That snow-caked beard. Her mouth went dry as dust even as her heart soared. "Rocco?"

He unsnapped the strap on his helmet, raised his goggles, then yanked it from his head and dropped it into the snow. His cheeks flamed red from the cold and a deep red goggle line ringed his eyes, but he was all smiles as he looked up at her. "Hello, Justine."

CHAPTER 26

"WHAT IN THE world are you doing? You don't ski!" Even as Justine stared at Rocco in disbelief, she was overwhelmed by how amazing he looked as he grinned up at her in the midmorning sunlight, surrounded by bright blue skies and snow-flocked trees.

"I ski."

"Barely! You could've gotten yourself hurt." He'd been maybe four or five times in his life, all with her. While he'd made it off the bunny slopes and onto the easier trails faster than most novices, he'd only tackled two or three intermediate runs. Never an expert run.

"It was the only way to get you alone." He tipped his head back as he heard Marit approach with his skis. "Or mostly alone. There's a crowd forming at the bottom of the run. Word has spread that you're here and there's a group hoping for photos of you and your coach. I was hoping to find you and arrange a private place to meet once you finished. I hadn't intended to wander into the middle of the run."

"Marit, meet my husband, Rocco Cornaro."

The tall Norwegian set Rocco's skis where he could step into them before raising her goggles to study the man in the snow. "You're kidding."

"I'm as shocked as you are," Justine said. "And yes, I married a non-skier. Rocco, meet my new coach, Marit Brekken."

Rocco pushed to stand, taking care not to tumble downhill, then shook the woman's hand. "The Marit Brekken? I'm honored. You're a legend."

"I could say the same to you. The Rocco Cornaro? You've been all over the news." Marit smiled, but her look was odd, as if she already knew Rocco. Marit turned toward Justine and was about to say something, but Rocco cut her off.

"I'm interrupting your training time. Now that you know I'm here, why don't we find a place to meet at the bottom—"

"Assuming you can get there," Justine told Rocco before she looked to Marit. "I hate to ask this—"

"We'll pick up tomorrow morning. Truth is, I didn't think you'd be in good enough shape to do as much as you've already done today. I had assumed we'd already be finished." Marit replaced her goggles and shook the snow from her skis. "Take it easy on the way down with him, then call me when you're back at the hotel and we can make arrangements for tomorrow. And take proper care of your leg tonight."

"I will. Thanks, Marit." Once the coach was out of earshot, she guided Rocco to a flatter area at the side of the run, then gave him a light punch on the shoulder. "What were you thinking? How'd you even get here?"

"I was thinking that I had to see my wife. I left two messages on your cell phone and you didn't call back. All I got was that text saying that you were in Hemsedal. I flew here, asked around, learned what run you were on, then studied the trail map so I could take one of the safer trails to find you. Apparently my map skills aren't what I imagined."

"You're crazy." Justine's hand went to her throat. "I kept it perfectly safe, but I knew that if I talked to you on the phone instead of making you see me in person, you'd just ask me to send it or you'd have Kos—"

Rocco edged closer to her, his ski boots sending a chunk of snow cascading down the slope. "What are you talking about?"

"The necklace."

Confusion clouded his eyes for a moment, then understanding dawned. "King Carlo's necklace? The star sapphire?"

Carefully, she undid the top button on her ski jacket and pulled the zipper to reveal the necklace topping her high tech undershirt. "It's on tight."

"You're wearing it to *ski?*"

"I wasn't going to leave it in a hotel safe. I knew if I kept it with me, you'd eventually have to come get it." She zipped her jacket and secured the button. "And here you are."

"You wanted me to come find you in Norway." His words were measured. "To see you in person."

"I didn't expect you'd put on a pair of skis and try to find me on a mountain." She brushed away a piece of snow that stuck to his beard. "Look at you!"

"Then what did you expect, Justine? That I'd find you at a hotel, reach around your neck and…what?" He removed his gloves and dropped them to the snow, then spanned either side of her neck with his hands so his fingers danced along the area where the necklace was fastened. "Take it?"

"I don't know what I expected." She hated how her voice shook on the last word. It hadn't been that long, but she missed his touch. The curve of his lips as he spoke, the sound of her name spoken in his rich voice. She physically ached for him.

"What if I told you I didn't come for the necklace?"

She hesitated. "You didn't?"

His grin warmed her as thoroughly as his tender touch. "I haven't given the necklace a second thought since I tried to return it to Carlo. I even forgot I left it in your purse. I came to apologize, you nut. To swallow my pride and beg you to give me another chance."

The movement of his thumbs along the column of her neck made it hard to think. "You decided this…without coming for the necklace?" On his own, without seeing her first?

"I thought I was doing what was best for you by staying away from you. I even went so far as to contact coaches you'd mentioned to me over the years and told them you'd been cleared to ski. I know they'd have contacted you soon enough on their own, but I wanted you to be safely away from Croatia when news of my relationship to Carlo broke."

She shook her head. That's why she'd received so many messages so quickly. It wasn't her former coach's doing; it was Rocco's. As always, his instinct was to protect her.

"I felt responsible," he added. "I didn't want the complication of my past to hurt you or your career."

"I told you, it won't."

"It will. But it doesn't make me love you or want you any less." His hands slid up, capturing her face between his warm palms. She yearned to lean into him, to kiss him into silence, but he held her too far away. "What I've learned is that I have to let you be hurt and trust that you are strong enough to deal with it. I know that's selfish…but if you choose to be with me, I will do whatever I can for the rest of my days to make up for the downsides."

Her mind swirled. "The…downsides?"

"There will always be those who'll judge you based on your marriage. People who'll gossip. Who may or may not hire you if they know you chose to stay married to me with the scandals of my upbringing." His perceptive brown eyes searched hers. "All your life, you've worked to be at the top of your sport. To build a career that will last beyond your competitive days. If you stay with me, you risk that. *That* is the downside."

She felt the pressure of his palms against her cheeks as she smiled. "And here I thought you were going to make another joke about the horrid sex."

"Justine." Despite the censure in his voice, he smiled. "Be serious."

"I can't live without you, Rocco. You're the calm in my crazy, high octane, competitive life. I knew it the minute I asked about your schnitzel that night in Garmisch. Everyone else in that pub disappeared when I spoke to you. The hardest thing I've ever done in my life was move out of the villa when you refused to tell me what was going on with your mother."

"And then I refused to talk to you again the night Carlo came to visit."

She nodded. It'd devastated her, even if she understood it. "It's not every day a grown man meets his father, let alone a father who's a king. You had a lot to digest. But I knew in my heart that if you saw me again, if you had time to breathe and to think, you'd realize that you can't live without me, either. I had to believe that if you saw me face-to-face, you'd talk to me, really talk to me, no matter the circumstances around us. That you'd trust me with what you believe are your faults."

She dropped her poles and reached up to cover his hands with her gloved ones, wanting to pull him closer, to convince him for once and for all that they belonged together. Forever. That it was what she wanted, too. "They're not faults at all, Rocco. You're honorable. You wanted to honor your mother, but found she'd put you in an impossible position. Rocco, I respect that. And I respect that you went to Sarcaccia to support King Carlo at his press conference."

"Read about that, did you?"

"I saw it. Watched the whole thing online. Read as much as I could afterward." Leaning uphill, she pressed a kiss to his lips. With her forehead only a few inches from his, she said, "You are a remarkable, magnificent man. That was a good thing you did for Carlo."

"It was good for me."

Rocco kissed her once more, gently, resisting the urge to crush her to his body and pull her down into the snow.

"You really think so?" Her blue eyes flashed in the late morning sun. "You heard Marit. You've been all over television."

That much was true. Since the news conference, reporters crowded the street around his villa and thickened the usual foot traffic in the square near his office. They'd stopped everyone going in and out of the building and even grilled the elderly man who ran the kiosk downstairs about Rocco and his habits. Enzo and Lina had suffered a similar barrage of attention, though it was Rocco's face that was now the most familiar, since media outlets had footage from the press conference to paste all over their reports.

"I'm not a fan of the coverage." He ran his hands down her shoulders, grateful to have her close. "I meant that it was good for me to be there. I spent time with King Carlo afterward. He gave me a tour of the palace and grounds, and we talked. Then I stayed for dinner. A family dinner."

Astonishment filled her gaze. "With all his children?"

"Prince Bruno had to return to school, but yes. It was...eye-opening." He thought back to the boisterous evening. It hadn't been anything like he'd expected. "There's an immense aura that clings to every one of them. I suppose it comes with the trappings of the palace and the royal titles. But they're all very human, too. Massimo is quieter, more contemplative than the others. Alessandro does everything full bore. He reminds me of Enzo. Sophia is the center of their world but also the butt of their jokes. Vittorio has a deep sense of responsibility, and Stefano—I swear—Stefano could be Father of the Year. He's crazy about his wife and kids. He seems to want nothing more than to spend time watching his daughter show off goodies she's baked herself while he holds his new son."

He'd gotten a good sense of all their personalities that night as, gradually, they relaxed around him.

"They're good people," he continued, wanting Justine to understand the significance of the time he'd spent in Sarcaccia. "They have every luxury, but don't act entitled. They treat the palace staff like family. To a person, you could tell that everyone who worked in that building was happy to be there. The Barralis were good to me, too, though I know the princes and Princess Sophia weren't comfortable with my presence. They couldn't hide that, not completely. But it came from a protectiveness toward each other rather than a distrust of me in particular. For all their differences, they love each other. They love their parents."

Wonder and a hint of pride colored her grin. Her hands slipped around his waist. "You genuinely liked them."

"I did." In spite of everything. "Not because of their fame or even what they've done for their country, though it's obvious when you look around that they've put their hearts and souls into improving the economy there. I liked them for what they've built together."

This was the part of what he had to tell her that was most important. What he'd spent the last few days mulling over, wanting to get exactly right when he saw Justine. "To say that Carlo and Fabrizia had a rocky start to their marriage is an understatement. Carlo nearly ended it early on because, even though he'd fallen in love with Fabrizia, he thought it'd be better for her in the long run given all that had happened with my mother. He told me that while he gave me the palace tour."

"Thought he had to let Fabrizia go for her own good, did he?"

Rocco exhaled and nodded. Tears rose in Justine's eyes, but she seemed too caught up in the moment to care. "He told me that Fabrizia asked him to trust in her strength, that she could get through anything. I know Carlo was trying to tell me not to give up on *us*, but I was so concerned by what being married to me would mean for you that I told myself he was wrong."

"But?"

"But watching them at dinner, how they behave when they're behind closed doors…" The happy sounds of that night came back to him in a rush. Alessandro and Sophia's laughter echoing through the king and queen's private apartment as they teased each other, Anna's screeches as her aunts and uncles tickled her, the love he saw between Vittorio and Emily, Massimo and Kelly, Stefano and Megan. All because Carlo trusted Fabrizia when she asked it of him, despite his instinct to protect her.

"I wanted that, Justine. The way Fabrizia looked at her husband…I want that with you and I want it for the rest of my life. I knew as soon as I walked out of the palace that I'd move heaven and earth for it. If Carlo and Fabrizia can do it, if they can both be that happy, so can we. If only you can forgive me for being such an idiot. Again."

The tears in her eyes finally spilled over. Her hands fell away from him as she blew out a breath and looked up at the brilliant Norwegian sky.

His hands tightened on her arms. "If you've taught me anything, Justine, it's that when you want something badly enough, you find a way to make it work. It's the reason I tracked you down on a black diamond ski slope in the middle of Scandinavia. It might not be easy. It might involve tough choices. But it is *possible*. It's all a matter of how much you want it."

Finally, Justine lowered her gaze to his. Her voice choked, she said, "That's what you came here to tell me? You didn't come for the necklace. You came to tell me that anything is possible."

"Yes."

"You're an idiot."

"I know. I shouldn't have—"

"You could've gotten yourself lost or hurt before you could tell me all that!" He froze, dumbstruck, as she continued, "You were forgiven the moment you drove off from my apartment the other night."

"I shouldn't have been."

"You had to come to terms with the situation yourself." She leaned forward, fitting her body to his, and smiled. "By the way, I'd say, 'Next time, wait for me at the lodge.' But there won't be a next time."

"I'll make damned sure of it." As the breeze picked up, causing the tree branches overhead to mist them with snow, he kissed her again. "I love you, Justine. More than life itself."

"And I love you, Rocco Cornaro. I want you to know it before I risk both our necks trying to get us down this slope." She let go of him and bent to adjust his skis so he could step into them without tumbling. "You're going to have to trust me."

"Says the woman wearing the million-dollar necklace to ski." At the fiery look in her eyes, he held up both hands and laughed. "I trust you. Now get me down to the lodge so I can express everything else I feel."

"Slowly and safely, all right?"

"Slowly and safely?" He couldn't help the wicked grin that spread across his face. "Mrs. Cornaro, I'm not sure you fully appreciate what I have in mind."

EPILOGUE

THE COOL AIR within the centuries-old stone building was a welcome relief after the heat of Rome's cobblestoned streets.

It'd taken four months, but Rocco finally lived up to his promise. He and Justine had spent three spectacular days in the Eternal City. They'd toured the city's ancient catacombs, people watched on the famous Spanish Steps with gelato in hand, and lingered in front Bernini's life-sized sculpture of Apollo and Daphne at the Borghese Museum. Justine had sighed over the smooth curve of Daphne's arm as the nymph reached for the sky and the contrast with her fingers, which had grown into branches and leaves as she was transformed into a laurel tree.

Rocco could hardly wait to see Justine's reaction to the gift that had arrived at the villa while they'd been in Rome. Kos had called Rocco to report that an armored car had arrived with a surprise gift for Rocco and Justine from King Carlo and Queen Fabrizia: an original Degas painting of a horse standing in a dew-kissed meadow at sunrise. The handwritten note accompanying it had said, *Remember the story of kindnesses given and accepted. Make this your legacy.*

Rocco intended to mount it above the mantel in his study, just over the framed photo of his mother. He hadn't completely forgiven her, though he hoped he could in the years to come. More and more each day, he appreciated the sacrifices she'd made so he, Enzo, and Lina could lead normal lives.

He still loved her. And now, by the grace of God, he had Justine to love.

Better than the days in Rome had been the three blissful nights in the luxury apartment he'd rented near the Piazza Navona. The comfortable bed with its decadent linens, the sprawling marble bathroom, and the elegant, sink-your-toes-in rugs had made Justine sigh with delight the moment she'd crossed the threshold.

He'd ensured those sighs transformed into more impassioned, gratifying sounds with each night they spent in the apartment, making love under the massive skylight that offered a spectacular view of the stars. It was his every dream come true, and witnessing Justine's wide-eyed joy as they savored Rome renewed his spirit.

The press hadn't caught wind of where they were staying, which gave him peace of mind. Private time with Justine needed to be just that: private. When they were out and about, it was a different story. There was no avoiding the attention that came their way when one or both of them were recognized. They'd been photographed several times, both by passersby and the local press, but Justine didn't seem to mind. When a group of Austrian teens asked for her autograph during dinner in Trastevere one evening, she'd not only obliged, she'd thanked them for being fans of the sport and posed for pictures with them.

Rocco was the one who'd had to adjust to the increased attention. Justine had guided him in the art of identifying and dissuading those whose speculation ran toward the salacious while showing kindness to those who were merely curious about him, or who—in a surprising number of instances—were longtime admirers of the royal family. Justine insisted there was a knack to speaking with well-meaning strangers in a way that kept the conversations brief, yet left them happy at having met a celebrity.

"I'm not a celebrity," Rocco had insisted.

"You are now, like it or not," she'd retorted. "But you can set limits to how much access the world at large has to you."

It sounded very much the way Carlo had described Fabrizia's adjustment to fame. Rocco was learning, thanks to Justine. To show his appreciation, he had one more stop planned for their trip. It meant a long wait outdoors in the sunshine, where anyone and everyone could take their photo or approach to make comments or ask questions, but he knew it was the spot in Rome Justine most wanted to see.

First, though, Rocco had business in the heavily guarded building on the outskirts of Rome's central tourist district. There'd be no cameras, no press. No curious looks except, perhaps, from the man he'd arranged to visit inside.

"You're sure you want to do this?" he asked Justine.

"I'm here, aren't I? And you said you had a surprise for me afterward, so let's get it over with."

They showed their identification to the uniformed man who sat behind a thick glass window, then waited to be buzzed in through a fortified door. Once inside, they passed through metal detectors, were given a briefing by a stern-faced officer, then were escorted to a room at the very center of the building, one with no windows, only a few long tables and benches that were bolted to the floor.

"The air's stale," Justine commented quietly. "Does anyone even use this room?"

At that moment, a door on the opposite side from where they'd entered beeped, and a man in jeans and a plain gray T-shirt entered. In the corner, a camera swiveled to follow his movements as he took a seat at one of the tables.

Without lifting his head to meet Rocco's gaze, he asked, "Why are you here?"

Rocco crossed the room to sit across from Viktor Radich. Justine followed, sliding onto the bench beside Rocco.

"You're still awaiting trial."

"And?"

"I'm curious about a few things."

Radich snorted. "If you think I'm going to bare my soul to you in an attempt to have charges dropped, you're wasting your time."

"You have a daughter."

Radich finally lifted his head. His dark eyes flared. "How did you—"

"I learned that your girlfriend gave birth while you were at MIT. About a month before your graduation, she ended your relationship and cut off access to your daughter. I believe it's because your father had started pressuring you to join the family business. You didn't fight her because you didn't want the nature of your father's work discussed in court. You were afraid if that happened, he'd take out his anger on them."

The stunned expression on Radich's face confirmed that Kos's research and his own conclusions about Radich's background were dead accurate.

The Russian sucked in his lower lip, then exhaled. "I quit seeing my father after I graduated high school and the courts could no longer force me to go. I haven't visited Russia since. If you know so much, you should know that."

"That's true," Rocco said carefully. "But your father's reach is long and you have skills he covets. He wanted you to work for him from the time you were a young boy and didn't take well to losing you as an asset. He threatened your ex-girlfriend and daughter."

Justine leaned across the table, but followed the prison rules and refrained from touching Radich. "Your daughter is diabetic, isn't she? What you told Rocco's mother was true."

Radich's eyes darted to the camera, then back to Justine, but he said nothing.

"You read medical journals on the latest technology and came across my name. You befriended my mother, hoping you could learn enough to steal my newest design when it was finished and possibly copy it to help your daughter." Rocco waited a moment, gauging Radich's reaction to the accusation. "Whether you could copy it yourself or not, you knew you could use the money your father paid you for it to help your ex and daughter escape him for good. If you could send them into hiding, they'd no longer be his pawns. You were hoping that if you pulled off this one job, you could escape him, too."

"I'd be insane to confirm any of that. As you pointed out, I'm awaiting trial."

"I understand that Karpovsky has cut a deal to testify against you. He's fighting extradition to Russia on charges he murdered his sister-in-law," Rocco said.

"That's what I'm told."

"You and Karpovsky are two different breeds."

Radich remained silent, though his set jaw and the grim lines at the edges of his mouth made it apparent he was fighting an internal battle. Radich and Karpovsky had both threatened Rocco's life and Justine's, but in his gut, Rocco doubted Radich would've gone through with it, even to protect his ex-girlfriend and daughter. Karpovsky, on the other hand, might've killed them just for sport.

Radich folded his hands in his lap. He looked from Justine to Rocco. "I'll ask you again: why are you here?"

"The pump you attempted to steal is being readied for testing and eventually a clinical trial. There's a long way to go until it gets there, but when it gets to that stage, your daughter's name is on the list, should she still be eligible to participate. "

Radich's expression changed. "You've spoken with her doctors? How is she?"

"I haven't, no, but a few calls were made from Johns Hopkins to her primary care physician. They asked targeted questions to see if the doctor had any patients who were good candidates for the trial."

"He suggested Lexi." At Rocco's nod, Radich's hands started to shake. He clutched them tighter to hide his nerves. "I assume I'm to confess in order to secure her place."

"No. You don't have to do anything." As Radich frowned at him in confusion, Rocco stood and Justine followed suit. "I imagine it's difficult being estranged from your daughter by simple reason of your birth and family connections. Consider this a kindness from someone who understands."

Rocco turned and went to the door, pressing the button to signal the guard. As the door opened, he heard Radich say, "Mr. and Mrs. Cornaro? Thank you. I won't forget this."

"Good. Learn from it. Make yourself the kind of man Lexi will be proud to call her father someday."

A few minutes later, when they were outside the building, Justine nudged him with her hip. "You're a good man, Rocco Cornaro."

"It was your idea."

At her look of confusion, he said, "On the flight to Baltimore, you told me to imagine I had a child with Type I diabetes. You said that if I were in that situation, I'd risk anything to save that child. I imagine that's what Radich felt he was doing. Even if he couldn't use the pump itself to help her, Radich hoped the money he might've gotten from his father could."

"I suppose I did say that."

He paused and turned to face her, taking both her hands in his. "You know, you're a brave woman. That man threatened to kill you, yet you didn't flinch at going to see him in prison. In fact, you spoke to him with a great deal of compassion."

Justine let go of one of his hands and reached up to smooth his hair back from his forehead, then caress his jaw, running her thumb over the close-cropped beard she'd asked him to keep...for now. "People will do anything for someone they love. He was trying to help his daughter and his ex-girlfriend. He was completely misguided in the manner he chose to go about it, but I understand the motivation."

"I hope he fights at trial. Not that he doesn't deserve to be punished, but I'm afraid part of his reticence lies in his belief that if he's in jail, it'll be safer for them. His father won't be interested in them if he can't use Radich for his own purposes."

"Maybe his father will see that Radich isn't a very effective criminal. We escaped him twice. You broke his nose. And he got caught."

"We can only hope." But that battle was Radich's to fight. Or not.

An easy smile lifted Justine's lips. "You told me you had a surprise for me."

"We still have one place in Rome to visit before we meet up with Marit in Austria tomorrow." And begin what was sure to be a whirlwind World Cup season.

"Where?"

He tucked her arm through his and led her toward the Metro station. "I thought we could go to the Vatican. We'll see St. Peter's, then the museum is open if we're willing to stand in line."

"We can skip the museum."

"It's the best way to the Sistine Chapel."

"Rocco—"

"You've wanted to see the Sistine Chapel ceiling for as long as I've known you. To see the separation of light from darkness, God's creation of Adam, David slaying Goliath—"

She shook her head vigorously enough to make her hair bounce. "You aren't comfortable when you're trapped. You know that line runs all along the outer wall of the Vatican. Once we're in it, we can't leave without giving up the chance to see inside. It'll take at least an hour, maybe two or three. It's not like sitting on the Spanish Steps or walking around the Colosseum, where we can simply move to another spot if there are too many gawkers or paparazzi."

"Then it'll be a good test of what I've learned from you about how to handle celebrity." He grimaced on the last word. He still didn't like using that term to describe himself or what his public life had become.

"You're going to hate it."

"It's Michelangelo. How much can I possibly hate it?" He paused at the top of the steps leading to the Metro station and drew Justine into his arms for a long, romantic kiss. "Trust in my strength. If you're with me, I can handle anything."

When he finally released her, she rewarded him with a smile that made his heart soar. "Onward then, my dear husband. Heaven awaits."

Thank you for reading *The Royal Bastard*. If you enjoyed this book, please consider leaving a review at your favorite bookseller or book club website.

Read on for a preview of the next Royal Scandals book, *The Wicked Prince*.

ACKNOWLEDGMENTS

Many thanks to Douglas Onsi of HealthCare Ventures, who took the time to walk me through the stages of preclinical product development for Rocco Cornaro's diabetes pump and answered my (innumerable) questions about Rocco's education and career path as an independent biomedical engineer. Any errors are entirely my own.

I also owe a great debt to my wonderful editor, Valerie Susan Hayward, who has worked on the entire Royal Scandals series to date. Valerie, your insights have proved invaluable. May you enjoy your retirement. You'll be missed.

THE WICKED PRINCE

Eighteen Months Ago

Prince Alessandro Barrali wasn't one to consume expensive champagne in feeble sips, but with several hundred people to fool tonight, nursing his drink was a matter of necessity.

Habit brought a polite smile to his face as he stood beside the bar at his sister Sophia's annual Christmas party and surveyed the well-to-do crowd. The usual suspects were present. Near the doorway, wealthy patrons of Sarcaccia's national art museum gathered in a knot around British billionaire and adventurer Jack Gladwell. Many of King Carlo and Queen Fabrizia's friends were in attendance, along with a smattering of Sarcaccian government officials and Italian socialites. But Sophia had shaken up the guest list this year, giving it a Hollywood spin by including two A-list British actors and their spouses, an American hip-hop star, three supermodels, and last year's Oscar-winning director. Instead of the usual orchestra, a DJ spun dance music at the far end of the palace ballroom, transforming the atmosphere to that of a youthful, energetic club. Many of Sophia's former college classmates danced under the sparkling chandeliers, one—lucky man—with an up-and-coming pop princess.

It was a setting in which Alessandro was in his element. One that allowed him to spend the night bantering with clever women and dancing with those who most interested him. After a flirtatious moonlight walk through the palace gardens or along one of the island's glorious Mediterranean beaches, he'd take one back to her hotel for a wondrous, no-strings-attached romp.

Unfortunately, tonight he wasn't Prince Alessandro. To all but his immediate family, he was his quiet, contemplative, identical twin brother, Prince Vittorio, the crown prince of Sarcaccia. There'd be no women, no carousing, no adventure. No *fun*. Certainly no second glass of champagne.

He took another paltry taste and cursed himself for creating the situation. Not that he'd have made a different choice, given the circumstances.

Vittorio's former girlfriend, a much-loved Spanish actress named Carmella Rivas, had died by suicide in early autumn, shortly after Vittorio ended their relationship. A private, heart-wrenching note arrived for Vittorio only hours after her death. In it, Carmella confessed the many ways she'd secretly deceived Vittorio during their relationship and apologized for her lies. She also claimed that she was pregnant. She said she'd told no one, but felt she owed Vittorio the truth after all she'd done.

Alessandro and Vittorio had been alone in Vittorio's palace apartment when the letter arrived. In the moments Vittorio's eyes scanned the page, Alessandro witnessed his normally stoic brother's complete devastation. The breakup itself had been difficult for Vittorio. Enduring both the heartbreak and the scandal surrounding Carmella's death while he remained in the public eye—and with the private knowledge she carried their child—was inhumane. Convinced Vittorio needed time alone, Alessandro suggested the switch. Vittorio refused, determined to keep Carmella's secrets and fulfill his duties despite his emotional turmoil, but Alessandro insisted that not only could it be done, it was the best choice for Sarcaccia. He talked his brother into a two-week trial run, during which they'd attended Carmella's funeral as each other.

It had worked. Alessandro urged his brother to leave the country and get his head on straight so he could be the crown prince Sarcaccia deserved.

Unfortunately, what Alessandro thought would be a week, maybe two, had now stretched to ten. There was no indication Vittorio would return home anytime soon.

Not that Alessandro could blame him. Vittorio didn't trust easily and the experience with Carmella had gutted him.

The crowd parted and Queen Fabrizia made her way to Alessandro's side. With her gaze on the guests, she asked, "Are you enjoying yourself, darling?"

He answered with a sidelong glance.

"You're too distant," she warned quietly. "I know you had a long day preparing for your trip to Istanbul, but your brother would circulate. Make casual conversation, dance with a few of Sophia's friends. Ask about their holiday plans."

"Once I finish my drink, I'll do that."

"Thank you. Now smile at your mother."

He did so, then leaned down and kissed her cheek. After a final civilized sip of his champagne, he set the half-empty flute on the bar. He might be the spare, but he'd learned the lessons of the heir. Duty before all else.

For the next hour, Alessandro made his way through the ballroom. He kept his shoulders square and expression placid, as Vittorio did, and commented on only the most mundane topics, such as Sarcaccia's unseasonably warm December weather or the flattering cut of his sister Sophia's glimmering silver gown. As had been the case since Vittorio departed, no one suspected that the twins had switched places. In fact, three separate guests asked if he'd heard from Alessandro, whom the whole world believed was off on another expedition to Nepal, the wilds of Africa, or a similarly isolated location. Or, a few of the bolder guests mused, perhaps he was hidden away at a friend's palazzo with a female or two.

Oh, how he wished.

He thanked each of them for asking, admitted that he hadn't heard from his twin, then repeated what his father recently said in a press conference, explaining, "Alessandro often travels to areas where communication is unreliable. We expect him to return soon, full of stories." He smiled each time he said it, then promptly changed the subject. The entire time, he took care to avoid the single women in attendance. Alessandro had long ago mastered the art of capturing a female's attention with nothing more than an appreciative glance that lasted a heartbeat longer than was considered casual. It had become such a part of him, he wasn't sure he could smother the reflex. It'd give him away as surely as if he wore a name tag.

In his peripheral vision, he caught sight of one of his mother's close friends zigzagging her way through the crowd. Lacking the energy for another round of small talk, he shot a meaningful glance at his younger brother, Prince Stefano, then subtly angled his head toward their mother's friend. Stefano took his fiancée's elbow, then guided Megan toward the older woman for an introduction.

Alessandro returned to the bar and ordered what he really wanted: a tumbler of sixteen-year-old Aberlour. Between the hard work he'd done for Istanbul today and the inane chatter he'd endured tonight, he'd earned it.

"Tired of talking about the weather, Your Highness?"

Alessandro looked in the direction from which the question had come. An unfamiliar brunette with wide, jet-black eyes stood a few feet away from him and smiled at the bartender as he handed her a glass of red wine. Her black gown skimmed her trim figure, but wasn't flashy. She showed little décolletage and the gown's leg-baring slit was a modest one. Even her jewelry was demure. She wore nothing but a pair of diamond studs. No necklace, no glittering bracelet. As she turned to face him, he also noticed she wore minimal makeup. Odd, since Sophia's annual party was a night to see and be seen, and this woman dressed as if intent on flying below the radar.

He eyed her curiously. For all her simplicity, she was quite pretty. "The weather is always up for discussion in Sarcaccia, is it not? Our tourist trade relies on it."

"It does. I simply thought that, given your recent pursuits, you'd have other topics on your mind."

Wariness snaked through him. He couldn't put a finger on why, but the woman struck him as highly intelligent, and as the type who could read people quickly. Surely she didn't know of the twins' switch? He resisted the urge to touch the spot under his left eye where a small scar—currently covered with concealer—differentiated him from his twin, and extended his hand. "I don't believe we've been introduced. I'm Prince Vittorio."

"I'm sorry. Francesca Lawrence." She met his greeting with a firm handshake. "I attended the Sorbonne with your sister. Her flat was across the hall from mine during our last year there."

He released her hand to accept his Scotch from the bartender, then turned to her with a smile. "I believe Sophia's mentioned you. Francesca is one of my favorite names. Hard to forget." Sexy. Romantic. A name far more suited to Alessandro than Vittorio. A name that made him wonder if she had racier gowns in her closet.

The woman's dark brows drew together. "I'd be shocked if she referred to me as Francesca. I go by Frannie."

Frannie? Considering the stiff tone in which she corrected him, he revised his assessment of her. She'd be perfect for Vittorio. The woman probably thought he was flirting simply by mentioning that Francesca was a favorite name.

Then again, he supposed he was flirting…by Vittorio's standards.

He raised his glass and said, "Frannie, then," before taking a sip to gird himself for more small talk. "Did you study art history with Sophia?"

"Economics, though I did manage to squeeze in one art history course. Can't avoid studying art in Paris." Her gaze moved over the crowd, then settled once more on him. "I understand you were in Cairo with your father a few weeks ago as part of the Mideast peace negotiations. And that you're traveling to Istanbul soon to continue the talks."

"I am."

"I think that'd be far more interesting to discuss than the weather."

He laughed, both because it came naturally and to buy himself time. Enticing as it might be, talking politics at a party while he acted the role of Vittorio was akin to tiptoeing amongst landmines. No matter how careful one might be, the slightest misstep would trigger an explosion.

From the day Alessandro suggested the switch, he'd spent every minute of his private time studying his brother's diplomatic and charitable work. Despite that effort, there was no way he could remember everything his brother had said and done over the years, particularly since, for many of those years, Alessandro had been out of the country following his own pursuits, none of which would be categorized as either diplomatic or charitable.

Testing his knowledge against Miss Economics wasn't worth the risk.

"It's Christmas," he finally said. "Most people prefer to discuss peaceful topics."

That brought an intriguing curve to her lips. "I see. You're a born diplomat."

"Any talents I have in that area are due to my parents' example, not any natural ability."

She took a thoughtful sip of her wine, then set the glass on the bar. "Your parents do a lot of good work. Sophia and I were just discussing your mother's morning visit to a home for abused and troubled teens."

"It's a cause Queen Fabrizia has supported for many years. She believes their needs are often overlooked." He wasn't sure why, but he got the feeling Francesca—correction, Frannie—was feeling him out for a reason. Perhaps she *did* suspect that he was Alessandro, in which case he needed to change her line of questioning.

The DJ transitioned from the boisterous dance music he'd been playing to a romantic holiday song about peace on earth, then encouraged guests to find a partner. Alessandro set his glass beside Frannie's on the bar and offered his elbow. "Care to dance?"

Her hand flattened against the bar. "With you?"

He flashed his most disarming grin and made a show of looking around. "Does it appear I'm asking for someone else? That wasn't my intent."

He waited. Felt like an idiot holding his arm in front of her. After a few beats, she said, "It'd be my pleasure, Your Highness." She tucked her hand in the crook of his arm and allowed him to escort her to the dance floor.

He assumed her hesitancy came from either nerves or inexperience, but quickly discovered that Frannie was light on her feet, as if she'd danced at soirees like Sophia's dozens of times before. She fit in his arms perfectly, matching each of his steps as if it were second nature. Despite the cautious nature of their conversation at the bar, this felt natural. Easy.

Heads turned their way as he spun her around the periphery of the dance floor. It occurred to him that Frannie's hesitation likely came because *he* hadn't danced tonight. In fact, no one had seen Vittorio dance since he'd been with Carmella. If anyone snapped photos, they'd likely appear in tomorrow's papers.

Well, so be it. Perhaps Vittorio would catch wind of it and decide to return home.

Alessandro glanced at Frannie. She was more self-contained than the effervescent, curvaceous women with whom he usually danced. Her hand felt small in his, and her touch at his shoulder soft, yet she didn't strike him as fragile.

In fact, she had a good deal of lean muscle, as if she kept fit for a living.

"Did the Christmas party bring you to Sarcaccia?" he asked. "Or do you live here?"

"I came on business, but I have a small flat here in Cateri. My mother is Sarcaccian." She gave him a small smile. "She actually went to school with your mother, though mine was two years behind yours."

Interesting. Since his mother had attended a rather exclusive school, one filled with children of the wealthy and well-connected, it explained why Frannie navigated the party with such ease. Then there was her last name. Lawrence. Though nearly everyone in Sarcaccia spoke English, Frannie didn't have a Sarcaccian accent. "And your father?"

"American. He works in finance and divides his time between London and New York." One of her shoulders lifted, then dropped. "They divorced when I was eight."

"I'm sorry to hear that."

"It was for the best. My mother's a globetrotter at heart and my father's job doesn't permit that. They've remained friendly and I'm close to each of them."

"Divorce doesn't always work that way."

"No, it doesn't. I'm fortunate."

She angled her head and smiled up at him. A hint of playfulness—or subversiveness—twinkled in the depths of her eyes. Perhaps she wasn't as straitlaced as he'd imagined. Or perhaps he was getting desperate after long months of walking in his brother's shoes and saw what he wanted to see.

"You're close to your family as well, Your Highness?"

"Very."

Her dark eyebrows lifted. "Sophia's always said you're a tight group, but that it was a challenge growing up with four older brothers and a younger one. You all wanted to tell her what to do. Even Prince Bruno."

He grinned at that. It sounded just like Sophia. "I wasn't that bad."

That drew a laugh from her. "She claims you're the worst of all."

True, Vittorio was the worst. "I've laid off recently."

"Prince Alessandro apparently pressures her the least. Fascinating, given that you're twins."

"Perhaps because he's around the least." Alessandro moved Frannie closer to the center of the floor, where the crowd blocked them from anyone with a camera who might be lurking around the edges of the room. "What about you? Do you have brothers?"

"Only a sister. She's five years older than I am."

"Are you close?"

"Yes, though we don't see each other as often as I'd like. She's married and lives near London."

The song ended, but the DJ transitioned to another slow tune intended to keep dancers from scattering. Etiquette demanded that he escort Frannie from the floor, as Sarcaccia's Old World customs still meant that dancing with royalty twice in a row indicated romance was in the air, but his curiosity kept him from releasing her.

"You don't mind, do you? I'm enjoying our conversation." Now that they weren't talking about politics or the weather.

She didn't answer, nor did she pull away. After a moment, she said, "Your twin has been gone a long time."

He felt his smile tighten. Before he could give her the same line he'd given everyone else about Alessandro, Frannie added, "I understand he's spent time in the South Pacific."

"The more remote a location, the more it seems to attract him."

"There's a lot to be said for traveling outside one's comfort zone. Seeing parts of the world that are unlike Sarcaccia, understanding a different way of life."

Just like that, he was in familiar territory. "I've learned more from traveling than I have in any classroom. I believe Alessandro has, as well."

"You must travel a great deal as crown prince. Environmental talks, economic summits, that sort of thing." Instead of pursuing the subject of economics, as he expected, she added, "I imagine when you're not in meetings, you're escorted about on carefully planned tours."

"It's not the best way to see a new location, but in those circumstances security concerns often make it necessary."

"I suppose that's true."

The music grew louder as the song hit its crescendo. When it quieted again, she asked, "When your brother's away, where does he stay? Does he stick to luxury hotels, as you must on your travels?"

He scoffed at that. "Alessandro isn't the luxury hotel type. It's not his constitutional role to involve himself in matters of state, which means—fortunately for him—he's not usually tied to those accommodations."

She was quiet for a beat before asking, "Does he pursue charity work when he's abroad?"

The question was asked casually, but he suspected it was a test...

though he wasn't sure whether she was testing Vittorio or Alessandro. He spun her away from a couple who'd maneuvered to a spot within hearing distance. "Would it be terribly rude of me to point out that you ask the strangest questions?"

One side of her mouth lifted. "As long as you don't mind the questions, in which case, I don't think you'd have asked me to stay on the dance floor."

"Touché."

Her smile blossomed at that. "Your family has a long tradition of philanthropy. I simply wondered if Prince Alessandro gets involved in local charities when he's away. When he's not, ah, socializing."

Ah, so it was a test. For some inexplicable reason, he wanted to pass, though he still couldn't fathom her reasons for asking, given his reputation for, as she put it, socializing. "Alessandro spends much of his time away either diving or climbing and keeps the details to himself until he returns. The only exception was when he summited Mount Kilimanjaro to raise money for the International Red Cross. That was—by necessity—quite public."

Her gaze lit on a spot behind his shoulder before shifting to him. When he circled so he could see that side of the room, he noticed his mother was watching them. Queen Fabrizia angled her chin in question, but Alessandro ignored her when Frannie spoke again.

"There's an island in the Pacific called Kilakuru. It's rather isolated. No airstrip, so it's only accessible by helicopter or an hour-long boat ride from neighboring islands. Ever heard of it?"

"I have." It was said to be a diving enthusiast's dream, well worth the effort to travel there. He leaned back and gave her a look to say, *You're still asking strange questions.*

She grinned, reading him correctly, but her voice turned serious as she said, "A tsunami recently wiped out much of the island's infrastructure. It seems like the kind of place the Barrali Trust would assist, so I wondered if that's where Prince Alessandro went. That's all." Her gaze darted toward the doors leading to the ballroom's reception area. "Jack Gladwell is spearheading the construction of a shelter for those orphaned by the disaster. He's also funding repairs to the island's emergency services facilities."

"I didn't think Jack Gladwell publicized his donations."

"He doesn't, but he's sailed in that area and felt compelled to help. I noticed him speaking with your father earlier and assumed Jack convinced your parents to finalize—" At Alessandro's open look of surprise, she explained, "I work for Jack. Well, I do for another two weeks. We spend a great deal of time discussing his charitable objectives."

Jack Gladwell operated a massive business conglomerate. Stefano's fiancée, Megan, once headed business development at one of Gladwell's many hotels. Few people could claim to work for the man directly. Far fewer referred to him by his first name. Frannie intrigued him more with each passing minute. "Why for another two weeks?"

She shrugged. "I was presented with a new opportunity, one that will take me out of my comfort zone. With Jack's blessing, I decided to take the leap."

Though he wondered what she did for Gladwell—and what she planned to do next—he couldn't help but tease her. "It was the fact he acquired an American baseball team, wasn't it? You hate sports. Can't work for a man with a financial interest in such nonsense."

She flashed a dazzling smile, one that made his breath catch. "I happen to love baseball, though the fact he now owns a rival to my Mets is a point against him."

"Rugby would've been a more appropriate British pursuit. Or polo. Baseball is surprising."

"Jack does love to surprise."

The song wound down and the DJ announced he'd play one more slow number before ramping up the beat. Frannie stepped out of his embrace. "Thank you, Your Highness, for allowing me to monopolize your time."

He covered his disappointment with a smile. "I invited you to do so."

"Still, I suspect others wish to dance with you."

He suspected as much, too. Women always flocked to Vittorio, though for different reasons than they flocked to Alessandro. With Vittorio, they hoped for marriage and a happily ever after as the future queen of Sarcaccia. With Alessandro, they simply wanted to get laid. Any woman who approached him tonight would be out of luck on both counts.

Before he could stop himself, he took Frannie's hand and raised it to his lips. "It was a pleasure to meet you."

Her eyes widened momentarily. "And I enjoyed meeting you, Your Highness. Have a happy Christmas."

He returned to the bar, pausing along the way to make small talk with his youngest brother, Bruno, while pretending not to see the women who'd subtly placed themselves in his path. When he finally reached his destination, he discovered his Scotch had been cleared away.

For the best, he supposed. His fascination with Miss Economics and her employment situation was a clear sign he craved a diversion tonight. Alcohol would only make matters worse. He'd been about to dance with her a third time, and he knew better. Vittorio wouldn't have danced with Frannie a second time, and she was exactly Vittorio's type. Intelligent, proper, and lacking flash.

Alessandro turned to face the room and schooled his features into the same placid smile he'd worn earlier. Another fifteen or twenty minutes and he could make a polite exit, claiming matters of state needed his attention in the morning. The fact it was true—and that he was beginning to find the complicated dynamics of the Mideast far more interesting than palace parties—proved he was slowly losing himself to the role of Vittorio, and that would not do. Even if he wanted to jump into the political fray, it wasn't his place.

His place was to show up for the occasional family or charitable event. Otherwise, he need only play backup to his father and twin brother.

The minute Vittorio returned to Sarcaccia and Alessandro was free, he estimated it'd take less than twenty-four hours to find a buxom, carefree woman willing to do absolutely anything he wanted in bed for as long as he wanted to do it. *That* was a role he'd enjoy.

ALSO BY NICOLE BURNHAM

ROYAL SCANDALS

Christmas With a Prince (prequel novella)

Scandal With a Prince

Honeymoon With a Prince

Christmas on the Royal Yacht (novella)

Slow Tango With a Prince

The Royal Bastard

Christmas With a Palace Thief (novella)

The Wicked Prince

One Man's Princess

ROYAL SCANDALS: SAN RIMINI

Fit for a Queen

Going to the Castle

The Prince's Tutor

The Knight's Kiss

Falling for Prince Federico

To Kiss a King

BOWEN, NEBRASKA

The Bowen Bride

A ROYAL SCANDALS WEDDING

More Royal Scandals titles will be available soon. For updates, please visit nicoleburnham.com, where you can subscribe to Nicole's Newsletter.

Subscribers receive exclusive content, including the short story *A Royal Scandals Wedding*, an inside look at the wedding of Megan Hallberg and Prince Stefano Barrali from the novel Scandal With a Prince.

ABOUT THE AUTHOR

Nicole Burnham is the RITA award-winning author of over twenty novels, including the popular Royal Scandals series.

Readers may visit Nicole's website and subscribe to her newsletter at nicoleburnham.com.

facebook.com/NicoleBurnhamBooks
twitter.com/NicoleBurnham
instagram.com/nicole.burnham